'Worlds Apart'

An historical novel set in Rural Hampshire, England in 1625

Colin Edwards

Illustrations by Pearl Hailstone

Published by C J Publishing

cJp

© *2009 Colin J Edwards*

ISBN: 978-0-9561549-0-3

The Tilly Family Tree in 1625

John Tilly = Emily

William	John, the less	Ruth	Sarah	Richard	Mary	Peter	Susan	George
18	17	16	15	12	10	8	2	10m.
River Boatman	Fisherman	in Service			At Home			

Other significant people in the story;

Next Door Neighbours	Other Fishermen	R. Avon Project	Sopley Hall		Sarah's Friend
Jo & Mary Watts	Jo Watts	Eddie Otter	Sir Richard Tichbourne		Nick Swanton
	Thomas Hayward	James Proudfoot	Lady Susan Tichbourne		

William's Friend/Wife	Carpenter	Congregation Leaders	Assistant to Governor
Miriam Hayward	Joe Witchell	John Stott	George Pengellan
		Hattie Stott	

'Worlds Apart'

Forward

This story of the Tilly Family of Hampshire, England is one set in a context of poverty, riches and extremes of religious thought. They wanted nothing more or less than to live as a family according to their conscience, but society in the 1600's thought differently.

We know that the family of one John Tilly lived in this Hampshire town at the time, with some family members emigrating to Newfoundland during the seventeenth century. We also know that they were fishermen, attracted to the North Atlantic by rich shoals of cod and other fish. However, we do not know anything about the detail of their lives. This story describes the social and religious circumstances of this period of history as they affected the family of John Tilly. Particular members of the family lived in both Hampshire and Newfoundland but not necessarily all of the characters described in this story.

For over two hundred years, various members travelled between the two countries. Their lives are recorded in both England and Newfoundland with certain individuals becoming significant in many walks of life on both continents. This novel is a testament to their faith, integrity and determination.

England at that time was one of religious intolerance. In the previous century there had been the break with the Roman Catholic Church by King Henry Vlll with subsequent changes of fortune between Protestants and Catholics. During the reign of James I, there arose a dissenting minority which gave birth to the Pilgrim Fathers and other separatist groups. In 1625 Charles 1 was crowned king, ushering in a new era of uncertainty. In this context, our story unfolds

'Worlds Apart' describes the challenge to a group of individuals in the face of religious and political persecution and their response.

Acknowledgements

"Extracts from the Authorized Version of the Bible (The King James Bible), the rights in which are vested in the Crown, are reproduced by permission of the Crown's Patentee, Cambridge University Press".

The 'Mason Map' is reproduced by kind permission and courtesy of the 'Centre for Newfoundland Studies, Memorial University Libraries', St John, Newfoundland.

I wish to thank all those who have assisted in the research, in the helpful comments and in the proof reading of this book. In particular I would like to thank, Mary Bashford, Jane and Chris Edwards, Nicky Mc Isaac and Alison Morse.

I would also like to thank Pearl Hailstone for her excellent art work which adds considerably to the interest of this book.

I acknowledge with love and gratitude the patience and assistance of Valerie, my wife, over the months that this book has been written and prepared.

Colin Edwards   2009

Contents

	Forward
Prologue	*The Family*
One	*Exciting News*
Two	*Preparation*
Three	*Ruth and Sarah in Different Worlds*
Four	*A Summer Festival - A Masked Ball*
Five	*William at Home on the River Avon*
Six	*Emily – a Woman beset with Problems*
Seven	*Arrest and Trial*
Eight	*It could never be quite the same again*
Nine	*The Homecoming*
Ten	*A Winter of Difficulty*
Eleven	*Is new life possible?*
Twelve	*Decisions, Decisions …*
Thirteen	*'New-Found-Land'*
Fourteen	*It wasn't quite as easy as they had thought*
Epilogue	*Worlds Apart – 'Yet One Family'*

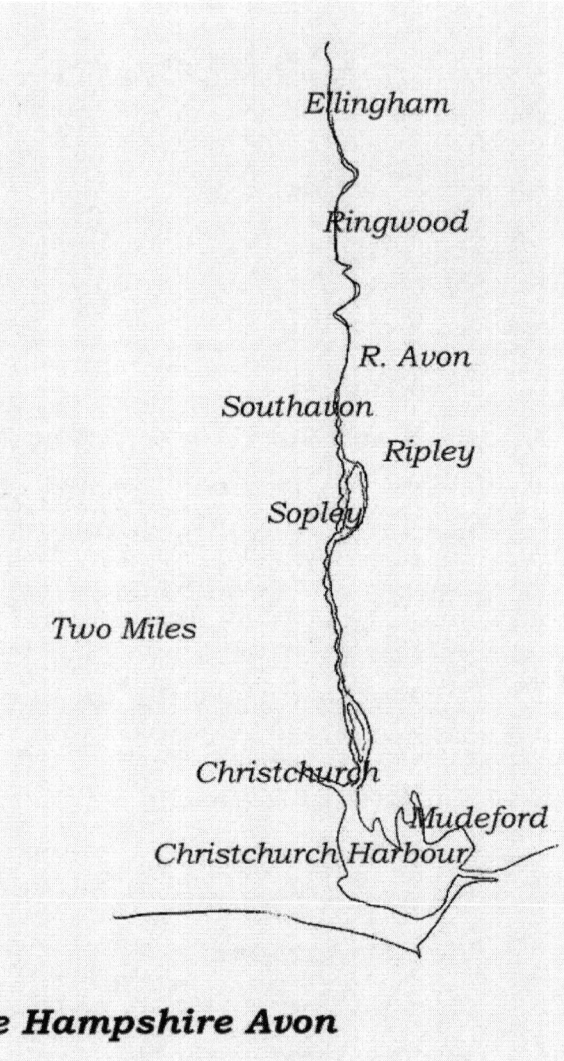

'Worlds Apart'

Prologue - 'The Family'

It was a family of individuals. The members of which were independent in thinking and lifestyle. A family who were hard working, yet still relatively poor. They were men and women who were guided by conscience at a time when an individual conscience was not allowed.

It was in June of 1625 in Ringwood, Hampshire, England when the family of John Tilly, started to think seriously about the alternatives to their lives of poverty, uncertainty and religious intolerance. They were fishermen by trade, freethinkers by religion and hardworking by nature. It was a family of nine children aged between ten months and eighteen years, their parents and grandmother.

The parents were John and his wife Emily. John was a fisherman, working long hours at sea in a dangerous job with his son and three other local men. He was a man of quiet resolve, given to thinking, but not often sharing his thoughts. He was strong in his faith and clear in his resolve to provide for his family.

His wife also worked long hours feeding her brood and trying to maintain their rented cottage. A woman with a warm hearted soul always caring for other people. Always believing that 'others were more important than herself'.

The eldest son, William, was just turned eighteen and 'worked' the river from dawn to dusk. He looked after a small boat, called a 'wherry' which was used on the River Avon from Ringwood to Christchurch and upstream towards Salisbury.

The 'wherry' could be sailed or rowed to ferry people to Christchurch and to move stores and fish up and down river. It also enabled William to fish with line for trout. Unfortunately, William, six months earlier had been involved in a serious accident at Ringwood Mill. There he had been crushed against a wall with the result that his right arm and leg where both badly damaged. He now limped and could not safely go to sea with his father. However, he was an intelligent man, listening carefully to the banter and gossip of the passengers as he ferried them on the river.

The next member of the family was known as John the less. He was his father's right hand man. He was not only named after his father but in character was also like him. He was a strong, silent man who was reliable, tough and able to withstand the rigours of ocean fishing which he shared with his father. At seventeen years old, he was a tall figure of man whom all the girls of the area admired. He had had a brief affair with one such girl but it had not come to anything, Fishermen were away from home for long periods at a time and when they returned, they were not very adept at social niceties. John the less was his mother's favourite. She tried not to show it but she always listened to his words with respect and admiration.

The next child was Ruth, a strong-willed sixteen year old girl who worked in service at Sopley Hall. She disliked the notion of working for someone else and challenged this at every opportunity. She worked hard in the kitchens and was very popular, particularly with the new owners, Sir Richard Tichbourne and his wife Susan. She worked long hours, rising before dawn and walking the six miles to the Hall, returning late at night. Ruth was outspoken at home, annoying her parents and challenging her brothers and sisters. She was often embroiled in arguments. Yet she was also very kind, emulating her mother's concern for people less well-off than herself, she was often visiting the sick on her way home from work. Recently she had sought the help of Lady Tichbourne in saving a family from eviction from an estate cottage. She was a girl who disliked hypocrisy and any kind of pretence, preferring to speak her mind, whatever the consequences.

Sarah was totally different. At fifteen she was aware of her responsibilities in life, a serious minded girl who was also extremely attractive. Sarah was very intelligent having taught herself to read with assistance from their next door neighbour. Everyone in the family and many others were dependent upon her for reading official documents. She was very much, 'an old head on young shoulders' yet at the same time, with a winsome smile and beautiful soft auburn hair that shone in the sunlight. She already had many suitors. The lads in the village and beyond viewed her with awe, knowing that she was beyond their reach. However, various suitors sent messages to her regularly but she declined them all, recognising that her responsibility lay at home with the family. Whenever possible she tried to teach the other children and her parents to read and write but without very much success. She helped her mother care for the younger members of the family. She did any buying or selling for the family and kept the accounts for her father. She was indispensable to everyone. Her parents worried about what they would do, as and when she left home.

The next child was Richard who was nearly thirteen years old. He was always in trouble, just couldn't help it; he was just made that way. He had recently been caught stealing from travellers passing through Ringwood and had been apprehended with his friends trespassing in the grounds of the manor. He had once been caught throwing stones at the horses of passing traffic, causing chaos. Richard was a likeable rogue with a commonsense approach to life but who was bored with life. He always completed his household tasks quickly and efficiently and had realised that the quicker they were done, the quicker he could go off with his friends. Recently he had been expected to do more at home and had been given the job of cleaning the fish that his brother caught. He had been taught how to smoke fish, mend nets and repair the sails. Work which he did not enjoy.

Mary at ten years old was a sickly child. If there was any sickness in the village she caught it! Several times her parents had feared for her life as she lay in a fever, coughing and wheezing. Mary was, however, very good at the domestic chores. She was always one of the first to be out of bed, as if lying in bed was a crime when there was work to be done. Mary was very competent at getting the fire lit in the mornings with little fuss and even less smoke. She cleaned the cottage as well as possible whilst looking after a small vegetable plot growing some excellent vegetables, the surplus of which was sold in the market. She was also an expert on 'medicinal herbs' for which she was locally quite famous. Mary was a quiet, unassuming girl who knew her place and got on with her work.

Peter was eight years old, quick witted and quite sharp. He assisted his sister Sarah in her tasks but did not want to concentrate on difficult things. He liked to be able to complete something quickly and move on to the next task. He was finding that he enjoyed words but didn't like learning how to read. Instead, he liked to argue, using new-found words to annoy everyone else. His dream was to travel to London and beyond, to see the world and to be successful. He dreamed of owning horses and carriages, of chartering ships and discovering new countries. He dreamed of challenging everyone and everything.

Two other children had been born to John and Emily but one was stillborn and the other died within a few weeks of being born, causing much sadness and heartache. Subsequently, two further children had been born, Susan and George.

Susan was two years old and into everything. She was a very determined little girl who was frustrated like many another two year old. But one who always seemed to get what she wanted by fair means or foul!

George was a little boy of ten months. A happy contented lad, who seemed to be able to amuse himself without causing chaos in the household. Everybody loved him and he loved everyone. He was a charmer who was already showing signs of being a diplomat, making and keeping everyone happy.

This was an interesting family yet no different from many others at that time. A family whose first priority was survival but also one deeply concerned about spiritual matters. A family, who in the months to follow were to be tested almost beyond endurance.

This book is the story of the Tilly family during a period of two years. Describing their difficulties and their response according to their religious convictions.

Fishing in the North Atlantic

'Worlds Apart'

One – 'Exciting News'

They had not stopped talking for days! Each had their own contribution to make, each their own viewpoint. So what was it which had so captivated the attention of this family?

The two John's, father and son, had just returned from an amazing fishing venture to the New World. They had sailed their small boat for weeks through storm and high seas. John, the father, was saying for the hundredth time;

"There were just thousands of them, the water just boiled with fish. We just couldn't stop; just dunked the bucket over the side and it was full. Full to busting, lovely big fish. We just couldn't stop collecting them – even at night it was just so easy. John, interrupted his father to exclaim – "I have never seen anything like it".

Sarah added her thoughts with conviction; "That one catch will pay all the bills for the past year, we can walk tall – we can pay our debts!"

Then mother cleared her throat and spoke quietly in simple words, full of emotion. "But you were gone for three months, we did not know whether you were dead or alive. I don't think that I can stand another such absence. It's just not right to leave us all to cope without you. Three weeks of a normal trip is bad enough but three months to the end of the world …"

"Not the end of the world, Mother" cried Richard, "It's the New World and I want to go there now!"

"Well you can't" said Ruth, "You have to grow up first. You have got to learn to work hard before you can go anywhere." "I will go, one day," said Richard, "and not to fish but to make my fortune, to be famous."

"I think we ought to go back immediately," said Father. "If we left next Monday we could be at the fishing grounds in a few weeks. We could work all hours and then return home in September. We would be back before the winter storms. The trip would change our lives forever. We would have enough money to feed us all and keep this house warm. It would change everything."

"But what happens if you don't get back or if you have an accident or if you can't find the fish or …." said mother, her voice trailing off in despair. Mary added her plaintive cry; "But I just don't want you to go!"

William interrupted the family discussion with a more reasoned and articulated series of observations;

"I hear that a John Mason has presented a report to Sir John Scott in Edinburgh about a New-Found-Land which is near to the fishing grounds. He reported 'that in some parts the salmon and cod were so thick that you couldn't row a boat through them.' If that is true, then we need to be part of this 'New World' fishing fleet. The boat is in good shape, the sails are all repaired, and we can easily prepare enough food for the voyage. I believe that the rest of the crew are keen to make an attempt. I will look after everything here. It's summer time so I should be able to earn enough by my fresh fish sales and ferry work to keep us all until you return. I think you should go. Besides, the political scene is changing. With a new king, new laws and new taxation, we shall need to earn as much as possible while there is opportunity."

"I suppose we do need to think more about the future," said Mother, "we don't know for how long we shall be able to continue to worship with our group of friends. Although we have got one of the new Bibles and our dear friend Mary is able to read to us from God's Word, it may not last. Persecution and even worse may come. We need to be prepared for the worst. We may all need to travel to the New World to escape persecution if King Charles makes matters really difficult for us."

"I hear that the 'Puritans' who left a few years ago on the 'Mayflower' have settled in New England, they have been able to build new homes and have found freedom from persecution," commented William. "Only last week, I ferried two men down to Christchurch who had returned from New England. They were talking about new crops which grow plentifully and about lots of fish and furs!"

"Let's not get too carried away", said Father. "It's a long, long way to these new places and the sea crossing is not easy."

"I understand that many of the original passengers died on the crossing", replied Mother, "and that when they arrived many caught diseases. In the first year there was no food and there were Indians and …."

"That's enough talk about gloom and doom", replied John, "Let's talk to our friends about a return trip to the fishing grounds. Then, we will decide."

With that comment, they moved to get on with their respective jobs around the house, each mulling over in their minds the problems and the possibilities.

The cottage where the Tilly family lived was typical for the period. It was small with little room for the ten people who lived there. The front door opened on to the street with two rooms on the ground floor and two rooms upstairs. There was no kitchen or bathroom, no separate bedrooms – all the rooms were used for living and for sleeping. The ceilings were low and the stairs went directly out of the front room. The cottage had a rough stone floor with a coarse mat by the front door. The room at the front was furnished with a rough wooden table with two benches which almost filled the room. A shelf on the wall provided a place for an oil lamp and Sarah's accounts and a few books. Below the shelf was a wooden frame with string fastened across it in a cobweb-like pattern. A straw mattress was fastened to the frame with the whole structure held upright against the wall by a wooden peg. At night this was laid flat on the floor and used as a bed for John and Emily.

In the rear room was a large hearth and chimney with a fire beneath which had to be lit each morning. The fire provided the warmth for the cottage, enabling water to be heated for washing and cooking. The smoke from the fire was directed up a chimney but much of it filled the whole cottage. In summer, the cottage was hot and smoky and the children if they could, slept outside under the stars. In the winter it was cold as there was no glass in the windows, merely pieces of wood which could be twisted to keep out some of the cold and rain. Again, a wooden frame was fixed to the wall which at night was made into a rudimentary bed. A wooden bench and table were kept along one wall which was used for preparing the fish for market, preparing food for eating and as the general workbench for the family. There was, of course, no running water. This had to be fetched from the river or from the well in the centre of the village. There were no toilets that we would recognise as such, except a rough shed at the end of the garden with a bench inside with a round hole. The waste emptied directly into the stream which fed into the river!

Upstairs, the ceilings were even lower and the rooms were very small with tiny glassless windows. Storage of clothes and personal belongings was minimal. The only clothes in the cupboard were their 'Sunday Best', a change of clothes for each member of the family. Otherwise, it was what they 'stood-up' in. The beds upstairs were similar to those downstairs, here the younger children slept in one room and Granny with Sarah and Ruth in the other.

At the back of the cottage was a small yard with a narrow plot of land which ran down to the stream, where Mary grew her vegetables. There was no privacy in such an environment, any discussion or dissent was known to everyone, not only in the cottage but to all of the people in the street.

Waterside Cottages, Ringwood

The road at the front of the cottage was made of cobbled stones covered with soil and the droppings from the horses and other livestock. When it rained heavily, the road turned into a sea of mud, when it was dry, the dust swirled around and blew into the cottage.

Next door there was another family of fishermen, an even larger family of twelve children by the name of Watts. Here Joe Watts and his wife Mary lived. Jo was the oldest friend of John Tilly, they had grown up together, played together and married on the same day. They worked on the same boat which they now jointly owned. It had taken them many years to save enough money to buy the boat that had once been rented. Joe could be quite dour at times, he was somewhat pessimistic and saw the problems in life.

Like the Tilly family and like many fishermen over the centuries, they were religious, More than that, they were 'dissenters'. They believed in 'freedom of conscience' which meant that their belief and worship style was dictated by their own personal convictions and not by the established churches of the day.

Jo's wife, Mary was educated. Her parents had lived at Sopley Hall as Housekeeper and Coachman. Mary had been tutored with the daughter of the House. She could therefore read and write which was very unusual in those days. She loved reading and thinking, particularly about religious matters. In fact, she had been able to read the new translation of the Bible commissioned by James I, the so called 'King James Bible'.

In Ringwood at this time, a group of 'dissenters' met each week to worship God and they were called 'Congregational Puritans', these people met as a group or congregation of believers. They were convinced that decisions made by the local congregation were more important than those sanctioned by the state and its religious courts. Under King James, many such believers had been arrested, fined, jailed and even executed. Under a new king there was much uncertainty. Mary Watts was one of the leading members of this group and her influence affected the thinking of her husband and the Tilly family next door.

John Tilly went to sea as a fisherman, with other men who were old friends. One lived in the nearby hamlet of Ellingham and the other in the village of Sopley. Firstly, there was Thomas Hayward who lived in Ellingham with his sister. At this time he was unmarried but lived in the old family home and assisted in the care of his sister's family of nine children. His brother-in-law had been killed in a fishing accident two years earlier. Thomas was a hard-working man, the local expert in gutting and smoking fish. Secondly, there was John Hayter from Sopley. He was the navigator who could read the stars in the sky, plotting their location with significant accuracy.

There were therefore a total of five regular fishermen who worked as a team together, hiring casual workers as and when necessary.

Although the family conference had been closed, the discussion went on into the small hours. John Tilly, John the less and William left the cottage, walked down to the Millstream, to the local inn where they could discuss the practicalities without the women and younger children being involved. After purchasing their usual tankards of beer they sat in the evening dusk continuing their discussion.

"I think that there are four things we need to consider," said William in his usual serious manner; "the financial needs of the family, the excellent fish stocks off New-Found-Land, the uncertain religious situation here in England and the possibility that we may have to flee for our lives. All of this suggests to me that you ought to go immediately, catch as much fish as possible, find out a bit more about the land and return before the winter."

"It's alright for you," said John the less. "You cannot go because of your injuries but the voyage is extremely dangerous. I didn't emphasise it with the women present but the journey is tough, we are totally at the mercy of the weather. The storms can produce enormous waves. There is always the possibility that we might not return. If we don't, it's your responsibility to feed and clothe everybody."

"I know the risks but I still think it's a risk worth taking. It just might provide a way of escape from possible persecution. I don't like what I am hearing. I think we could be returning to the bad old days of execution without trial. Even now, people are being arrested in Oxford and London for 'dissenting' from the laws about worship. I am sure that it will come here before the year is done."

"You may be right" said Father, "it's a risk we are being forced to take. However, it may be God's way of testing us. Do we have enough faith in Him so that we can 'face the storm' and return to our loved ones? I believe that we should put our trust in Him and go forward."

"We really need the money from a good catch", observed William, "Sarah and I are really worried about buying fuel for next winter. There is a rumour that we shall not be able to collect fallen timber in the Forest anymore. If that is true and we have to buy wood for the fire, then we might have to go without food. I don't know which is worse, to freeze or to starve."

At this point, across from the Inn came their two colleagues, each with a tankard of beer, Thomas Hayward and Joe Watts, as usual, Jo was talking and Thomas was listening.

"I don't want to return to the fishing grounds, I just want to stay here in the warm summer sun, I like it here and that is that!" stated Joe defiantly. "With the size of those waves, if you went overboard, you would be gone for ever. The air is so cold it freezes your insides as you breathe. Even when you land it's so bleak and barren. Even the trees when fully grown are just sticks, like wizened old men with lichen and moss growing all over them."

"I see your point", replied Thomas, "I didn't like it either but I have ten mouths to feed and my sister can't get any work. She has her hands full just looking after the tribe. It's been terrible this past year. I must earn some money this summer to keep us all fed next winter, let alone keeping us all warm."

"Evening all" spoke the Tilly family as one man. "I hear you're talking about New-Found-Land and whether or not we return to the fishing before the winter closes in", said John the less. "Yes, that's about it" replied Thomas. "Well, we think we ought to return – we don't think that there is any choice in the matter. It's either fish for plenty or fish for nothing. It's either accepting God's will or dying here of starvation or persecution." said John, speaking for his family.

"Well, you could be right, but I am not convinced. I shall have to talk it over with Mary, she's the brains in our family. If she is prepared to struggle through the summer without me and if she thinks it's a wise move, then I'll consider it." said Joe.

They all sat still for a time, contemplating the future. On the one hand, worried and uncertain but on the other, excited at the prospect of sailing and fishing in unknown waters.

Then the conversation moved to other matters; the weather, the political scene and the cost of flour and milk. Subjects that have always engaged the minds of men in English villages, men with a drink in the hand and time to talk.

The next morning was fresh and beautiful. There had been a shower of rain during the night and now everything was washed clean. The light green leaves, the flowers in the back garden, the street freshly washed with the cobble stones shining, all clean and new in the morning sunlight.

Ruth had risen from her bed as the sun rose in the sky. She dressed quietly and quickly in her long dress, mop-cap and flat simple shoes. Outwardly she was the very epitome of a country serving girl but inwardly she was angry at having to get up so early and work such long hours. Grabbing a crust of bread she set out on her long walk to work. If she was honest, she actually enjoyed the walk, it gave her time to think and dream of the future. That particular morning she had lots to think about – everything that had been said the previous night, her own future and the future of her family. Yes, she had plenty to think about and in no time at all, she was knocking quietly on the kitchen door at the Hall.

Mary had had a good night for once, she had slept well and she also had risen early. She had lit the fire and it was now burning brightly ready to heat the water for washing. She and Richard had to take the water buckets to the village well where they had to wait until it was their turn. Between them they could wind up the bucket full of water and fill their own buckets. They had to carry the water, without spilling it, back to the cottage. By which time, father and the boys were up and had used the toilet and needed water to wash and shave as they stood talking in the back yard. Breakfast was eaten on the move, a chunk of bread, a piece of cheese and mug of beer. The family did not sit down for this as there was too much to do and they did not have time to sit and talk.

As usual, Susan the two-year old, was getting in the way of everyone else, wanting something to eat, trying to gain attention whilst Mother was looking after baby George. The whole house was alive and active as any family of nine children would be in one small cottage.

It was agreed that the men should make contact with their fishing colleagues and decide together what to do. This would be quite easy as they would all be coming to Ringwood Market during the day. Meanwhile, the children, under Mother's guidance, packed away all of the bedding and tidied the house.

It was Wednesday, Market Day. Mother and Sarah sorted out their items for sale while John the less, carried the table out into the street on which to set-up shop. They had smoked cod, brought back from New-Found-Land and fresh trout, caught the day before. There were slabs of hard cheese and packets of soft cheese collected from a local farm. There were also bunches of herbs which John the less had hung on a couple of poles. Mary had grown these in the garden and dried them. They were invaluable in cooking, as medicine for illness and generally around the house. The family were hoping for a good day's sales.

Other stall holders were setting up their tables and displaying their wares. There were weavers with their course clothing for sale. Various baskets and wattle fencing-panels made from local willow were displayed in prominent positions. The leather workers had travelled from nearby towns with their belts and wallets to tempt the village folk. There was a candle-maker offering candles and soap made from lye and wood ash. The grinder with his stones and his collection of newly made knives and daggers, an ever popular stall with the men of the area. Across the square were pens for animals and wooden cages for chicken and ducks. The noise of the animals being brought for sale gave a background feel of rural life. The street musician brought the whole scene alive with his playing and singing. By mid-morning, there were probably a hundred people around the stalls, some from Ringwood, some who had walked from nearby villages and others who had ridden from further afield.

William had been busy from early morning on the River Avon. He had been meeting passengers' up-river and ferrying them to the market with their vegetables, livestock and belongings. Unfortunately, there was little wind that morning and this meant that he had to row. But he struggled on and was ready for a break when he was called to join the fishermen in their discussions.

The men met outside the Inn for their meeting. With a tankard of ale in the warm sunshine they were ready to talk and make decisions. Each stated their point of view, their doubts and uncertainties but also their hopes and expectations. Jo had talked to his wife, Mary. She had persuaded her husband to 'trust in God' to find a new life where the family could enjoy peace.

After an hour or so of discussion, it was obvious that they had reached agreement that they would be leaving the following week. By now it was lunchtime, the market had finished. People were taking their purchases back home and clearing away the stalls. The Inn was filling up rapidly, the Tilly men-folk returned home for lunch.

Lunch was the main meal of the day consisting of meat or fish with several vegetables in a broth-like stew. While the market had been busy, Mary had stayed at home preparing lunch. She had pulled onions, carrots and beetroot from the garden and collected potatoes from the straw-covered store at the bottom of the garden. She had peeled the vegetables, cut them up, and cooked them with lentils and barley together with several different types of beans. She had also boiled salted beef which was cut up into small squares which she added to the broth. This was a rare treat in honour of the men being home on market day. The meal was served on rough pottery plates and eaten with bread being used as a rudimentary spoon.

While this was being served, Sarah had found a corner in the front room and was busy counting out the coins which they had earned that morning. When she was satisfied that her addition was correct, she lifted her ledger from the shelf, the quill with its ink container and carefully wrote in the book the sales details. The page was without blots, everything was in neat columns and it all added-up correctly.

Mother was also pleased with the morning's business. She had been able to sell all of the fish and most of the cheese. All the herbs had been sold, apparently they were reckoned to be the best in the district! Everybody was excited by the smoked cod – the flesh was said to be thicker and meatier than anything anyone could remember. She could have sold it for much more money but she was conscious that people who really needed the fish could not afford to pay any more. Times were hard.

However, Father was quite concerned that lunchtime, as he now had to inform the family what the men had decided. He knew that there would be tears. However, he gritted his teeth and told the family what had been agreed. They reluctantly accepted the situation which the older members knew was inevitable.

The rest of the day was a blur – everyone was busy talking and planning for the forthcoming fishing trip. It had been agreed that departure would be on high tide the following Monday, thereby allowing the family to meet together on the Sunday to ask for God's blessing on the venture. The next three days would be very busy, sorting, packing and loading.

John, the less, decided that he ought to go to Sopley Hall and find his sister and explain to her in person the reasons for the decision. If she found out when she arrived home late that night, she would be very angry. He wanted to spend a few minutes with his sister but he also planned to use the opportunity to see a new stable girl at the Hall. The girl had been at Christchurch harbour when the fishing expedition had arrived home and she had smiled and waved enthusiastically to him. He was sure that she liked him and he wanted to explain how necessary the planned trip really was. That he would soon be back home and hopefully able to stay at home for most of next winter. That was his dream, at least. His brother was able to take him by boat down the river to a point where he could walk across the fields to the Hall.

He knocked tentatively on the kitchen door, Ruth answered the door as she had been busy preparing vegetables in the kitchen for the evening dinner.

"Oh, my handsome big brother, what a surprise!" she exclaimed. "It's not bad news, is it?" "Well not exactly," he replied. "But, it's been decided that we will return to the fishing grounds off New-Found-Land. We are to depart next Monday on the high tide."

"I knew it," Ruth cried, "You are going off again, leaving me to work all hours at this place, at the beck and call of everybody. Do this. Do that. Then at the end of a long day I go home and have to do all the things that no-body else wants to do. It's just not fair! Why can't I come with you? I can cook and sew and even smoke the fish on this New-Found-Land, whatever it's called. I don't see why girls have to work in service, why can't we do a proper job like you and William?"

John the less, let her calm down and then picked her up and twirled her round and round in his big muscular arms. She buried her head in his shoulder and let just one tear fall on his shoulder before she shook her head and defiantly stated; "One day, I will work for myself. I will choose my own husband. I will show all of you that I can do it by myself!"

At this moment, around the corner of the stable block came the new stable-girl. John the less came to an abrupt stop, dropped his sister to the ground and went scarlet with embarrassment. He wished the earth would open in front of him. He managed to stutter; "Hello, I was just coming to find you".

"Why?" she asked. "I am afraid that we are going to leave Christchurch next Monday and we are going to be away for at least three months," he replied. "We are going to return to the fishing grounds off New-Found-Land and I'm going to miss you …" his voice tailed away as he suddenly realised that he had said more than he had planned. His sister looked at him quizzically. She caught his eye as she smiled to herself. "I had better get back to my work and leave you to it," she said meaningfully to her brother.

When the door had shut behind Ruth, the girl, whose name was Bess, was also embarrassed not knowing what to say or do. She just cast her eyes to the ground and looked away. John the less, felt it was time to go before he made any more blunders. He just stuttered, "I must be going, I will see you sometime – bye." With that, he quickly walked away and was soon out of sight across the fields, walking towards the river.

Back home in Ringwood, John and Emily were sitting down in the front room of their cottage with Sarah. They were thinking and talking about what they would need to load on the boat. Emily was listing all of the domestic items they would need whilst Sarah was trying to write them down, without much success. John was thinking, and occasionally interrupting the women about what equipment they would need. "We need some new knives for gutting the fish, some metal hooks, skillets and salt for packing the fish," thought John out loud. Whilst Emily was saying that they needed a change of clothes, strong, waterproof boots as well as beef, pork, eggs, cheese, vegetables, bread and flour.

Sarah, knew that they had did not have any money for any of these items. She started thinking about a loan but recognised that the money-lender would require an exorbitant rate of interest. Money they could not afford. If the men did not return, then they would lose their home and all of their possessions to repay it.

Emily saw the worried look on her daughter's pretty face and stopped talking to hold Sarah's hands before giving her a big hug. "Don't worry," she said, "The Lord will provide, doesn't scripture say, "Take no thought for your life, what ye shall eat, or what ye shall drink nor yet for your body, what ye shall put on. Is not the life more than meat, and the body more than raiment?" If this is God's will then he will provide all that we need." "I know", said Sarah, "but I still find it hard to have such trust in a God whom you cannot see. You can read His words but cannot hear his voice." "You will learn, you will learn," said Father with quiet assurance. "When you have been in such terrible, violent storms as I have and survived, you will know that there is a God who hears and who is near every one of us, even if we cannot see or hear him."

Out on the River Avon, William was working hard. It had been a long day and his arm was aching painfully. Yet it had been a good day, because it had been market day there had been many ferry passengers. He could charge a higher rate on market day to take account of the produce and animals which he transported. A good day's work.

It was also a beautiful day – blue sky and a warm June sun. The river was at its best, with the clouds mirrored on its surface and the breeze just gently picking up the reeds along the river bank. The wetland wildflowers were out in full bloom, the meadowsweet and the scabious with the hay meadows beyond almost ready for cutting. On the river, the white fronted geese, the ducks and great crested grebe were everywhere. He loved it.

His boat was small and flat-bottomed with a protruding wine-glass shaped bow which overhung the river bank enabling people to board easily. It had a single sail which William could manage on his own and a long single oar at the rear, by which he could steer and propel the boat forward. He could transport two or three people at a time or a man and his sheep, pig or chicken. William not only earned money from his work but it provided a form of easy transport between the family home in Ringwood and the harbour at Christchurch where the fishing boats were moored.

After the discussions and decision reached at lunchtime, there was much to occupy William's mind. He took his brother down to Sopley and then some other passengers to Christchurch, he was able to think carefully about the options available. He would have liked to have gone fishing with his father and brother but it wasn't easy with his injured arm and his being lame. He would probably be more of a liability than an asset. Besides which, he did have the family to look after in his Father's absence. That was not always easy, either.

On the way back from Christchurch he saw his brother John the less, running across the fields towards him. It was good to be able to spend a little time together as they made their way back up-river. John, the less, was quiet and contemplative – must be a bit worried, thought William. In reality, John the less was thinking what a fool he had been that afternoon, Bess must think him to be a total idiot who couldn't talk to girls let alone do anything else! The great shame was that she was actually very attractive and he wouldn't be able to do anything about it for at least three months, by which time she would be someone else's. Ah' well, that's life. he thought.

As they neared Ringwood, they could see that there was a commotion on the bank! "It looks as if there has been a fight and someone's been ducked into the river to cool them off", said William, "Yes, I bet I know who it is," said John the less, "It looks like young Richard, he just can't keep out of trouble." As they got nearer they could see that it was indeed young Richard. They pulled the boat into the bank and John the less grabbed hold of his brother by his ragged shirt, cuffing him lightly in the process. "What have you been up to this time?" asked his older brother, "You just cannot keep out of trouble for five minutes, can you?"

Not waiting for an answer, he launched into a lecture; "I have told you before and I am telling you again, that you do not get into fights, whatever the reason. You know what Mother and Father will say. It is wrong to fight, you must 'turn the other cheek'.

Richard interrupted his brother, "But, but it was not fair, little Johnny from the bakers' has had smallpox and the bigger boys were throwing stones at him, saying that he was evil and that he must go away from the village. I challenged them and they attacked me." "All right, I was possibly a bit harsh on you but Mother still wouldn't agree with you, she would say 'A soft answer turns away wrath," said John the less.

"I know, I'm sorry" replied his younger brother.

That night, the members of the Tilly family were a little subdued over their supper of bread, cheese and dried fish washed down with their regular beer. Each had their own thoughts, each their own concerns and worries, each their own dreams and hopes for the future.

Busy in the Kitchen ...

'Worlds Apart'

Two – 'Preparation'

For the next three days, it was frantic mayhem. Everybody in the family had their jobs to do. Mother was in charge directing operations from the kitchen. Large baskets were open on the table, they were packed, one for food, one for clothes and one for New-Found-Land. Each basket was lined with oiled sailcloth to keep everything dry.

Mary Watts was in and out of the kitchen all the time. She was baking and sorting out the items of food which were coming from neighbours and friends. The whole village had become involved in 'the voyage' as it was now called. Someone had provided pork, pickled and salted. Another had provided a large cheese and yet a third had brought a large basket of dried peas and beans. A local farmer had brought a basket full of hens' eggs – these were handled with great care as they were both fragile and a valuable source of nutritious food.

Ice was a problem, both finding it and keeping it frozen. It was vital for freezing the fish when caught. Ruth plucked up courage to ask Her Ladyship for the ice from the Ice House down near the lake at Sopley Hall. The request was granted, two of the lads from the village took a horse and cart, axes and a load of straw. At the Ice House, they hacked out some ice, packed it in wooden boxes, covered it in layers of straw and carted it down to the boat at Christchurch Harbour.

Another problem was of finding suitable clothes, particularly something that would be waterproof or at least protect the crew from the worst of the weather. The normal practice was to paint outer clothes with duck or goose grease, but this took some time to do and they did not have time. Then a friend from another village, hearing about 'the voyage' rode across to Ringwood with several cloaks and breeches, oiled and prepared for use. Footwear was also a problem. It was not easy to find anything which would keep out the water. The normal shoes of the period were pieces of leather wrapped around the foot and laced from the toes to the ankle. These were useless for life on board a fishing boat. Many of the deck-hands worked barefoot, but this was not ideal in the cold of the north Atlantic! The problem was discussed at length with no immediate solution.

Another family offered to prepare a cauldron of pottage, a thick soup containing meat, vegetables and bran. It would be allowed to set in its fat and could be used over several weeks. At least this would provide nourishing food on the outward voyage. Bread was another problem. It was enjoyed as a staple food but after a week or two it would grow mould. In addition they were to take a quantity of flat oatmeal biscuits which would last longer. Even the Lord of the Manor at Ringwood made a contribution of salted venison from his food-store. This was highly prized and would be invaluable as a change from their fish!

On Thursday morning they heard from a travelling peddler who reported that in Romsey, there was a cobbler. He apparently made boots from separate pieces of leather stitched together with a rigid base, which he could make reasonably waterproof. It was therefore quickly decided that John the less and Sarah should borrow a friend's horse and ride to Romsey to buy some boots for the men.

Early on Friday morning, a grey mare was brought across to the Tilly household. A rough blanket had been thrown over its back and a simple bit and bridle had been fitted. "Don't worry," said the owner, "she is a gentle old lady and will take you to Romsey. She knows the way herself." John the less, although muscled and strong was a fisherman and not used to horses. He clambered onto the back of the mare with difficulty but he was able to pull Sarah up easily. She sat side-saddle although there was no saddle to ride! She held on to her brother, glad to be able to spend some time with him before he left for distant places.

There were no roads in the New Forest as we would recognise them today. Instead, there were muddy tracks from village to village, sometimes laid with stones to enable traffic to pass in the winter. The simplest way to get to the town was to travel across country, using whatever tracks they could find.

It was about twenty miles to Romsey, quite a long way for such inexperienced riders, they had to stop several times en-route to give the horse a rest.

They did not know Romsey at all. As they rode down the hill into the town, it seemed a very busy, noisy place full of people, horses and carriages. This was a strange, alien environment as they saw only one or two carriages a week. They stopped at an Inn to ask for directions to the cobbler. They tied up the horse outside and ordered a beer at the bar. It was twice the cost of beer in the village and took all the spare money they had.

They asked for directions to the cobbler who lived on Abbey Street. Eventually they found the right house and the right man. "Yes", he said, "We do have several different styles of waterproof boots, please come in and try them."

"We do not have much time and cannot wait for boots to be made," replied Sarah, as she proceeded to describe the planned voyage to the other side of the world. John the less, tried on several boots and at last found one that fitted reasonably comfortably. "We will take two pairs of your boots," said John. They paid the bill which meant that everything they had earned on Wednesday at Market had now been spent.

The ride home proceeded well until their steed began to gallop down a particularly steep slope. Sarah found herself slipping, before she could correct her position she had slipped further until she was flying through the air.

She fell awkwardly, hitting her arm and her head on the stones which littered the side of the road. Meanwhile, John tried to bring the mare to a halt but she was having none of it. She was going home and having shaken off one person, she had a much lighter load to carry. Eventually, he managed to rein her in but not until he had gone a mile or so beyond where the accident had happened. After a battle, he managed to get the mare to walk back up the hill that they had just flown down. He eventually found his sister. She was sitting on the side of the road with an old woman bending over her, trying to help her to stand.

"I think that she is just winded," cried the woman. "I saw her fall and have been nursing her since. She is slowly coming round."

Sarah started to struggle to her feet as John held her arm, then uncharacteristically, gave her a hug, saying, "I thought you were dead, thank God you are alive." But, although she could stand, her left arm was at an odd angle. John the less, tried to straighten it but Sarah screamed with pain. "We will have to find a branch to use a splint; it looks as if it's broken." Whilst the woman held Sarah she bit her tongue in pain. John searched the surrounding area for a tree with a suitable branch. Meanwhile the woman had been tearing strips of cloth from her skirt and these they used as a rough bandage to fasten the piece of wood to Sarah's arm.

As it was mid-afternoon, they eat their lunch before commencing the difficult journey home. They shared their bread and cheese with their new friend before bidding her "Good speed", thanking her profusely for her help and kindness

After what seemed like an eternity, they rode into Ringwood, Sarah clutching her brother with one hand and the other immobilised by the wooden splint with the boots slung over the horse.

Everybody crowded round as they helped Sarah down to the ground. Emily helped her inside the cottage. Sarah was in real pain. Here was a very real cause of concern, if Sarah developed a fever, she could become seriously ill and even die! They carried her upstairs between them and laid her on one of the beds "Keep her warm" was the cry as they loaded blankets on her and fed her from a mug of broth. "We will get 'Bill the Healer' to come and have a look at you and prescribe a poultice for your bruises". If you develop a fever we will get some leeches," said Mother. "Oh, not the leeches", cried Sarah, "I hate them."

In spite of the chaos surrounding the returned travellers, the preparation for 'the voyage' had been progressing all day and continued to unfold during the evening. Earlier in the day, William had ferried his Father and young Richard to Christchurch harbour where they had met Jo and Thomas. Their first task was to engage a group of ten or twelve fishermen who would act as deck hands on the voyage. These men would do most of the actual fishing work, gut and smoke the fish in readiness for the return trip and hoist the sails. They selected men that had been with them before who commenced immediately in getting the boat ready for sailing.

While this was taking place, William and his brother Richard went back up the river Avon to fetch several loads of stores. The men worked from 'stem to stern'. They checked every item of equipment, every rope, and every piece of timber. They examined the hull of the boat carefully to see whether or not it was damaged. This was done as the tide went out leaving the hull of the boat almost totally exposed. On deck, the woodwork was checked to make sure all of the planks were secure and any splinters were rubbed down. The sails were carried on shore and spread out on the stone quay side – several holes were repaired before they were furled and roped so that when required they could be raised easily. Special attention was paid to the halyards, a new one which had been bought some months ago was fitted to the jib mast. The storage space in the hold of the boat was scrubbed clean and several new poles were fitted. These would hold the storage baskets in place when full of food on the way out and fish on the return voyage.

There was an air of excitement abroad during the Friday as the boat was made ready. This was heightened as the boys delivered their first load of stores on to the dock side. The wooden boxes of ice, packed with straw were stowed first below the water-line so that the ice would not melt too quickly. Next, the barrels of salt and the other items of equipment that would be needed when they arrived in New-Found-Land. Finally came the food – first the larger items like the meat and the vegetables followed by more delicate items like eggs and cheese.

By the time they had completed two trips down the river and packed stores into the boat, it was late. Thomas stayed on board with two of the hired men to make sure that the boat was secure whilst everyone else returned home for the night.

When the men reached Ringwood, they were met with the news about Sarah; her fall and broken arm. However, John was very pleased about the boots as he had had major problems on the last trip with his feet being constantly wet and cold.

Sarah was resting, Mother had given her a sedative, a mixture of herbs which had made her relax and sleep. They had bound her arm with strips of cloth to a wooden splint. Hopefully as she was young and fit, she would quickly recover with no long term ill-effects. What particularly worried Emily was that her beautiful daughter would be disfigured with a crooked arm and consequently not eligible to be a suitable bride. But this concern she quickly dismissed from her mind. She had more important things to consider, she had to accept that whatever was God's will had to be accepted gratefully.

Supper was a hurried affair, so much to do and so little time to do it! Then bed for the children, talking for the adults. The events of the day were reviewed in detail; the trip to Romsey, the checking and provisioning of the boat, the concerns about Sarah. All of these things occupied their minds as they got ready for bed and a well earned sleep.

Saturday was the last full day to get everything ready. Everyone was up early; Even Ruth had been able to negotiate the day off work by offering to do extra time the next week. Only Sarah was incapacitated. William had promised, however, that later in the day when he had transported all of the goods down to Christchurch, he would take her as well. The oiled cloaks and breeches were now loaded together with the perishable items of food – the bread which had been baked early that morning, the ham that had been boiled. A large basket of fruit that the village boys had picked – plums and greengages, the apples, pears and soft fruit which were not yet ripe for picking. These were not too popular with the fishermen but were important, everything had to be cooked, fresh fruit was thought to be bad and unhealthy.

Finally, the large cauldron of pottage and the barrels of beer were loaded on to the small boat by John the less and William, and were carefully transported down the river. On the quay side a small crowd of onlookers had gathered to watch the final loading and preparations. Christchurch harbour was quite a busy place in those days. Although small fishing boats were commonplace here a major trip was very much the exception. The crew of the boat was drawn from local families so there was a particular interest in this adventure.

By late afternoon, all of the Tilly family and all of the Watts family had arrived on the quay-side and were talking excitedly with the families of the crew. They had brought food for their men-folk and personal items, all of this had to be stowed below. Finally, the boat was fully laden and ready to depart early on Monday morning. But first, 'the voyage' needed the blessing of God and they returned home to worship God on Sunday, the Lord's Day, when they would seek divine support for their venture.

Sunday morning dawned bright and clear but within a couple of hours it was raining. It was a fine rain which was almost mist and made everything damp. No work was to be done on Sunday by our friends in Ringwood. They were part of a new trend in religious thinkers of the day, they were what might be called; 'Congregational Puritans'. Following the previous century's conflict between Roman Catholic and Protestant Christians, the Church of England had been established. Under the Act of Uniformity in 1559, everyone was expected to conform to the rules of the established church. Failure to do so could result in fines, imprisonment or even death.

On that particular Sunday morning, the Tilly family and their next door neighbours rose early and prepared themselves for the Lord's Day. They did not do any kind of physical work on that day, believing that as God rested on the seventh day from his work at Creation, so should they. They had a family breakfast together. Sarah seemed a little better that morning and came downstairs to share in the meal. They were all dressed in their Sunday best, the men; clean shaven wearing a long linen shirt and baggy knee-high breeches, the women wearing dresses and a head covering of a coif (bonnet). After breakfast, the rain had stopped and they were all able to walk across the village green to the home of John and Hetti Stott. They were yeoman farmers and had larger house with a more suitable room in which twenty or thirty people could meet. The children all sat on the floor at the front, the older folk on benches around the wall. The dining table had been covered with a white cotton sheet and on it was a pewter plate with a piece of bread and a small flagon of wine.

John Stott sat in his chair, the only one in the room, and led the service. He began by welcoming everyone and reminding them of the imminent departure of three significant members of the congregation. He then stood and led the worshippers in prayer. This was not read from a prayer book nor spoken in Latin but a prayer given in his own words as he felt moved to pray. Following this, they all stood for a hymn which they had learnt together from the book of Psalms. As only John Stott, his wife, Mary Watts and Sarah could read, these four took it in turns to read from the Bible. They had only just been able to obtain their own copy of the new 1611 translation. They were finding it quite amazing and exciting to be able to read God's word for themselves.

There followed quite a long sermon, based on the care that God gives to those who follow his teaching. They all listened with careful attention to the words which were so pertinent to the whole company. Another psalm was sung followed by a reading from the record of the 'Last Supper'. The actual communion of bread and wine was introduced by prayer and then the bread was blessed and passed around the adult members who all shared in the celebration. The sharing of wine followed a similar pattern. After prayer and a period of silence they moved round the group, greeting each other with a hug and a kiss or a handshake.

Before they left, there was a special prayer for the fishermen, asking especially for God's blessing on those travelling and those left behind.

When the service was complete they bid each other 'farewell' and walked to their respective homes for their last lunch together. At the Tilly household this was a meal shared in a feeling of uncertainty. Yet in the knowledge that they had now committed themselves to God's care and that He would protect them.

Each member of the family had their own thoughts, John Tilly, was apprehensive about going back into the unknown, sad at leaving home again, excited by the forth-coming challenge. Emily was worried at having to bid farewell to her husband yet reasonably confident in faith that he would return safely. Ruth, jealous of the men travelling to far off places, reluctantly resigned herself to her life of servitude. Sarah, still in pain, worried about the future for herself and for the family.

These thoughts and many others crowded into their minds during that afternoon and evening as they all tried to make the day last forever.

Early on Monday morning, while it was still dark, the family were up and about as were many other families in Ringwood and the surrounding villages. William took his father, John the less and Sarah down in his boat first of all, Sarah had determined whatever else, that she was not going to miss one moment of this day. William then returned for the rest of the family. All of the crew were ready and waiting together with Joe, Thomas and many of their families. Some were emotional, others embarrassed whilst some were cracking jokes to conceal their fears. What was apparent was that there was a high degree of emotion amongst everyone on the quay side on that June morning in 1625.

The crew made their way on board, each with his own kitbag of personal things plus some item of food his mother or wife had prepared; a meat pie, a fresh loaf of bread or a container of eggs. Each man found a little bit of personal space below deck and marked his space by leaving his bag and food there.

On deck, all of the ropes, sails and other items were stowed away neatly, ready to be used when required. Each man had his task, each his responsibility.

At last, all of the families were on the quay side. All of the men went ashore for one last time to say goodbye to the respective wives, girl friends and families. There were many tears. The fishermen tried not to show that they were as moved as their women-folk, but often to no avail.

John Tilly, as captain gave the command; "All aboard" and slowly but surely all of the crew gave a last hug to their loved ones and jumped aboard. The small jib sail was hoisted and as the wind started to catch the sail, the ropes were undone on the quay side. The boat slid away from the stone wall and gently moved out across the harbour.

It was difficult to navigate out of Christchurch harbour. There were many sandbanks which changed their position daily and had to be negotiated carefully. Slowly, the boat moved across the harbour past Mudeford Quay and towards the sand bar across the entrance to the harbour. This had to be cleared before the tide turned otherwise they would be grounded before they had even started. Fortunately, everything went well and open sea beckoned, 'the voyage' had begun.

'Worlds Apart'

Three – 'Ruth and Sarah in Different Worlds'

Even before the fishing boat was out of sight, it began. Ruth and Sarah were in disagreement. "How could you make such an accusation, with Father and John the less, barely out of the harbour?" said Sarah. "I tell you its true", said Ruth, "On Thursday when you and I were so busy working hard. There was John, flirting with the new stable girl at Sopley Hall. He only used me as the excuse; he really wanted to see her. I saw the look in his eyes when she appeared. If I hadn't been there, he would have been in the hay barn in two seconds." Sarah was embarrassed and quickly defended her brother; "You mustn't speak like that – it's not nice." said Sarah. "He is a good man and I won't have anything said against him."

Emily suddenly realised that her two daughters were bickering on the quay side in full view of everyone else and that most people would have heard what had been said. "Shush you two, let's get back home and back to work. Ruth, I thought that you were due at Sopley Hall by mid-morning. If you're late, you will not get any money this week. We need every penny, we've spent everything we had and much more on getting the boat provisioned." "Yes Mother," Ruth replied with barely concealed irritation. "Why is it that I have to work long hours whilst Sarah, Richard and Mary barely do anything and the men go sailing off on a voyage of discovery? Why me and not them?"

Emily did not reply, this was an old argument and she had no intention of getting tangled up in it today, of all days. She called across to William; "If you can take Ruth, Richard and Mary back up-river it would be appreciated. If you drop Ruth off at Sopley she can walk across the fields to work. We will sit here and spend some time with the families of the crew." Ruth sighed and knew that she could not win the argument today, so back to work. At least a good part of the day had gone, it wouldn't be too bad. She was dropped off near Sopley Mill and she made her way to the kitchen door of the mansion.

Sopley Hall 1625

Sopley Hall was built in the style of a country house of the period but of modest proportions. It was a three-storey red-brick house with the typical design of Elizabethan houses. Tall chimney stacks dominated the skyline with each wing having large windows to the main rooms. The effect was one of symmetry and power in a rural landscape, speaking of city money amongst rural ignorance and poverty.

The main entrance was up a short drive off the road. A modest frontage hid its more imposing interior that could not fail to impress. Oak entrance doors gave access to a magnificent hall, dominated by the regal sweep of the grand staircase. It was impossible not to follow its curve to the upper floors where the public rooms lay. Heraldic history clothed the walls of the long Elizabethan corridor which connected the library, dining room and main bedrooms. These official rooms demonstrated the status and wealth of the Tichbourne family of Sopley Hall.

A further staircase led one to the quieter sanctuary of the private rooms well away from view. Here the family lived, served by the various members of staff, some of whom lived on the premises, having rooms in the attic. All of the staff, however, shared the kitchen, scullery and the basement rooms during the daytime. Ruth's work was in the kitchen, preparing vegetables, meat and poultry for cooking as well as washing clothes and bed-linen. It was tiring work but the worst thing was not the work but the cook. Claude-Philippe was a very tyrannical but extremely competent cook. He had been coerced by Lady Susan on a recent trip to France to come and work for her at Sopley. Having left his beloved France he now bitterly resented having come to England. Everything about it was 'just awe-full' – the weather, the food and the staff. Not least of which was Ruth, who although quite hard working was often challenging him and disobeyed his instructions because 'she thought she knew better.'

On this Monday morning when Ruth arrived late, he was not in the best of moods. "Why come to work if you can't arrive on time?" He exclaimed. Ruth replied, "You know that my father and brother were leaving England for a long fishing trip this morning. I told you last week that I would be late this morning," with a degree of irritation. Claude-Philippe cut across her excuse; "Anyway, now you are here, her Ladyship would like to see you in the Long Room. You had better smarten yourself before you go upstairs; you look as if you have been to sea yourself."

When Ruth heard this, she trembled inwardly. She couldn't lose her job, not today of all days. Mother would be devastated. It was better than nothing, at least, it paid a little and she had most of her food free! She looked at her face in the polished pans on the rack and grimaced. Her hair was all over the place, her face red and her hands really raw from all the kitchen work. She was a mess. If only she had hair like Sarah and her looks! She wouldn't stay in Ringwood one minute, nor work in this place; she would be off and away. But still, that wasn't to be. She had better go upstairs and present herself before Lady Susan. She washed her face, tidied her hair and went through the servant's door. She passed into the hall of the back stairs, climbed up the stairs to the second floor where she paused to compose herself. Then she pushed open the door on to the corridor. This was an unknown area of the house, she was very, nervous. Worrying as to why she should be summoned in this way.

She paused outside the door into the Long Room, knocked gently and waited trembling for the answer. "Come in", called the voice from within, "Come in and stop shaking girl. I'm not going to tell you off or anything like that. Come over here where I can see you properly." Ruth did as she was told and wondered what on earth her Ladyship was going to say next. She could not have been more surprised.

"I would like you to become my maid-in-waiting," she said. "I have had good reports from the housekeeper about you. The chef says that you have a good head with your own opinions, which is good. I need a new maid. I need someone who can be trusted but also one who has ideas and opinions. Would you like to do that? It would mean, however, that you would have to live-in for most of the week and be at my beck and call. Whenever I want you – I would expect you to respond immediately. However, I would be prepared to pay a little more than you receive now."

"I am honoured to be asked", stuttered Ruth, "Of course I would love to work for you, and I shall be pleased to work for you."

"You will need to smarten up your appearance. You will need to get some new clothes and have your hair cut. You will need to stop trembling in front of me and particularly in front of Sir Richard and any visitors to the Hall we may be entertaining. We are going to teach you some decorum and I am quite looking forward to it" stated Lady Susan with a grin.

"Yes, your Ladyship" said Ruth, backing out of the room with as much confidence as she could muster. The rest of her day was spent in a whirl, the peeling of potatoes and the trimming carrots and beetroot was done in minutes. She even asked the cook if there was anything she could do to help him. When her work was complete, she hung up her apron and took off her mop cap for the last time and left for home. She ran and skipped and sung all the way back to Ringwood, utterly forgetting that earlier the same day they had all said goodbye to her father and brother, John the less.

As soon as she arrived in Ringwood, she ran to the cottage, bursting in and shouting; "I'm free – I have got a new job, Lady Susan has asked me to become her new maid and I won't have to peel potatoes or clean or wash dirty sheets ever again, and …." Her voice trailed off into uncertainty as she saw the look on her Mother's face. "Have you forgotten that your father and brother are at this moment battling with the wind and waves. Facing that awful weather and will not see land for weeks, even months and all you can think about is yourself? If you think that is the 'end of service', then you have another think coming. You will be at her beck and call every moment of the day and night and where are you going to sleep, pray?" "She has offered me accommodation at the Hall during the week. I won't have to walk home each day – that will be great!" replied Ruth.

"I am not quite so sure about that", said Mother, "I am not at all keen on you sleeping at the Hall, you will be mixing with all sorts of people. Most of whom do not believe in God, let alone worship him in the way we believe to be right. I am not at all sure that father would approve of what you are proposing to do. It is so worldly at the Hall with their drinking parties, and their friends from London coming to stay. Some of whom bring women to stay who are not their wives!" said mother with a worried frown on her face. "Oh, Mother, don't fuss – it will be alright, you'll see," replied Ruth as she dived up the stairs to tell her sisters.

By contrast, Sarah was feeling very low, her arm ached abominably. She was already missing her big brother and life just seemed to be getting worse each minute. She couldn't go out easily and she couldn't concentrate at home either. Then Ruth had come bounding up the stairs with her good news, that just made matters worse. There were just so many problems in life and she couldn't find any answers.

The following day Ruth was up as usual before dawn, but this time she was humming to herself. She packed her little bag with some personal things, her nightshirt and her Sunday best clothes, just in case she needed them. She said good bye to the rest of the family. They were just getting dressed and washed as she left the house. The road had suddenly become much shorter as Ruth made her way to her new life at the Hall. On arrival, she was shown her new bed in the attic, next to the stable girl, Bess who her brother had made a pass at the previous week – how long ago that seemed, just five days ago but it seemed like eternity.

She was given a long list of instructions, most of which she could not remember ten minutes later! Her first task was making all of the preparations for her Ladyship's bath and toilet arrangements. Water had to be carried from the kitchen up the back stairs to her Ladyships' bedroom. The copper bath tub also had to be carried upstairs and then the various items of clothing and undergarments had to be prepared. She had no idea which dress and shoes would be required, but hazarded a guess. She then invited her mistress to have her bath, the first she had had for several months as she had had no maid to prepare it for her and the fact that no-one was particularly bothered about washing – anyway.

Breakfast had to be prepared and taken up to the bedroom, bread rolls and tender pieces of chicken and venison with a tankard of ale. It was now beginning to dawn on Ruth what she was going to have to do as a lady's maid. It was not going to be easy. But it was better than being a scullery-maid in the kitchen, at the beck and call of the horrible Claude-Philippe.

Once her mistress had risen, completed her toilette and breakfast, Ruth had to clear the away the water, the bath tub and everything else, but before that could be finished. Lady Susan called her and wanted her opinion about which brooch matched her dress and did Ruth like her new painting on the wall in her room? Ruth found this very difficult as she had never been asked her opinion before on jewellery and art. She just responded in her normal honest way, saying that she did not like either. That art was vulgar, that it was often irreligious and should not be displayed. She then stopped, having realised that she should not have been so out-spoken. She went scarlet and stammered an apology for her inappropriate comments. Susan laughed; "That's why I hired you, I have had enough of hypocrisy. You are like a breath of fresh air in this place – you are honest and straight to the point. Thank you for your observations."

The next few days went like lightning – Ruth was so busy that she did not have time to think, but it was fun. She was allowed into rooms she didn't know existed, she was privy to information that no-one else knew about. She learnt some of the darker secrets of the lives of the rich and famous. She learnt that another Manor, by the name of Southavon had also been bequeathed to Lady Susan as well as Sopley. That 'The Will' had just been accepted by the probate court. In celebration of this windfall, there was to be a masked ball in early August at Southavon Manor. This was a really exciting piece of news; this was the stuff of dreams.

Ruth made her way home on Saturday evening, her mind full of all the things that she had seen and heard during the week. She had not given her mother or her brothers and sisters one thought, definitely not even considered her Father and brother on the high seas since Monday. Now, walking home she started to think about home – her mother's situation, the narrow confines of her family's existence, yet at the same time there was a peace and a trust that she loved. There was a certain confidence that life was for-ordained by God, that each person had a role to play. Each had a job to be done and that God was in control of life. Therefore one had to respond in thanks, prayer and praise and she certainly had much to be grateful for this week. On reflection, she realised that she was looking forward to their weekly religious service at their friend's house.

When Ruth arrived home there were questions from everyone and Ruth tried hard to answer them all. Yet at the same time she wanted to know how they had coped with market day, how William had been getting on and so on. It seemed as if she was now missing home for the first time in her life. Somehow, she had suddenly grown up. Her Mother thoughtfully reflected, "I like this new Ruth, she's nice, she is becoming aware of the wider world and of her responsibilities. Maybe her new job will be good for her after all."

Sarah, by contrast had had a very different week. First of all there had been her broken arm and all the bruises. Then on Monday, her Father and brother had left for 'the voyage'. Then on Monday night, her sister had come home all excited about her new job. Sarah was frustrated and unhappy. She had tried hard not to moan but it was hot and unpleasant in bed. But if she got up, she couldn't do anything. Most of the household tasks were beyond her. For the first time in years she was of little use on Market Day. So, she just read, thought and talked. She had so many questions to ask and the answers did not satisfy her.

Why couldn't people give her straight forward answers to her questions rather then evading or prevaricating? On Thursday morning she was so frustrated that she decided to go for a long walk on her own, to find a quiet place in the forest. A place where she could try to think and sort out in her mind some of those bothersome questions.

She put together some bread, cheese and pickle with some freshly-squeezed lemon juice, packed them in her bag and off she set, saying to her mother that she would be out for an hour or two and not to worry. She walked down to the Millstream, crossed over by the bridge and down the track towards the woods. She kept walking into the country. Soon all she could see were the sheep and the ponies, but they took no notice of her. The bluebells had come and gone, all the primroses and buttercups were in full flower and the sun was shinning through the young fresh leaves. She thought that it was good to be alive! After about an hour and half, she spotted a large tree, fallen by the side of the track, she made her way to this and sat down to think.

She tried to analyse her thoughts into broad areas but she realised it was well nigh impossible. All the questions seem to bubble up one after the other; Why was she alive? Why did people suffer? Why were some people very rich and others very poor? Were women really inferior to men?

Sarah was a bright young woman with lots of questions troubling in her mind. The real problem was that nobody wanted to answer her. Most said; "Shush – young women shouldn't bother their heads which such things. Things are meant to stay as they are, that's the way God made it and we should accept it." But, Mary Watts had taught her to read and think for herself. Mr Stott on Sundays had also challenged her to think, even if he wasn't very keen on her asking questions in public. He said that "Women should be in silence,' as Scripture clearly stated!"

As soon she started to think about Sundays, a whole barrage of new questions assailed her; Were the priests right in saying that they were appointed by God, possessed by the Holy Spirit and were they the only people who could explain God's teaching? Why were people so cruel to each other, particularly in the name of religion?

Sarah in thought ...

For a moment, sitting there in the peace of a summer's morning with the birds singing, the sun shinning through the leaves with the sheep and ponies in the background, she felt to be at peace with herself. Although she had all these questions fighting for answers, in reality, the world was a beautiful place and life was good and she thanked God for it.

Life was strange, she mused. On the one hand; there was suffering, bloodshed and death caused by man – his selfishness and greed. On the other hand: there was purity, peace and beauty – designed by God? Was this what Mr Stott had been talking about when he described a future Kingdom of God upon earth, when he had quoted the prophet Isaiah; 'The desert shall blossom as the rose. It shall blossom abundantly, and rejoice with joy and singing.'

What a wonderful picture, she thought, something to hope and pray for, something to imagine in the midst of their life of hardship and suffering.

Then and there, Sarah decided that she had to focus on the future as well as the present. This would help her to cope with the problems of her daily existence. Life at home with all its hard work and life without her father and brother was difficult. Even if she didn't have any answers to her questions, she could at least accept the present drudgery if she concentrated on future peace and happiness, she decided. She then remembered another quotation, a quotation she decided would be her motto; "Having food and raiment therewith be content".

With these words ringing in her ears, she unpacked her lunch and contentedly ate. She sat for ages just watching the birds, the squirrels, the many insects and butterflies, marvelling at their beauty and design. By mid-afternoon, she realised the time and guiltily got up and made her way back home through the forest. Although she hadn't talked to anyone, she now felt more at peace in her mind than she had for weeks. For the next few days she worked to the best of her ability despite her injured arm. She worked hard, helping her mother and the rest of the family with the household tasks. Accepting in good grace her responsibilities.

The next Sunday was a strange day without the two Johns, Emily felt really alone although William was very good in the absence of his Father, but he was not her husband. Both of the older girls were happy, the one having obtained a new exciting job, the other having found a certain peace of mind. As usual they all rose early and prepared for their Sunday service in their best clothes, breakfasted and walked across to the house of their friends, John and Hetti Stott.

On this particular Sunday there were some visitors at the service, a middle aged couple from Fording bridge and a young man who was obviously dressed in city attire. Smart and well-spoken, he seemed very much at ease in his doublet and hose. Mr Stott introduced the visitors to the others present. The young man was a Mr Charles Tyler, he was staying with the Stott's for a few days and would be giving the talk. After the usual Psalms, Bible readings and prayers, Mr Tyler was asked to address everyone. "Good Morning", he began, "I would like to talk about obedience this morning, the ways in which we should obey our conscience and be obedient to the teaching of the Bible. The Bible says; "Do not steal, do not commit adultery, do not take the name of God in vain." Sarah listened intently and thought him a wonderful preacher answering some of her questions. He stated that man was on this earth to obey and not to question, to develop a conscience in order to know right from wrong, to be able to obey the teaching of the Bible. By the end of the talk, Sarah was ready to commit herself totally to a life of obedience, then and there.

Lunch that Sunday was an animated affair, without Father and John the less to modify the extremes, the two girls were volubly expressing their opinions; "I thought he was very interesting", said Sarah. "An educated man who taught from the Bible, I thought it was a wonderful talk," she stated. Ruth immediately challenged this with; "He was a hypocrite – he doesn't know anything about obedience – he has never had to obey anyone else. I think, that he has always been asked if he would like to do something. He doesn't understand the first thing about living. He is just a clever man who has simple answers to difficult questions." She was now into her stride and kept going in even stronger tones. "He doesn't actually know anything - if he did, he would know that a conscience is something within your own mind and it is not just about obedience to certain rules. In fact, I think that each individual should act individually as each of us will have to stand before the Judgement Seat of Christ on our own. Isn't that right Mother?"

"Yes, you are right Ruth, we do need to listen carefully to what other people tell us, just because they sound right and dress well, does not mean that they always speak the truth. When you are a little older Sarah my dear, you will understand."

Ruth, feeling that she had scored a point over her clever sister felt superior for once. Yet at the same time wishing that she did not have these jealous thoughts about Sarah, who could not help being clever and beautiful. That was just the way it was. She suddenly realised that she had better get moving in order to walk back to Sopley Hall before dark. William offered to row her down the river to save her the walk, this she gratefully accepted and soon they were on their way.

Sarah, stung by the mild rebuke at the dinner table, tried hard to concentrate on the various domestic duties, not allowing her emotions to surface. Although Charles Tyler didn't really answer her questions, she thought that he was rather a nice man, she liked his educated eloquence and manner.

Ruth arrived quite early back at Sopley Hall to find that outside the house were parked several carriages and horses. Inside the house it was quite full of people. People that she didn't know or know anything about. She crept carefully upstairs to her room, changed her shoes and put on her maid's uniform. She thought that she ought to go and find her Ladyship and see what was happening and if she was needed. She carefully wended her way through the crowd of smart city folk that all seemed to be drinking glasses of wine and laughing. They were all dressed outrageously for a Sunday, she thought, the ladies in gowns with low, plunging necklines, the men in doublet and hose in bright colours with shoes sporting polished buckles. It was a kaleidoscope of colour, a pageant of clothes and money. Ruth was amazed as she carefully searched and found her mistress in the centre of a group of admiring men and women.

"Madam, I am sorry that I wasn't here for you, is there anything I can do?" she blurted. Scared that she might easily say or do the wrong thing. "Why hello", said one of the men near to Ruth. Turning to Lady Susan he continued; "Is this the girl you were telling us about, the one who has her own opinion on everything?" "Yes", replied Lady Susan laughing. "Yes, Ruth comes from a family of 'Separatist Puritans'. She has been taught to think for herself and although dangerous, it does make for a much more interesting time. She has strong opinions on fashion, art and politics as well as on religion."

"You must be quite a smart girl", said the gentleman who spoke first, "We shall have to ask your opinion on what is happening in London, you may be able to enlighten us all," he said with a twinkle in his eye.

"Ruth, these ladies and gentlemen have been staying at Braemore House for the past few days. We have all been to Christchurch Priory this morning to service. Afterwards, everyone came back here for lunch." "I am amazed", replied

Ruth, "I have never seen such finery in all my life. It's just amazing." She looked around a little more carefully and gasped at the splendour. A lady over by the door was dressed in a rich purple skirt, a full bright canary yellow blouse with a spectacularly embroidered linen jacket. Another lady had a bodice of scarlet with slashed sleeves showing vivid blue beneath with large pantaloons with a pair of high boots. The men were equally dazzling with a white linen shirt, a cape over the shoulder with brightly coloured doublet and hose. They were also wearing their hair quite long in a way that Ruth found quite captivating.

"I see that you're not frightened by such people," said Lady Susan, "that is good, I knew that I was right in asking you to be my maid. I have high hopes of you my girl. Now go to the kitchen and check with the cook so that he can provide something for supper before everyone goes home."

Ruth was so excited, "Fancy Lady Susan making those comments about me", she thought as she made her way to the kitchen.

The rest of the evening passed very quickly. Ruth was sent on one errand after another until she was quite dizzy, but she was happy and content. This was quite different from being a scullery maid in the kitchen. This was being an assistant to the host. When everyone had departed home, she made her way to her bed, knowing that she would have to be up early, very early in the morning.

The new week began for the two girls in totally different surroundings. The one - young, intelligent, able to read and write but living in a poor rural environment. Having many questions but with few answers. Determined to be 'content with her lot' but with no possibility of change. Her sister however, was not so intelligent or attractive but more outspoken. She lived in a servile situation but in a wealthy environment with new opportunities.

'Worlds Apart'

Four – 'A Summer Festival and a Masked Ball'

In early August that year, two events took place which were to influence the lives of Ruth and Sarah. The first was the Summer Festival at Ringwood, the second, the Ball at Southavon.

Every year for as long as anyone could remember, Ringwood had staged a Summer Festival. This was part market and part show. It was the opportunity when everyone had a break from work. It's planning occupied people for weeks ahead. Everyone was affected. The event brought many visitors to the area from far and wide. Amongst them were a large number of visiting showmen who travelled around the countryside, exhibiting their wares or presenting their extravagant shows. There were giants and dwarfs, there were insane and deformed folk, everything was on public display in order to earn their families a few extra pence. There were wizards and fortune tellers, there were performing bears and talking parrots – everything that could be vaguely described as entertainment. Sporting events crowned the occasion with one village challenging another in a 'tug of war', and 'climbing a tree' competitions.

The other main event, which was really the purpose of the Festival, was the sale of animals. It was an annual market when sheep, cattle, goats, pigs and poultry could be bought and sold. Most village families had at least one animal, be it a cow or a pig, this provided a basic supply of food, but if the cow had two calves then it made sense to sell at least one of them. If the flock of hens became too large, then the sale of some chicks or hens would come in very useful indeed. Ponies would be rounded-up from the Forest and some of them would be sold and the money divided between the 'commoners'. In the week before the Summer Festival, animals would be driven into Ringwood from all over the Forest and penned around the village, thereby adding to the Festival atmosphere.

As there were no shops In Ringwood or in any other of the villages or small towns in the area, the only items which could be bought would be limited to those sold on the few stalls at the weekly market. Therefore, many items could only be bought at the Summer Festival, items such as, cloth, leather, buckets, farm tools, clothes and cheap jewellery.

This was a very important period of the year for the Tilly family, not only was there extra trade for William but Sarah's skills were in constant demand. Mary's herbs were much sought after as she prepared hundreds of bunches ready to be sold. Emily had great difficulty in keeping her brood together both before and during the Festival as everyone had their jobs to do. Richard managed to avoid much of this being out with his friends most of the time.

Sarah's arm was mending slowly as it was strapped to a piece of wood. Otherwise, she had fully recovered from her fall. One wet July morning, there was an impatient, violent knocking on the door of the Tilly cottage, "Richard, open the door please," called Mother from out the back. Richard went to the door, lifted the latch and in-bound an amazing dog, long legged with an arched back and sharp ears. Behind it followed its owner, an equally long-legged young man. He was dressed in course flannel breeches with a brown, dirty shirt and a leather jerkin, two sizes too small for him. "Oh, I am so sorry" he said apologetically, "I was told to come here for some posters to be painted for the Festival. The door opened and in my dog came and here I am. Sorry to have disturbed you."

At the sound of this commotion, Sarah came downstairs, curious to know who the man was who spoke so interestingly. He took more than a glance at her and grinned," I have been told that someone here paints posters and writes messages," he stated, looking enquiringly at Sarah. She blushed from ear to ear, and stammered, "Yes you have come to the right house and the right person; I would love to do some posters for you." She suddenly realised what she had said and almost fled back upstairs, but something stopped her. This man looked interesting, she wanted to know more about him. It transpired that he was with a group of travelling players who had come to Ringwood to play at the Summer Festival. They had thought that posters displayed in Southampton, Salisbury and Winchester would attract people to the Fair. It was agreed that the following morning Sarah and he would meet. He would bring paper and she would prepare some paints and ink. Sarah was really excited at this new development but Mother cautioned her against developing any ideas in her head about befriending this young man. "You don't know where he comes from, you don't know whether he is Puritan, Catholic or Protestant. You don't know whether be believes or whether he is ..." "Oh, Mother, don't worry," replied Sarah. "I will do this work for him, then he will return to his travelling around the countryside."

For the rest of that day, Sarah busied herself preparing some ink and paint. The ink she made from soot collected from the chimney and mixing it with glue and water. The paints she made from using the juice from various vegetables and herbs, carefully mixing each colour with linseed oil to make a paste. The crimson she made from using cochineal powder mixed with linseed oil. The yellow from concentrated cow's urine mixed with mud. I hope he brings some paper, she thought, we haven't any and it's very expensive.

Early the next morning, before they had even finished breakfast, he was at the door, bursting with energy, his dog bounding around him. Under his arm he carried a bundle of paper. It was a dirty grey colour, course and rough, probably made from old clothes and other rags. "Come on," he called to Sarah, "we have a job to do, we are going to paint posters. It's a lovely day and you're going to show me how it's done." His enthusiasm and excitement were contagious. Sarah found herself excited as she rushed around completing her tasks and collecting her materials together. A task which was not easy with one hand bandaged. "Here, let me help," he cried as he picked up some of the quills and feathers which would be used for painting and writing. "Let's go."

At last they were outside with all their bits and pieces; "I know the ideal place where we can work", said Sarah, as she led the way down the village street to the river. She led him to the place where the washing was often done. A place with large flat stones, here they spread out the paper and weighted the sheets with large stones collected from the river.

"By the way, my name is Nick," said the young man and gravely stood and bowed to Sarah who replied equally seriously. "And mine is Sarah," she said and then burst out laughing. He joined in as they shared a few moments together with a mixture of embarrassment and excitement. The rest of the morning went like lightening, Nick said what he wanted. Sarah painted the larger words and wrote the details at the bottom of each poster. They didn't really talk, they just seemed to get on very well together. After they had completed the work, Sarah stated that she would go home; collect some food and return. They could then sit on the bank of the river and talk while their work dried in the sun.

She brought back a fresh loaf of bread, some cheese, pickle and a leather bottle of ale. "Wow, this is a veritable feast; more food than I have seen in weeks." He exclaimed with a twinkle in his eye. "I have brought food fit for a prince", said Sarah. "I would wish to share it with my princess," was his swift rejoinder. So began, a conversation which lasted all afternoon. It ranged far and wide over all many topics, including the inevitable religion and politics. She learnt that he was an itinerant musician, playing the fiddle for a group of folk singers and dancers. That he had been attending University at Oxford but had decided not to graduate, finding that it was 'just a drunken orgy' for most of the time. He had been sent to Oxford by his father, the Earl of Swanton who lived in Northumberland with his third wife and his many children.

She learnt that although the family were historically Catholic and had supported Queen Mary, he was in fact a Protestant and supported the Royalist cause of Charles I. He explained that he believed that a strong Protestant King who, together with the Church, was necessary. "In order that stability and peace can be achieved, so that everyone can worship God according to the law of the land within the Church of England."

Sarah had never heard this point of view before. She had grown up with parents and family members who all felt that the established church was wrong, that a person's conscience should be the determining factor in matters of religion. Here was an educated man challenging all her preconceptions and prejudices. However, more than that, she was just amazed that here she was, a poor fisherman's daughter talking to the son of an Earl. A man who would in all probability inherit wealth and property. Moreover, she didn't feel out of place but rather challenged and stimulated to think for herself, for once.

Sarah raised all sorts of questions with Nick, questions which she had had for a year or two but no-one had answered her. Questions about life and death, pain and suffering, wealth and poverty. Nick didn't give answers to every question but at least he had also thought about such questions. She asked about the role of women and the education of women, subjects which were normally taboo in both of their worlds. Nick's answer was typical of him; "I have never thought about it so you need to help me," he said with a grin on his face.

"However, I must go," he concluded by mid-afternoon. "I promised to meet my musical friends and we are going to ride to the other towns tomorrow and put-up your posters. Just think about it, tomorrow, your writing is going to be seen and read throughout the region."

"Come back soon," she called after him as he strode off back through the village with her posters under his arm. "I will," he shouted and was gone, leaving Sarah excited by the side of the river.

The days before the Summer Festival passed in a dream for Sarah. She didn't see or hear of Nick until the morning of the Festival. Whilst struggling to move tables and fill them with food for sale, trying at the same time, to keep account of exactly what was on offer. He suddenly appeared at her side, grabbed her free hand and held it tight. "I'm back", he whispered in her ear. "I've missed you. We must meet again. What about tonight after we have finished playing and everyone is drunk with ale? Go down by the river to the stones where we did the painting. I will see you there when it gets dark." Sarah just looked at him, agreement in her eyes.

The rest of the day was spent in hard work by every member of the Tilly family. For them it was 'a once in a year' opportunity to make a little bit of money. Crowds of people came for the Festival, all dressed up, almost as smart as when they went to church. The animal market was an area fenced off with wattle hurdles containing pigs, sheep, goats and cows. There were also wicker baskets containing; chicken, ducks, geese and rabbits. All of these were auctioned off, section by section. The noise and the smell of the animals provided a farm-yard atmosphere for the Festival. This was added to by the stalls of produce and goods, some of which had come from the cities and towns around. All of this was brought alive by the performing artists, each shouting about their respective acts of entertainment. Around the edges of the festival area there were various tents with fortune tellers, magicians and other entertainers. Then finally in the centre of the whole colourful and vibrant scene were the musical performers with Nick in the centre of the group. During the day there were groups of villagers who would join together to dance and in the breaks from the music, there would be 'the tug of war' or 'climbing the tree' contests. It was a rare opportunity to laugh and be drunk, without worrying about food and the future.

Later that night, when most people where at the Inn, Emily resting after a hard day's work, with the younger children in bed, William and Sarah were talking outside. Sarah was weighing up the situation, trying to decide how to slip away without anyone knowing. At last she decided, "I'm just going for a walk to clear my head, I won't be long." "Take care", said William, as she disappeared into the dusk. She hurried to the river to the place of the stones.

The river could be seen as a black mirror reflecting the stars. She became aware of a shadow in front of her, with heart beating she whispered; "Is that you Nick?" In reply, the shadow moved to her side and materialised into a breathing, living person. He held her hand, pulling her towards him as he gently spoke; "Yes, it's me, who did you think it would be?" As they clung to each other in the darkness, they talked quietly about the day and its exciting events. After a little while, Sarah with great reluctance said; "I must be going, William will be worrying about what has happened to me and will coming looking for me, I must go." In reply, Nick asked; "When can I see you next? We are to leave this area soon as we are riding to St Albans for their Summer Fair."

"We could meet again tomorrow night at the close of the Festival. You could come to our service on Sunday at 'Byways' the home of Mrs and Mrs John Stott. You could see how a simple congregation worship without a Prayer Book and without a priest officiating. You could stay to lunch. I am sure no-one will mind. We could have some time together on Sunday afternoon before you leave for St Albans". Said Sarah in a torrent of words, not realising the implications of what she was suggesting "Yes, I would like that, it would be really interesting," replied Nick, with that a hug, Nick managing to kiss her briefly on the cheek. She departed to her family, he to the camp which he shared with his musical friends.

At Sopley Hall, Ruth had been kept very busy and was not able to squeeze even a short time to go home for the Summer Festival. She was bitterly disappointed as this was the first Summer Festival she had ever missed in her entire life! But Lady Susan was adamant, Ruth had work to do. They had much hard work to do in preparation for the Masked Ball which was to be in two week's time at Southavon.

The house at Southavon was not particularly large or attractive. Not much more than a farm house but it had a beautiful formal garden with a timber pavilion erected for the ball would make a wonderful location. It was only about two miles from Sopley Hall but on the other side of the river so one either had to have a boat to cross the river, or ride upstream and back. Not easy for the staff to transport all the furniture and food from one house to the other.

There were going to be one hundred guests at the ball which together with servants and staff would make a lot of people to entertain. Claude-Philippe had prepared the menu which was to be; boars head, venison, mutton, beef. with vegetables washed down with gallons of ale. Being French, he was introducing several unusual items into the meal, anchovies, ragouts and fricassees and a special white wine. He planned to present salads and fresh fruit which were very novel at that time. Of course, it was expected that there would also be many pies, cakes and puddings, all of which had to be made during the week before the ball.

The gardeners spent many hours preparing the grounds of Southavon which were laid out in the formal style. It was like a chessboard with many pathways around rectangles full of lavender and other scented herbaceous plants. It was the period of history for box and yew hedges, for avenues of oak and ash trees with the larger houses having grand avenues of cedar trees. This was not the case at Southavon, there was a formal garden framed by weeping willows on the banks of the River Avon. It was this wide grassy bank which provided Lady Susan the opportunity to have a pavilion built of timber covered in waterproof sail-cloth.

Ruth's job was to assist all of the other staff when required, as well as her normal duties for Lady Susan. But as the day got closer, she was preoccupied with assisting Lady Susan prepare her clothes for the evening. Lady Susan was going to wear black and white. A black full skirt, split to show her white under-skirt when she walked, A white silk bodice with tight fitting sleeves with a black jacket completed the planned wardrobe. Shoes were to be of black leather with silver buckles, a 'feather affair' as head-covering complemented by a feather fringed mask completed her Ladyship's attire. Ruth had never seen anything like it.

The whole scene was amazing, the food, the clothes, the setting for the ball. Ruth just reeled from the extravagance of the event and realised that by comparison, her family were very poor. What her Ladyship spent on just her own outfit could keep her whole family fed for a year.

The Masked Ball

When the day dawned, Ruth looked out on the rain which fell steadily all day, with despair. Fortunately they had moved all the furniture required the day before, all the food and the cooking equipment. Ruth had already persuaded her brother William, to ferry people across the river. However, they would still have to walk from the boat-crossing up to the house. They would just have to get wet.

In reality, it made the event more memorable, some people didn't arrive, presumably frightened of getting their feet wet, thought Ruth. To be honest, she realised she would not want her shoes wet and her gown spoiled by the rain, knowing how much the clothes had cost.

By early evening, most of the guests had arrived at Sopley Hall and were making their way through the wet grass, across on the river and on to Southavon. It was different, it was beautiful; the birds in full voice and the fields fresh and green. The air had been washed clean by the rain. Ruth really noticed the scent of the August evening, usually, the smell everywhere was just awful, village streets were public sewers but that night was special – clean and fresh. She accompanied her Ladyship, holding her skirts, keeping her as dry as possible and making sure the mud did not splash on her. Sir Richard was also accompanying her Ladyship. He had returned home from London to celebrate his wife's inheritance.

As they neared the gardens of Southavon, Ruth became aware of the guests, each in their beautiful gown each masked. The men in white linen shirts with brightly coloured doublet and hose. Most of the them wearing quite long hair and some with the occasional moustache – something that was new to Ruth. By now the rain had eased and it was just a light drizzle. Music was being played gently in the background as they made their way through the gates and into the walled garden. Everyone cheered and waved their hands in the air as Lady Susan walked carefully around the pathways and entered the pavilion. Sir Richard walked across and took her by the hand swinging her into the first dance of the evening. Everyone else followed, Ruth was mesmerised as she stood in the background not daring to breathe lest the dream be shattered. The colours, the sounds, the dresses, the men! It took her breath away.

She had to help with the food, making sure that the plates were replenished when empty, clearing away the empty glasses and the dirty plates, meanwhile, and keeping an eye on her Ladyship so that if she needed anything she was there at her side in a second. As darkness fell on the company, there was a move towards the river, drinking and shouting as they went. Just before midnight a flotilla of boats came sailing along the river, all painted in different colours with dancers, acrobats and musicians performing. As they passed the assembled throng, fireworks were let off with many a bang and flash of light. Everyone cheered and flung their hats into the air at the same time whipping off their masks to reveal their true selves. There were many gasps, as people realised with whom they had been dancing during the evening.

The dancing and drinking continued till dawn when breakfast was prepared for those wishing to eat. However the majority wended their way to back to the boat to be ferried back to Sopley Hall and their awaiting carriages. What a night, thought Ruth. As she, along with the rest of the servants, cleared the debris and repaired the damage of a hundred revelers. Eventually, it was time to accompany Lady Susan back home, caring for the dress and her gifts of jewellery.

It took time to re-gain normality at Sopley Hall. In a way, things weren't quite ever the same again for Ruth. It was if Lady Susan had adopted her as her daughter and in so doing, changed the way she spoke to her. Ruth became aware of this change a few days later, when, while she was combing Lady Susan's hair, she was unexpectedly asked; "Why don't you go to your local church to worship God, I'm curious?" Ruth was a little taken aback and was not sure how to answer, particularly as her mistress was a Royalist with strong religious views. But after a moment or so to think about it, she replied; "We believe that everybody is responsible for their own salvation. We believe that everyone should worship God as their own conscience dictates, just as the Bible teaches."

"But how do you know what the Bible teaches, if you cannot read?" questioned her mistress further. "I suppose I depend upon what my parents have taught me and that which our friends and neighbours teach when we meet together. It's also a matter of simple logic, I have to think about what I hear, then compare that with life and what I observe," stated Ruth, gaining more in confidence as she explained her faith. "If Jesus and the Apostles taught a way of life which was to keep away from evil and to do good at all times, if the church leaders cheat and lie, if they kill people when Jesus said, ' do not kill'. Then they are being hypocrites and I do not want to follow them or worship in their churches."

"That is alright if what you say is sanctioned by the king and by the courts of the land, but it is breaking the law to speak as you do. The punishment is imprisonment or even hanging," said Lady Susan with feeling," I have some sympathy with what you are saying but do not let my husband hear you or he will have you arrested and imprisoned. Your secret is safe with me. I think that it would be helpful for you to explain to me how you understand these matters and in return, I will teach you how to read and write," offered Lady Susan.

So it was agreed that Ruth was able to talk to her mistress about her faith and Ruth would learn how to read. Each morning, they would have an hour or two talking about religion. Lady Susan had her own copy of the King James Bible. Ruth learnt how to read the words and she would then explain the passage as she had been taught at home and at the services she had attended.

Back in Ringwood, Sarah had been explaining to her Mother about her friendship with young Nick. About how she thought he was wonderful, that she could listen to him explaining things for hours and not get bored. "He's interesting and intelligent, he's learnt to write and studied books and can answer all my questions," defended Sarah. "But," said Mother, "he's not one of us, he does not worship God in the way we believe to be right. His family do not worship God acceptably. What did you say his name was?" questioned Mother with some trepidation. "Nick, I think that is short for Nicholas and his family name is, er... er... Swanton from the north of England."

"No", cried Mother," it cannot be the family 'Swanton' who supported Queen Mary, if it is, then this lad's grandfather provided safety for Queen Mary, Bloody Mary, as she made her way south to overturn Queen Elizabeth.."

"But that's all history, it's years ago," said Sarah, "Nick says that his Father is a strong Protestant, he was a supporter of King James and now of King Charles." "Yes, but that could be fateful for us," challenged Mother, "he will support the teaching of the clergy and the courts, they will lock us up in prison for worshipping God as we do."

"No, I don't think you should worry so much," cried Sarah, "he's not involved in politics, he's merely playing his fiddle with a group of travelling musicians and … I like him."

"If we end up in prison – you may want to think again," concluded Mother in a tone of concern. Anyway, we need to get ready for Sunday, we shall see what your Nick thinks about that."

Sunday was overcast with cloud threatening to obscure the sun all day. Ruth had not returned home the previous night due to her work, preparing for the ball. Sarah was very excited, not quite sure whether Nick would attend their service or not. If he did make an appearance, she wondered how everyone else would react to him. She was sure he would win over the womenfolk but she was not quite so sure about the men. If he said anything about the way in which they worshipped, there would be a strong reaction.

They all dressed as usual in their Sunday-best and made their way across to the home of the Stott's. Everyone was there including the family of urchins who now attended regularly. Just as they were about to start, the door opened quietly and in slipped Nick. He made his way carefully to where Sarah was sitting on one of the side benches, aware that everyone was silently watching him. He nodded acknowledgement to Mr Stott and Mrs Tilly and sat down. The service proceeded as usual with Psalms, Bible Readings, Prayer and a talk from one of the other men present. When it came to the sharing of the bread and wine of the communion, Nick did not take part but sat quietly, with head bowed. He seemed lost in thought, as Sarah took a sideways look at him. After the service, Sarah introduced Nick to everyone present. They welcomed him into their midst, several saying that they hoped he had enjoyed their service.

As they walked back across the village, Nick seemed to re-gain his usual effervescent personality. Teasing and laughing with the younger children whilst challenging Sarah to respond to him. But it was not until they were all sat down to lunch that William asked the question which they were all burning to ask; "Well, what did you think about our service this morning? Are we all heretics?"

Nick took a moment or so before replying carefully, "It was strange; no priest, no incense, nothing in Latin, no prayer-book, no altar, just a simple meeting of friends talking about God. I liked it, but I don't think it was right. It still seems to me that you need a divinely appointed priest who has been educated, who can lead and instruct everyone else."

William replied; "That's interesting because we do not believe that any of the items you listed are needed for worship. The Bible teaches that in the First Century they met in houses and according to Acts 2:42, they shared in 'the Apostles doctrine, and fellowship, and in breaking of bread and in prayers'. There is no mention anywhere of priests, incense, Latin, prayer book or altars. These have all been invented by the established church. Mostly by the Catholic Church and the Protestant Church has not relinquished these traditions of men."

At this point, Ruth interjected," As for being educated at university before you can teach others. I hear it said often that only a few at university learn anything. Most spend their time in drinking and womanising. With the schools of Divinity being the worst offenders. Even then, for those graduating and seeking a church – most are appointed because they have friends in high places, not because they have any spiritual wisdom and desire to teach their congregation."

After these comments, Nick became animated; he sensed that in this family there was intelligence and understanding of matters which had concerned him for many months. Here were people who cared about life, who had principles and put them into practice, even in defiance of the authorities. Nick launched into a series of observations about religious worship as he had seen it at home and at university. Each member of the Tilly family joined in the conversation in their own way. Peter expressing his thoughts simply, "You should always speak the truth, whatever the cost" and even Mary, normally shy and retiring, contributed her thoughts by saying that, "If you work hard, if you think carefully and do what is right, God will be pleased with you and will bless you."

The afternoon went all too quickly and before anyone realised it, the evening was upon them. Nick had to leave, as the following day he and his friends were travelling to St Albans. Nick bade leave of the family, thanking them for the day which had been so illuminating. Sarah whispered to him that she would meet him when darkness fell at 'The Stones' where they had met before...

That night as it grew dark, Sarah, having escaped some of the domestic tasks, made her way trembling to the place of meeting. Excited and a little scared at the prospect of meeting Nick and the possibility of a more intimate time with him. She lingered at 'The Stones' but no-one came. With her heart hammering and her thoughts full of dread and uncertainty, she waited until she knew that he wasn't coming. She collapsed in a heap and sobbed bitterly. She was still there an hour later when William found her and led her home. Her big brother guiding her, speaking softly and gently to her, giving her support that only a big brother can do.

What became of Nick, Sarah was not to learn for several months. In the meantime, she gradually recovered her self-esteem and immersed herself once more in her work at home. She often rehearsed the events of that week in her mind, savouring each moment, believing in her heart that she would see Nick again and re-new their special friendship.

Meanwhile, at Sopley Hall, Ruth was working harder than ever. She was not only doing all the work as Lady Susan's maid but also helping the house-keeping staff with their duties. At the same time she was also learning how to read. Each morning, when she had finished her duties, she went to Lady Susan's room to share in discussion of some religious topic. They decided to begin with the Book of Genesis and see how they progressed. Ruth would read a few verses, then they would discuss what they had read. Ruth trying to remember what her Father had said about the passage and sharing those thoughts she could remember. After an hour or so, they both felt exhausted with the concentration, Ruth would leave to get on with her duties whilst Lady Susan would sit thinking about what she had heard.

Sir Richard had decided to stay at Sopley Hall for the time being rather than return to London. The city was such a foul, stinking place during the summer. He liked the river and the meadows at such a time in the year when everything was fresh and sweet-smelling. He was a tall, quite handsome man, always used to getting his own way as a man of influence and money. He had land and houses of his own in North Hampshire and in London. Now that his wife had inherited properties in South Hampshire he had decided to move there for the summer.

He mused about whether or not to build a new house at Southavon or re-furbish the house at Sopley. He quite liked Sopley Hall, but it really needed some money spent on it, some new furniture, some new tapestries and some paintings. if King Charles was to visit him next year, which he had promised he would do, he really needed to do some planning and spend some money.

Then there was the question of an heir. This matter concerned him all the time, they had tried for children but so far in their three year marriage, Susan had not become pregnant. It was very important for Sir Richard that the family line was continued, not least because he needed an heir to inherit his land and houses. In addition, there was also the small matter of the family title and heritage. He needed a male heir as a matter of urgency.

Sir Richard also had doubts about Susan herself. Although she was quite attractive and had brought with her an excellent dowry, he doubted her loyalty to himself and to the crown. He was a royalist, believing that the king was divinely appointed and that his laws were sacrosanct. The previous king, James, had pursued policies of neutrality, trying to balance the Protestant reformers against the Catholic extremists. He had reinforced the power of the Established Church and had demanded that everyone worship in a proscribed manner using the Book of Common Prayer. As a loyal Member of Parliament, Sir Richard believed it was his clear responsibility to maintain the status quo. However, he had picked up-rumours from the servants, that his wife was being taught heretical ideas from her maid, whose family were Puritan extremists. This was troubling Sir Richard considerably.

However, Sir Richard was rather smitten by the young maid himself, she was not attractive in the normal sense of the word, yet she had an inner strength of personality, she didn't seem like a normal serving girl. He carefully planned to trap the young girl into a situation and then observe her reactions.

One evening when Lady Susan had retired to bed early, Sir Richard waited in the shadows near the entrance to the back stairs. At last, Ruth came along the corridor and as she turned to open the door, Sir Richard grabbed her wrist with one hand and put his other hand over her mouth. Initially, she struggled, but he whispered in her ear to go with him quietly to his rooms. She submitted. Her heart was thudding violently and her thoughts were racing as she considered what might happen to her. She was led along the corridor and down the main-staircase to the Master bedroom. He seized the lamp from the stairs and opened the door into his room. Once the door was shut he released his victim and invited her to sit opposite him. 'If he was going to rape me, he would have got on with it and not allowed me to sit down', she thought gratefully.

"I hear that you have been teaching my wife about the Bible and putting all sorts of ideas into her head. Ideas that are false and illegal. Is that true?" He asked in an authoritative tone that could not be ignored.

Ruth thought fast, if she said 'yes', she would be dismissed, her ladyship and her family would be in serious trouble. If she said 'No', she would be a liar, denying her faith, her family and her God. So after second's hesitation, she replied carefully; "Please forgive me. I meant no harm. Yes, you're Ladyship and I have been talking about the Bible. She is teaching me to read, and I have been answering her questions."

Sir Richard angrily responded "What do you mean, answering her questions? You were using the opportunity to teach her falsehood. You were using your privileged position as Lady Susan's maid to teach matters which are heretical and illegal. You have brought damnable heresies into my house. You, infiltrator. You viper."

Ruth shook violently, she was frightened. She had not seen anyone as fearsome as this before. Then, as suddenly as it had erupted, Sir Richard's anger evaporated and he was calm and spoke quietly yet with a clear message to Ruth.

"If you stay here tonight, in my bed, you will be able to continue to work here and I will overlook your indiscretions. But only as long as you cease trying to convert my wife. If, however, you will not stay here tonight, then your employment is finished and you will be reported to the authorities," said Sir Richard.

Ruth quaked in her inner being, what a terrible dilemma. She had been taught to keep herself pure and undefiled until her wedding night. Yet if she did not accept his ultimatum, she and her family would be finished. They would lose everything and she might be imprisoned or even deported as a slave.

At that moment. There was a scream on the stairs outside the room. A tremendous commotion erupted. Sir Richard moved quickly. He pushed Ruth into a cupboard and locked the door. He flung open the door onto the stairs to find one of the other servant girls clutching her dress to her body as she screamed; "It's dark and I was attacked as I came up the stairs and ..." Sir Richard interrupted the frightened girl, telling her to go the kitchen and report the events to the housekeeper, asking her to investigate.

When he returned into the bedroom, he unlocked the cupboard and pulled out the frightened Ruth, who looked at him in absolute fear. He sat her down and spoke calmly yet with considerable authority, "You may go to your room, if you say anything about tonight's events to anyone, I will have you dismissed immediately and thrown into prison. When there is a more convenient time I will send for you. In the meantime there will be no more teaching sedition and heresy to my wife."

"Yes sir. I understand sir." said Ruth through chattering teeth. She fled from her master's room and almost ran, trembling and shaking to her room in the attic. But sleep would not come as she laid tossing and turning in bed, debating in her mind what she should do.

The following day was extremely busy and she just didn't have time to think out a strategy as to what to do. As it was Saturday night, Ruth finished her work and when Lady Susan had gone to bed, she carefully escaped down another staircase and slipped out of a back door to walk home. It was only then, that she was able to think about her ordeal the previous night.

When she arrived home, everyone was bursting with questions about her past week, about life at The Hall and the activities of the rich and famous. Ruth buried the thoughts of her recent experience in the depths of her sub-conscience until everyone was in bed, except her Mother and William. Then with her heart-in her-mouth, she asked William to walk with her down to the river. Once they were out of ear-shot, she sobbed violently on his shoulder as she poured out her story to her understanding big brother. He comforted her as he listened with growing alarm to the details. It took a couple of hours of talking to calm her sufficiently to return home and for her to be able to go to bed.

The next day was Sunday, the usual routine was completed with a subdued Ruth but otherwise a normal family. There were the usual disputes between the younger children but it was quieter and more serious day between the older ones, Mother and Sarah sensing that something was afoot but not knowing what it was.

They crossed the village and entered into the living room of John and Hetti Stott's house. It was a warm and muggy day, so they sat in their shirt sleeves and blouses fanning themselves, while the prayer and the Psalms were completed. John Stott began his talk by opening his Bible and reading from Psalm 64; "Hear my voice, O God, in my prayer; preserve my life from my enemy. Hide me from the secret counsel of the wicked: from the insurrection of the workers of iniquity."

As he read firmly and clearly there was the sound of horses outside, the unmistakable sound of soldiers moving according to commands. The crunch of boots on gravel and the click of guns being alerted everyone to the crisis. Ruth was visibly frightened. William reached for her hand and held it tightly. Sarah was in a quandary not understanding what all the commotion was about, thinking that maybe her beloved Nick had returned. Young Richard knew what it meant and he gripped the bench tightly with his hands, trying not to cry. Mary started to sob, whispering to her Mother, asking what was happening? Peter and little Susan were listening for the sound of the guns being prepared and thinking that this was going to be exciting. George merely whimpered not knowing what it was but realising that something was afoot.

The room fell-silent as the door was banged and a voice commanded; "Open this door or we fire."

'Worlds Apart'

Five – 'William at Home on the River Avon'

When the fishing boat left Christchurch and sailed out past Mudeford quay, William knew that his responsibilities for the family had returned. Whilst his father and John the less were at home, he could relax and enjoy his work on the river. But when they were away it was his job to provide for the family.

His main priority was to provide financially for the family. This demanded that there was enough money to pay the rent each week, having food on the table each day and firewood in the store. This was easier said than done.

During the summer, he could work long hours on the river, but it was very tiring, yet he enjoyed it. He enjoyed the outdoor life, he felt near to his Maker, at peace with himself and with everyone else.

William was quite a slim man with a shock of hair that refused to be tamed. His face and arms were tanned to a deep bronze. He wore his long, short sleeved shirt outside his breeches so that the breeze would keep him cool during the day. During the summer, he worked barefoot as this helped him maintain his footing on wet planks of the boat. His hands were calloused as a result of long hours with the oar. His face often creased into a grin with eyes that twinkled in the reflected light of the sun.

He was a thoughtful man, usually thinking carefully before he spoke. Then his words tended to be expressed slowly, deliberately, with a degree of logic so that everyone respected him. Sometimes people, who were quite important in the locality, would seek his opinions on matters of religion and politics. Sometimes those opinions would be voiced around the bar in an evening or in more significant locations in the salons of the country houses.

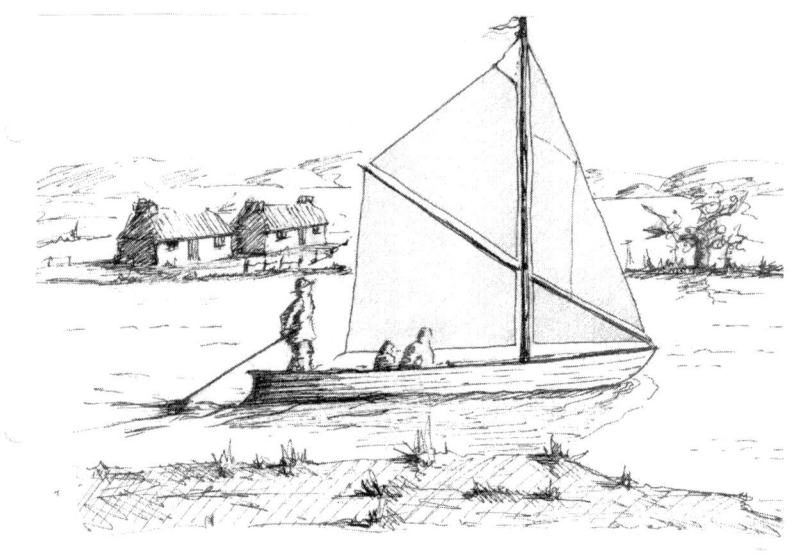

A 'Wherry Boat'

Each day, he would leave the family home as the sun was just beginning to rise. He would leave with a small loaf of bread with cheese or ham and walk down to the river. His boat would be moored not far from 'The Stones'. He would clean out the leaves and rubbish that had gathered overnight, untie and cast off from the bank. Whether or not he could use the sail was dependant upon the wind, its direction and strength. Otherwise, he would use the single oar to both steer and row the boat by a kind of swirling action.

William was a man quite happy with his own company. However, he was also interested in other people, he could take it or leave it. He was really interested in what they thought. He was not bothered by riches or by status.

He greeted all alike, whether a Lord or a commoner, whether a religious fanatic or an irreligious unbeliever. To William, all men and women were equal before God. All had a right to live and think as they wished. So often he listened without comment to the many viewpoints expressed by the travellers. William couldn't read or write but he could listen, think and express his thoughts with clarity and conviction.

It was therefore with mixed feelings that he ferried the family back home after his Father and brother had set sail for far-off places. He knew that he had to watch the two girls carefully, Ruth was now exposed to all sorts of situations at the Hall, people with different views of politics and religion. She was also not afraid to voice her opinions which might get her into trouble at any time. Sarah was growing up fast, she was so attractive that someone was going to be asking to marry her or worse. She was rather naive in such matters, he must talk to her about the 'ways of the world'. Richard worried him, it was as if all of the teaching that Father had given him had not registered in his mind at all. He really must have Richard with him on the boat and teach him how to work. Peter, on the other hand, needed to be trained to read and write as he would most certainly need those skills in due course. Then there was Mother and Mary, they needed all the support he could give them in caring for young Susan and little George. Finally, there was mother-in-law who was getting steadily frailer and would one day fall asleep and not wake.

A family to be concerned about, yet at the same time one with which he could be proud. As for himself, what was he going to do with life? What was he going to do with his life? Was he going to spend all his energy on the family? What about finding a wife for himself and starting his own family? These responsibilities weighed heavily upon William's shoulders as he rowed up the river that summer's morning. However, his immediate concern was work – ferrying passengers and fishing for trout.

A few days later, he was fishing quietly near the mill stream that fed Sopley Mill when he heard a shout; "Hey, you. Row over here, I need a lift to Fordingbridge." William pulled in his line, shipped his oar and rowed the boat over to the bank for the portly gentleman to clamber in. This was done with some difficulty. The man was smartly dressed, obviously not used to the countryside or to muddy river banks. Eventually, he managed to clamber in, sitting down with much huffing and puffing. "I am not used to such forms of transport," he said after he had re-gained his breath and composure. "I like a carriage and horses, or at least a sedan chair to carry me. However, in this part of the world the roads are not very good and there are no sedan chairs! I suppose that's why I'm here." "Oh, that sounds interesting," said William anticipating that the man would explain himself further.

"Yes, I have been talking to Sir Richard at Sopley Hall about extending the road and subsequently the post to Salisbury from London. In due course, on to the West Country. In order to make that proposition worthwhile, I need to make this river navigable all the way up to Salisbury. Then I can open up the trade route from the coast to Salisbury using this river. As the river passes through his Lordship's land for the first twenty miles I have to persuade him of the benefits of the idea before I can proceed any further."

William was always amazed as to why complete strangers opened up to him. Maybe it was his quiet, unassuming manner, maybe it was just because he was alone and people trusted him. For whatever reason, people shared confidences with him. This particular piece of information however, was of major significance to both William and the whole river community.

"So, you mean you want to open-up the River Avon to freight traffic?" asked William. "Yes, I would need to clear some of the sandbanks, clear the weed, build some bridges, dredge the river up to Hamham and build a new wharf at Salisbury." explained the stranger. The man had got completely carried away with his ideas that he had failed to realise that he was talking to a river boatman. William kept quiet, just thinking about what he had just been told. Of course, it might be just a bright idea but on he other hand it could be something that would revolutionize life on the River Avon. At last he ventured; "It's an interesting idea, how far did you get with Sir Richard? Was he interested in your ideas?"

"Yes, I believe that he thinks it's an idea for the future. A way of developing this quiet backwater and bringing great wealth to the area," answered the visitor as they neared Fordingbridge. William brought the boat to rest near the beautiful, ancient bridge, assisting his passenger to alight without getting his feet wet.

As he manoeuvred his boat back downstream, he couldn't stop thinking about what he had heard. It could be the end of his business or it could be the start of something big. He wondered what the other boatmen would think if they knew about the idea. After a little time reflecting on this notion, William decided not to say anything to anybody for the time being. He would just bide his time.

He pushed away from the bank and rowed down stream for a mile or two. It was a beautiful afternoon with the sun reflected on the river, the occasional moor-hen popping out from the bank, the ducks squawking as a swan landed on their stretch of the river. The concentric circles caused by fish coming-up for air – it was beautiful. Without warning there was a commotion on the river bank. He was just near Ellingham when through the tall meadow-grass two men appeared shouting and gesticulating to William to get to the bank quickly. As soon as he was within reach, they jumped into the boat almost making it tip over. "Watch out," shouted William, "Just sit down and don't rock the boat."

The two men were dressed in good quality clothes but were a little unkempt and dirty. They were unshaven and their hair was long, the one wearing a beard. Strange, thought William, educated men fleeing from the law. William did not know them and his first thought was that these men were up to 'no-good' and the sooner he got rid of them the better. Before he could decide how to get rid of them without causing a crisis, a musket shot was fired from the bank, followed by another. The grass parted to reveal a farmer and a soldier. The latter had a loaded musket aimed at the men. The soldier shouted; "Turn your boat round William Tilly, return here with those two men. They are wanted for sedition and treason." One of the men in the boat whipped out a sharp dagger and jabbed it into William's neck, "Turn round and you're dead." he whispered threateningly into William's ear.

In a split second, William had to decide what to do. He swung his oar deep into the water to bite into the mud, he pushed with all his might on the oar, sending the boat directly for the bank whilst he clung to the oar and was left hanging in mid-air. The boat swung violently and was driven into the bank with the two men hanging on it for their lives. Meanwhile the soldier moved along the bank with his musket covering the two men as he commanded; "One move to escape and I will kill you." The boat rammed into the bank and the two men were grabbed roughly by the arms and marched off. "What about my boat?" cried William as he slid down the oar into the water. Fortunately, it was a warm afternoon and he was able to swim across the river, haul himself into his boat, return to regain his oar which was stuck fast in the mud and move off down the river.

What a day it had been. Some news that could change his world and his life threatened at knife-point! Most days were predictably similar. Different people but the same routine, different cargo but the same places. He decided to find out a little more about the plans for the river and who the escapees were and why were they wanted for 'sedition and treason'.

The next day, he decided to take Richard with him on the river. This would enable William to see if Richard could be trained to take over 'the wherry' someday. They started early one morning, a bright, sunny day. Their first job was to collect some timber which had been seasoned on the dockside at Christchurch. It was oak which had come from woods in the west country, brought by sea to Christchurch and was going to be used to make some oak chests and cupboards. Just beyond Fordingbridge there was a carpenter and this timber was destined for his workshop so that it could be made into some furniture for a smart city house in Salisbury.

On the way down-river, William showed Richard how to unfurl the sail, making sure that it was catching the maximum amount of wind. After a while, William shouted; "Can you hold this sail, it makes my arm ache?" Richard grabbed hold of the offending sail and fastened it to a cleat on the side of the boat. William also showed the lad how to use the oar to steer, he managed this for a time but the oar was too long for him to manipulate. Once alongside the low end of the quay, they loaded about twenty pieces of timber aboard the boat. On the return trip, William had to row most of the way which was tiring. Near Sopley Mill they stopped for a lunch-break, William using the opportunity to talk to his younger brother.

I think it's time you started to realise you're not a little lad any longer, you have just got to start being more responsible. You can't just disappear when you want to and go playing at the river. I think it's time that you learned about a real job. What really interests you? What do you want to do?" He asked Richard. "You have been learning to clean the fish, mend nets and general 'fish work'. Would you like to go fishing like your Father and John?

"I just don't know," replied young Richard. "Fish work is alright but it smells so and on the boat at sea it's often cold and you get wet. In some ways, I like forest work better, I like this timber that we are carrying, I was just looking at the way the graining has a nice pattern in that piece over there – it would be a challenge to make that into a piece of furniture."

"That's a good idea, when we get to Fordingbridge we'll have a word with the carpenter and see if you can spend some time at his workshop. You might be able to stay with his family and help him. But if you're going to work in wood you will have to learn how to measure and calculate in order to do the work," commented William. Thinking that it would be good to get the youngster involved in something sensible. It would really be helpful to everyone.

If I can do some real work then I will learn whatever is required – you just watch me," replied Richard with enthusiasm.

After their break, they continued up-stream. At the carpenter's workshop, William was as good as his word, asking if Richard could do some work for him. The carpenter agreed that after the Summer Festival, when William brought the next load of timber to the yard, then Richard could stay for a few days and try his hand in the workshop.

It was now only a couple of days before the Summer Festival, William was working all hours with his boat, ferrying goods up and down river. He was also preoccupied with thoughts about Nick Swanton who had come into the family scene the previous day with such a devastating effect upon Sarah. 'I hope she is not disappointed', thought William, 'she is such a beautiful, but somewhat naive girl.'

Whilst deep in thought, he was hailed from the river bank by Miriam, Thomas Hayward's eldest niece from Ellingham. She was sixteen and William thought she was 'a nice girl'. She was a quiet, serious girl, a 'Puritan' believer who attended their services whenever possible. The trouble was that they both had to work long hours to help their families survive. Miriam worked in the blacksmith's forge at Ellingham. This was the most important forge in the area and people came from many miles for the skills of Bill the Blacksmith. He did all of the usual tasks of shoeing horses, making the iron rims for wagons, making nails and tools for farming. He also produced finer works of art as he was also a gunsmith and a cutler. Often, he turned his hand to veterinary work when the animals which were brought for shoeing were unwell, tasks that Miriam loved to get involved in.

Miriam's job was to make sure everything was ready for the men. The fire maintained at the correct temperature, the water container kept full for tempering the metal and the various fluxes and pieces of metal in the right place. However, her most important task was to look after the animals as they were brought for shoeing. Keeping them calm and looking after any problems that they had. She was a strong, hard working girl who knew everyone and everyone knew her. It was a tough life but she enjoyed it, particularly when caring for the animals.

He was pleased to see and hear Miriam, she was kind, warm hearted and he liked her. There was nothing dramatic about her, nothing that would change the world, just a hard-working, honest reliable girl who would make a good wife for someone.

"William Tilly," she called, "We have some expensive goods to take to Ringwood for the Summer Festival, can you take them and look after them at your house?" she asked. "Bill and the men are taking the heavy goods by cart tomorrow. They will set up a stall at the fair, but the guns and knives are worth a lot of money, if you look after them it would be a great help." She explained, as William drew near to the river bank and held out his hand to help Miriam step across the mud. They were old friends and had shared many a happy and sad times together over the years. William would like to move the friendship on to something more but didn't know how to proceed. They were just good mates and she seemed content with that. He propelled the boat into the bank; William jumped ashore and made the boat fast so that they could transfer the boxes of metal goods. Once this had been completed, they rowed the boat into the flow of the stream.

After a while, William thought it would be good to stop for a short time. "I think its time for a break before we reach Ringwood", suggested William, hoping that he could encourage Miriam to be just a little more responsive. When they had navigated the boat into the water reeds, William became embarrassed, not sure how to begin the conversation or what to do. It seemed to him that his sister Sarah, so much younger than he, had much more intuition than he had about such matters!

"I understand that you were the means by which the two men were arrested a few weeks ago", said Miriam, looking at William accusingly. "I also hear that they have been executed, apparently they were hung, drawn and quartered at the Tyburn in London yesterday." She shuddered as she spoke; "I thought that you believed in freedom of speech and non-violence, I thought you were a free-thinker, supporting worship according to conscience." She challenged him with these straight comments that are only expressed between close friends. William thought, 'this was not the way he had intended this conversation to be going, he wished that he hadn't stopped the boat'. "What's got into you? Why are you so upset?" he queried with feeling, he was both annoyed and upset that she should so accuse him.

"Listen", she said. "Those two men were supporters of people like us. They had challenged the Bishop of London a few weeks ago. One had given a talk outside Westminster Abbey decrying what went on inside. He'd said; 'they were little better than papists, sacrificing conscience for popularity' and you have killed them. They were looking for a place of safety, they were looking for protection and you have killed them. You see, I hear everything at the blacksmith's shop, everyone comes to us and while their horses are being shod they talk. It's surprising the things that you hear."

William had never seen Miriam so worked-up before, normally she was a quiet, undemonstrative girl but now she was really agitated. He tried to explain the circumstances which had led to the two men being arrested and his own part in the events. That when one had drawn a knife, he thought that they must be criminals. She gradually quietened until William felt he could put his hand on her shoulder and give her a gentle brotherly-type kiss on her cheek. She didn't resist and suddenly he thought that he was making progress so he moved a little closer but she was not having it. "Let's get on with the work; I've lots more to do today and so have you, William Tilly."

It was therefore back to work for William. That was the story of his life for the next few days. The Summer Festival was very successful. William was able to earn a reasonable sum of money with many people and animals to move along the river. Sunday was an interesting day when Sarah brought young Nick along to the service, he was an intelligent young man, actually he was almost the same age as William but he seemed so much younger and more vibrant. Of course he came from a totally different background, one of privilege and education but for all that he was a likeable lad and they had all taken to him. However, his religious affiliations and ideas were worrying; William just hoped it wouldn't lead to problems. He was also worried as to why Nick did not return that night to say goodbye to Sarah. This was even more disconcerting. "I wonder what really happened to him", mused William.

The next big event was the Ball at Southavon. Ruth had co-opted William to act as ferryman at Sopley. This would be useful work but it was also hard labour as the current was much stronger down-river. He would have to row all night. After the ball had finished he would be required to ferry hordes of drunken revelers back to Sopley Hall. However there was one event which made the whole evening worthwhile for William.

In the early hours of the morning whilst the dancing was continuing, people were starting to drift away from the party and various couples had disappeared into different rooms of the house. One man had walked unsteadily towards William's boat and sat wearily on the river bank. William recognised him as the man, who weeks before had talked to him about the projected dredging and development of the River Avon.

"Good evening", said William, doffing his cap and bowing slightly to the gentleman. "Good evening or rather I think, good morning", replied the gentleman. "I am not one for dancing and carousing. I enjoy a good wine or a good ale but I am more interested in planning for the future, in creating something which will make money. I think you were the man I was telling about my plans for the river?" asked the gentleman. "Yes, you were and I found it very interesting. It was exciting to hear about such a new project." said William carefully, hoping that he would hear more from this man.

"Since, I have been here," replied the gentleman, "I have been discussing the matter with several other landowners in the area. Some are interested; others think it a waste of money. One is absolutely against it. However, I have also been talking in London with Members of Parliament. Lord Kilmuir, who represents much of Salisbury is very keen and would like me to draw-up plans for the development of the wharf in Salisbury. He would also like to obtain some idea of what is required throughout the length of the river, where the deeper parts occur and where it would require dredging. He would like to know whether or not the project is really feasible. I know what," said the gentleman suddenly. "You could be the 'waterman' in the project. You could use your boat to take my surveyor up and down the river, you know all about the currents, the sandbanks, the dangerous spots and what you don't know, you can learn. That's a brilliant idea, Hurrah. You will assist won't you?" asked the gentleman of William who was standing alongside him? William was stunned by the ideas and the offer. "Yes, I think so," said William.

"What do you mean, you think so? This is an opportunity of a lifetime; you will be a key part of a new development. You will be part of the plan, part of the plan to change Hampshire," confirmed the gentleman, a man not used to refusal "We will talk more of this in one week's time at Ringwood at the Inn by the river at noon. Now, you can row me back to Sopley Hall and I will be away."

When he had finished his work for the night and all the revelers had returned to their carriages, William quietly rowed back up the river. About half-way back home he was able to raise his sail in the early morning breeze and dream of his possible future, a dream of security and stability, a dream of a regular income and of responsibility. He suddenly realised that he did not know the gentleman's name. 'Ah, well' he thought, 'I shall know it soon enough'.

The following week was one of routine and work. Work at home with all the normal duties that William had to complete. With his work on the boat, he managed to squeeze in some fishing on Tuesday. For market the following day there were bright, fresh trout to sell. He had the usual amount of passengers to ferry, but his mind was on other matters, his forthcoming meeting on Saturday with the gentleman from London and the future of his relationship with Miriam. How could he repair the damage caused to their relationship and how could he move it forward? He just wondered whether it was the right thing to be doing anyway. He compared the excitement and obvious love shown by Sarah for Nick and his own sterile friendship and he wondered whether or not he was on the right course at all.

On Thursday afternoon, William had a fare to Ellingham, so he decided to tie up his boat and walk to the Smithy and see if he could have a few minutes with Miriam. As he got near to the Smithy, he could see that they were quite busy. There were several horses standing outside and the hammers were sounding loud and clear as Bill and his assistant hammered away at new shoes. He caught sight of Miriam and waved her to come across to him. "Have you got a few minutes to have a chat? Can we just walk down the road for a moment?" asked William. "Only a few minutes because we are quite busy. But as they have four horses to shoe and they have everything to hand I can come with you for a little while," replied Miriam. She went back to the Smithy and spoke to Bill before she joined William down the road. "What's the matter?" she asked.

"I am so sorry about the other day, I didn't know anything about the two men, who they were or why they were fleeing. I just knew that when they threatened me, I had to do something. I am so sorry that you were upset. You were right; anyone who stands up for 'freedom of conscience' needs our support. Please forgive me," beseeched William.

"Of course I forgive you. You are an honest and good man William Tilly. I now realise that you had good reasons for reacting in the way that you did," she cried, her red face glowing with excitement. She was filthy dirty from working in the Smithy. Her hands were black with soot and from handling iron but her eyes had lit up with something William and not seen before. He grabbed her face in both hands and kissed her with a ferocity he did not think he had within him. "I love you," he said. "We ought to be more than friends," he said, speaking rapidly and without really thinking what he was saying. "Wait a minute," said Miriam, "just slow down, it's the first time you have talked about commitment, let alone anything else. Let's take it step by step, shall we?"

"Yes, I am sorry," said William realising what he had said and the implications of what his comments implied. "Let's talk about it on Sunday after the service. We can have some time together on Sunday afternoon. In the meantime, we had both better get back to work."

Saturday morning dawned damp and overcast; William was up early as usual. He completed his domestic duties around the house before setting off to complete several ferry journeys during the morning. However, he made sure that he was back at Ringwood for noon.

He tied up his boat and walked across to the Inn where a couple of men were waiting. As he got nearer, he saw that the one was his gentleman acquaintance and the other a much taller, younger man, a man with a shock of auburn hair and a beard to match. His acquaintance held out his hand to greet William as a fellow business man much to William's amazement. "This is James Proudfoot, he is my surveyor, by the way, my name is Eddie Otter, you are?" asked James; "Er, er ,,. My name is William Tilly", said William haltingly, not used to being accepted on equal terms with the gentry.

"Let's go and get some ale and then we can talk", said James leading the way into the Inn. When they were settled with their drinks in a comfortable spot, Eddie began;

"At the moment we do not have a legal right to change the natural flow of the River Avon into a commercial waterway. We know however, that the whole river from Christchurch to Salisbury is navigable. Two years ago, one John Taylor and his compatriots did just that by rowing their wherry boat all the way. William have you ever rowed or sailed all the way?"

"No. I have gone up to Braemore House but no further." replied William. "But I understand that the river is quite navigable for flat-bottomed, small boats all the way to Salisbury. Although there are several areas of reed beds and shallower parts further up-river and the flow of the river is very rapid in parts."

"Good, that's the sort of information we need." interrupted James. "Before we can approach Parliament with a formal Bill and also apply to possible financiers with a proposal, we need detailed evidence. We shall need to complete a set of drawings for the whole of the river with depths and currents indicated. All bridges will have to be measured for height and subsequent clearance. We would be planning to use horse-drawn freight barges. We shall therefore need to look at access and provisioning facilities en-route. The real challenge is to be able to check on the 'fall of the river' so that we know if locks and weirs are required." explained James, with enthusiasm.

William just listened spell-bound to such comments. He could see and understand what was needed to be done but how could he become involved in such a grandiose scheme? He had no money, he had no time and above all things he had no education.

James saw his puzzlement and at the same time interest and excitement, he smiled as he motioned to his benefactor to explain.

Eddie looked to William and asked him; "We would like you to use your boat to ferry my friend James up and down the river. He will make the relevant notes, measurements and observations. We will pay you twenty pounds a year as our boatman, to be paid in weekly amounts. We would expect you to be at our disposal and not do any other work for as long we require your services. Would you be willing to do this?"

"Willing! Of course I would be willing, when do we start?" cried William.

"Not so fast, my young man. We need to work carefully and plot our work secretly. There are enemies out there who would sabotage our work if they get wind of what we are doing. As I said to you last week, I believe, one of the landowners in the area is very much against our proposals. He would not stop at anything to destroy this project," said Eddie with some feeing. "So we need to proceed carefully which also means not a word to anyone, is that agreed?" The other two nodded in agreement.

"I think we need to start at the Christchurch end of the river first of all. We need to draw up some plans of the Mudeford and Christchurch harbours with some ideas for extending the harbour wall," said James carefully. We then need to plot the first part of the river up to Sopley and Ringwood. Everyone in that area has agreed in principle to the plan so we shouldn't encounter any opposition. That will keep us going this summer and autumn, and then next spring we can start on the next stretch."

"What about the winter, what do I do during the winter months? I can't get paid for doing nothing," said William with concern in his voice. "Don't worry, if everything goes according to plan you will come to Salisbury with us. You will then learn how to draw and write in our offices. We are going to make you our clerk!" said Eddie with a big grin on his face.

"You see, I told you about our plans weeks ago and yet no-one has heard about them in this area which means that you can be trusted. I told you not to tell anyone and you haven't. So well done, welcome to the 'River Avon Project'. We will meet in three weeks time to start work.."

William ran back home as fast as he was able. He burst into the cottage, calling for his mother who came, wondering what on earth was happening. He explained his new found job, without divulging too much. Then he realised that he wanted to share his news with someone else. He put his boots back on, grabbed his coat and ran out of the cottage and down to his boat. He shipped the oars on his boat and rowed hard up-stream towards Ellingham.

By now, it was late afternoon and he hoped that his friend Miriam had finished her work and could spend a little time with him before she returned home. He reached the village, tied his boat to the usual stake and walked quickly to the Smithy. There were no horses outside, which was a good sign, nor was the furnace roaring as it was normally. Good, Miriam was still there clearing up and dousing the fire before going home.

"Miriam, I have got some exciting news to tell you, can you spare a few minutes before you go home?" he asked her carefully. However, she sensed from his face that this could not wait and she replied; "Just give me a few minutes to finish packing everything away and you can walk me home, William."

Ten minutes later they were walking down the road, he steered her across the field to her cottage so that they could sit down and talk.

"What's so exciting that couldn't wait 'til Sunday then?" she asked him with a quizzical look on her face. "Well, it's like this …" He began, and then it all spilled out like water from an overfull jug. He just talked and talked, describing the men and their ideas and his own part in them. Eventually, he ran out of words and was silent. "So, what's this got to do with me", she said enquiringly. "Well, er it means that I shall have my own income, we could rent our own cottage and ...." said

William tentatively, "it means that we could get married and have a family and live our own lives together." He looked at Miriam with expectation and desire. "Oh William, I would love to do that, my dream would come true and I would be happy for ever but it's not quite that easy." she said, breaking away from his embrace; "we have to be responsibilities, you have your Mother, brothers and sisters to look after, I have my Mother and family to look after whilst Uncle Thomas is away."

"I know all about that and I agree that it we couldn't get married until they return from New-Found-Land. I would want to be sure that father was in favour and that Mother and the rest of the family were able to look after themselves before I did anything. But, we can plan and if everything works out, then we could marry in October. What do you think?" asked William.

"Yes, I would like that. I shall have to talk to Mother about it and I don't know where we could live but I am sure that we could find somewhere. Of course, we might need to live in Salisbury, if what you say is true and everything works out according to plan. That would be really exciting," replied Miriam with enthusiasm. "I must be going, Mother will be wondering where I have got to and she will send out a search party."

"Don't say anything about the new job, will you?" asked William. "Of course not," replied Miriam. "Your secret is safe with me."

With that, they parted, both extremely happy and excited about what they had agreed. William ran back to his boat, cast off and quickly rowed back to his home, singing and shouting for joy. He was going to be married, he had got a new job and he thanked God for his goodness.

He had decided to keep his news secret for the time being, although they would all know that something had happened, it might be wise to bide his time.

Just as he arrived home, Ruth arrived breathless from walking from Sopley Hall, he sensed that she had news, but for her it was not good news. He knew that she would want to confide in him. He looked at her and nodded, they could talk when everyone else was in bed. The meal was ready for them all and on the table. Mother and Mary had been working hard and they all sat down to eat and share in conversation with the younger children. As soon as they children were in bed, Ruth whispered to William, "Can we talk?" They went out down to the river bank, Ruth pouring out her story of Sir Richard and his threat. William held her tightly , speaking gently to her as she sobbed on his shoulder.

He was worried, worried to death. This was serious. If Sir Richard wanted to, he could have them all imprisoned, confiscate their cottage and his boat. He could have Ruth condemned 'as an evil person, preaching subversive doctrine' and have her shipped abroad as a slave, sending her to Barbados or Virginia. William did not sleep that night. All thought of marriage and setting up a new business was banished from his mind. The exciting prospect of being part of a new project was all but a dream if the situation with Sir Richard got worse. What were they to do?

At last, the first vestiges of dawn were to be seen and William wearily rose from his bed and went for a long walk into the woods, trying to get his thoughts straight. On the one hand he was angry. At the very moment when he had opportunities in his own life, a new job, money and marriage. His world and that of his family could fall apart. On the other hand he believed 'that all things worked together for good to those who loved God'. In other words, his religious belief taught him to accept his lot and that if persecution came his way it was for his good.

He had seen the way his parents had coped with the death of two of his younger brothers, his father had said, "The Lord giveth, the Lord taketh away." His parents had accepted the consequences of this teaching but William did not know whether his faith was strong enough. He did not know whether he could accept his dreams being destroyed with possible imprisonment and other even more horrendous possibilities.

After walking for about an hour, he found a spot far into the forest where he could kneel down and pray for strength to guide the family. He prayed carefully and fervently his Lord's prayer which he had prayed in the Garden of Gethsemane; not what I will but what thou wilt."

Strengthened within, he returned to the cottage and helped everyone get ready for their usual Sunday service at their friend's house.

As they walked across the village, William had a sense of foreboding as he surveyed the members of the family. Mother was worried, Ruth was wearing a brave face but William knew that she was dreading going back to Sopley Hall later in the day. Sarah had had her brief few days of excitement but since then she had oscillated between hope and despair. William himself was all mixed-up. Dare he hope for love, marriage and a new career or was it to be prison, torture and death?

They greeted each of their friends as they entered the home of John and Hetti Stott and their service of worship began not knowing what was ahead of them.

Villagers at work

'Worlds Apart'

Six – 'Emily, a woman beset with problems.'

Emily had a lovely character. She was a good woman but unfortunately, had one shortcoming. She worried about everything. She tried not to, but her concerns always seemed to surface sooner or later. She worried about her husband, her family, and her friends, but above all she worried about her faith!

Emily was a very devout woman. She had grown up during the reign of King James. This had been time of relative peace and security, a time when religious thought was more moderate than the extremism of Elizabeth and Mary. But, King James had enforced his expectations of conformity by his rules for a 'state religion'. Everyone was expected to worship God in a proscribed fashion. However, Emily had been taught to think for herself by both her parents and her best friend, her next-door neighbour, Mary Watts.

Emily always wanted to please other people; everyone else always came before herself. If there was anything left in terms of food or anything else then that would do for her. She particularly wanted to please her God. Her religion was a very personal one. She believed that her Heavenly Father was active in every aspect of her life. He was the giver of all blessings. If misfortune occurred, it was because God was directing her life according to his purpose. Her task was to accept life as it was and maintain her faith whatever the circumstances. As she would often quote; "I have learned, in whatsoever state I am, therewith to be content. I know both how to be abased and I know how to abound: everywhere in all things I am instructed both to be full and to be hungry, both to abound and to suffer need."

At the same time, she worried. She knew that she shouldn't but she couldn't help it. As a fisherman's wife there was a lot to worry about. But as a mother she worried even more, about each of her children. She was particularly concerned that her quality of life was not up to the standard required by her God, that at the Day of Judgement, she would be found unacceptable. In the day-to-day hassle of survival these big questions didn't surface. It was only at night or on Sundays when these disquieting thoughts emerged and affected her. Normally, life was busy, so very busy.

It began early in the morning with the sounds of Mary rising to light the fire, of the chickens in the yard, of Richard and Mary arguing about the water buckets, of children next door rising from sleep. The sounds of a village coming to life woke everyone from sleep. Each family had to complete the domestic tasks before anything else was done; collecting water, lighting fires, going to the toilet, waking the children and preparing food for the day. Everything could be heard from house to house along the village street.

Food was one of Emily's main concerns. Basically, they tried to be self-sufficient but without success. Dried fish was their staple diet supplemented by cheese and very occasionally some meat. Vegetables were grown in the back garden. Bread and pastry were made at home but the flour had to be bought from the mill and this required money.

The other major worry was health. Any illness could lead very quickly to death. A stomach upset or a cold could lead to complications and an early grave. Remedies for illness were often bizarre and frequently made matters worse. There was no concept of disease being caused by bad hygiene. Houses were dirty and washing the body was considered unhealthy. Emily had already lost two babies, one was stillborn, and the other had died within three weeks of birth. Of the rest of the family, George seemed to be fit and well, but Mary caused constant anxiety, particularly during the winter. Mary was the present focus of her anxiety.

Mary was an interesting eight year-old girl, she was often sick and nobody could decide what was wrong with her. Even when she was ill, she always wanted to be up and about even if she was coughing and wheezing. Mary was a very determined girl.

Mary worked hard in the garden and had learned to grow many vegetables. Back in the spring, she had begged her sister Ruth to get seeds from some of the vegetables at Sopley Hall. She wanted to grow marrows and beans which she would be able to sell on market days. She had also experimented with a wide range of plants which had medicinal properties. These plants she grew carefully and used the foliage, roots or seeds. She had decided that this was going to be her speciality and that she was going to not only grow the plants but also to use them to heal people, if no-one could help her then she would help herself.

In her garden she therefore grew a range of plants and had tried out several of them on herself. This was dangerous but she didn't know that! She grew the common herbs like thyme, rosemary, sage, hemlock, fennel and St John's wort. But she also grew more unusual plants like chamomile which she had learnt had a calming effect when she was agitated. Horseradish which she found helped her to breathe more easily and rocket which eased her coughing. She was currently experimenting with spinach, yarrow and foxglove. Each of these she prepared in different ways according to her own experience and was then able to advise others. All of this information she carried in her head but sometimes she forgot the exact measurements which she had used. Sarah was therefore helping her to write down in a large book about the details of the plants. A description of the plant, what part of the plant was used for which ailment, the amount to be taken and the effects on the body. As Sarah had said; "It's important to keep a record for one's own information and also as a reference book for other people."

During this time, one wet and miserable day, they had a caller at the cottage. He introduced himself as Joe Briggs. A travelling salesman who had heard about the 'herb-girl' at Ringwood. He explained that he would like to buy several herbs and take them on his travels and sell them to the public. This seemed a wonderful idea to Emily and Mary. They therefore put together a bag of various herbs and sold them to the man. He left a very happy man.

Four days later he was back, this time, totally changed. Apparently he had sold several of the packets of herbs, including foxglove, to a man who was suffering from dropsy. The man had taken a dose of the powder and was now fighting for his life. The man's son, who was very important in the court of King Charles, said that if his father died he would imprison the salesman,

Sarah checked Mary's notes and suggested that if they tried chamomile then this may modify some of the bad effects. They sent the man off with a free supply of herbs which they thought would help matters. They heard several months later that fortunately, the man recovered and that his dropsy had been cured. This really made Mary aware of the need to have written records so she set about learning to write so that 'Mary's Book of Herbs' could be compiled properly.

At the Summer Festival, the 'herb-girl' was really in demand. They had tied up several hundred bunches of different herbs, each with a different coloured tie to differentiate the various plants. One of Sarah's jobs was to describe to each customer how to apply the particular herb and for what disorder it would provide a cure or at least some help. She still thought that even this procedure was one fraught with danger and would have preferred to have made notes on each bundle. But most country people could not read! So at least she tried to divide the herbs according to their effects. This helped matters but many items were used for more than one ailment and so even that proved difficult.

One of their customers was an elderly gentleman who was a stranger to them all. He was obviously rich, his clothes were of good quality and he had his own private coach. Not a normal visitor to a Summer Festival in rural Southern Hampshire. He seemed, however to enjoy the festivities and spent several hours watching the events. He paid several calls on the Tilly family stall, asking about their smoked fish, where it had come from and where the fisherman were now. Nobody thought this strange at the time, only on reflection did Emily remember this conversation. Eventually, he bought several bunches of herbs, a mixture for healing eye disorders, some deadly nightshade and fennel. He commented, by way of explanation, that his wife suffered from an eye disease.

No-one thought any more about this transaction until three weeks later, when in the middle of the morning a horseman in uniform came galloping into the centre of Ringwood. He was riding a beautiful mare with significant livery – outstanding and very official! The rider swung down off the horse and demanded to be shown the house where the 'herb-girl' lived. People pointed to the cottage where Mary lived, he strode across the street and hammered on the door. Emily opened the door cautiously; the man barked a question at her; "Is this where the 'herb-girl' lives?" "Yes," said Emily fearing the worst.

"The 'herb-girl' is charged with murder, she supplied deadly herbs to Sir Randolf Varney in July 1625 at the Ringwood Summer Festival from which Lady Elizabeth Varney has died of poison. The 'herb-girl' will appear at the Hampshire Court of Assize on October 10th 1625, if she does not appear, she will be deemed guilty and condemned to deportation." With these words hanging in the air, the man strode back across the village, mounted his horse and rode off. Leaving the women of the Tilly family, shaking in fear.

No wonder, Emily was worried about her family, Mary in particular! What could she do to challenge the court order? What could she do to prove that Mary was innocent? Her hard-working, frail young daughter Mary was only a child, how could she be guilty?

There were not only the normal daily worries of paying the rent, of feeding the family and caring for her children. There was now the added burden of Mary being accused of murder. In addition to Ruth working at the Hall, exposed to all sorts of evil (at this stage she knew nothing of Sir Richard's demands on Ruth nor of William's marriage plans) and of Sarah falling in love with a one-time Catholic family's son and heir. Emily had plenty to worry about.

At least Peter, one of her younger sons, was not likely to get into any kind of trouble. He was a dreamer. However, she had noticed that of late he was starting to stand up for himself. He had opinions and was not afraid to voice them. He liked to listen to his big brother, John the less, when he returned from his fishing trips. Peter was fascinated by places and people. He loved to hear about how other people lived, what they did, what they ate and what they wore. Peter was a very bright child who could remember vast amounts of detail and his mother was beginning to realise that when Peter became involved in an argument he always won. He was a lad who thought through the possibilities, evaluated the strengths and weaknesses of a situation and chose the winning argument. He had a way with words, even at eight, nearly nine years of age; he was 'more worldly wise' than most children.

At home, Peter was frustrated. He assisted Sarah in her writing and keeping records but was not allowed to actually make an entry into the ledger. He tried to assist Mary and Sarah in their labelling of the herb bundles but was told 'that he was too young to help'. He was frustrated! Everything he tried, he wasn't allowed to do. So he dreamed of travel, of riding to far-off places, of sailing the seas in search of adventure and wealth.

One particular day, when he had completed his household chores, he decided to go for a walk. He would see if there was anyone exciting to talk to in the village or even to do something different which he hadn't done before. He walked through the village along the lane to the village church. He had never been inside, he was not allowed to do so! He carefully lifted the latch and pushed open the large door. Inside it was quite dark with a musty smell with a hint of incense. He walked quietly and carefully towards the altar where he could see that a man in a long robe was praying.

The man finished his devotions, turned and seeing Peter said to him; "What do you want? Why are you here? "I was just looking," said Peter diffidently, "I have never been in here before and I wanted to see what it looked like." The man looked at Peter carefully and recognised him as one of the Tilly children, one of three families in his village who were 'dissenters'. These families could bring the wrath of the Church Authorities down on his own head and wreck havoc on the whole community. The priest, for that's who it was, thought that if he befriended this lad he might find out more about this group of people. He might even be able to discover some incriminating evidence which he could report to the authorities.

"Let me give you a guided tour around our church, come this way." said the priest to Peter. Taking him by the arm he showed him the altar, the altar rail, the pulpit and the vestry. He explained the different robes he wore for different occasions and why they were used. He explained the importance of tradition and the history of the communion, the chalice and the plate used for the communion service. He showed him the Book of Common Prayer and the

Authorised Version of the Bible and the harpsichord which had been donated by the Lord of the Manor.

He showed him the pews for the special families in the area and how one had to respect their position in society. Peter was over-awed by everything which he saw and heard. He was full of questions. Why was it done this way? What did this mean and why were there stone carvings of dead people on the wall and why were there gravestones with messages on the floor of the church?

It seemed to Peter that everything had a story to tell, everything had a message to impart. It was so rich with symbolism and history. He thought that the church with all its significance was like a parable containing hidden stories. Finally, he was taken by the stone plaque commemorating the travels of one 'John Blake, who had discovered an island in the West Indies in 1540'. "I would love to do that", he said wistfully.

The priest thought he had better give the lad a reason for returning to the church, so he suggested that if he came back in a couple of days time, he would take him up the tower and show him the whole village. Then he would be able ask some carefully prepared questions about his family, how and where they worshipped. He could then use that information to get them arrested, if necessary, thereby removing the problem of the 'Dissident Believers' from his village.

"I would love to go up the tower – I'll be back." said Peter, as he made his way out of the church and back home. Two days later he returned to the church, as agreed with the priest. True to his word, the priest met him at the door to the tower; he took a great key from his cloak and opened the door. It was quite cold and damp as they made their way up the spiral staircase to the top but the view was spectacular. Immediately Peter could see the row of cottages where he lived and yes, there was his mother and his sister by the back door talking to Mrs Watt next door. Peter was astounded. He had not seen anything like this before.

As they were going down the stairs, the priest turned to Peter and asked him; "Where did you say your family worshipped?" "Oh, we go to the home of Mr and Mrs Stott, we don't have someone like you to lead the worship. Any of the men lead it although it's normally Mr Stott. We don't have an altar and candles; we don't have fancy robes or incense. We just have a plain and simple service, singing the Psalms and reading the Bible, just like they did in New Testament times." Peter was rather pleased with himself for his clear description of what happened on Sundays.

The priest was equally pleased with the boy's comments, they were just what he needed. He would now be able report them to the authorities and have them imprisoned for sedition and heresy. He gave the lad a penny for coming back to see him. Peter was thrilled with his afternoon of discovery. He did not think for one minute of the significance of his comments.

Peter ran back through the village and into the cottage and into the arms of his concerned Mother. "Where have you been?" She asked, rather agitatedly, "I need you here to dig carrots, beetroot and prepare them for cooking tonight. We are going to have a meal with Mary Watts and her family. We thought that as it's been such a nice day we would all eat down by the river." "Do we have to?" asked Peter in that tone which suggested he would do anything other share the evening with the family next door. "Yes, we do and you had better get yourself organised – you have a lot of work to do before then." replied his mother, in a tone which could not be challenged, even by Peter.

He spent the evening in a state of heightened imagination. In his mind's eye he could imagine himself travelling to similar places; North Africa, the Levant, even to Virginia and the West Indies. He couldn't wait to return and hear more about those famous travellers. He was so wrapped up in his dreams that he did not hear Mrs Watts asking him; "And what have you been doing lately young Peter?"

Without thinking, he launched into a vivid description of his visits to the church. Of what the priest had told him about the history and traditions of the village church. He described the memorials and the famous people they commemorated. Finally, how he had been taken up the tower and had seen all the village laid out at his feet. As he came to a stop, he saw the look on his mother's face and he realised that he had done something terribly wrong.

Mrs Watt nodded to Emily as much as if to say, that she would explain the situation. She began carefully; "Peter, you know that we worship God in a simple manner in someone's home and not in a church, without all of the ritual that was described to you by the priest." "Yes, I know that," said Peter, "but why do we make such a fuss about being separate? Why can't we go to church like everyone else?"

"That is because we believe that you can worship God anywhere, not just in a special building," continued Mary Watts with considerable emphasis. "We believe that any man can lead the worship, read from the Bible and teach from it, not just special people appointed by the church. We believe that the bread and the wine are just symbols to help us remember the death and resurrection of Jesus and not literally the body of Jesus. We believe in the resurrection from the dead, the judgement seat of Christ and the Kingdom of God which is not taught in the church. The Church of England and even more so, the Church of Rome have substituted the truth of Bible teaching by the traditions of men. They make feast days, rituals of worship, bishops and the clergy of more importance than the religious belief they are supposed to preach. We have taken our stand as the apostle Paul wrote; 'Come out from among them and be ye separate and touch not the unclean thing.' We cannot have anything to do with their evil ways; we must separate ourselves from them. We must only share in fellowship with people of like-minded faith."

"You mean – Puritans?" interrupted Sarah who had been listening intently to the conversation.

"Yes," agreed Mary Watts, "We believe in purity of faith and purity of lifestyle. In order that we can confidently stand before the judgement seat of Christ when he returns to the earth. Knowing that we have done that which he commanded his disciples."

"But it's not quite as simple as that," added Emily quietly; "During the reign of King James it was illegal to worship separately from the Church of England. Since 1603 it has been a crime, punishable by imprisonment or even death, to worship separately. More recently many people in Yorkshire have had to flee from England to Holland and even to New England because of their beliefs and their refusal to worship as the state requires. So we have to be very careful whom we talk about our beliefs. How and where we worship, otherwise, we could easily end up in prison."

By this time, Peter was visibly upset when he heard what his Mother had said. He ran home, hiding his face in his hands. Sarah got up immediately and followed him into the cottage. When they got inside, she put her arm around him and asked him; "What have you done? What have you said? Did you tell the priest where we meet and what we do?" He nodded, not able to speak as he realised the enormity of his admission,

"God will look after us," said Sarah, talking quietly whilst she hugged him. "Don't worry, we shall be alright. Remember that "the angel of the Lord encampeth round about those that fear him, and delivereth them." She talked quietly to him for ages, explaining about the Bible characters that had denied their Lord and yet had been forgiven. He actually smiled when she talked to him about the Apostle Peter and the way that Jesus had told him to 'care for the flock of God' even after Peter had denied his Lord.

By the time the others had returned home and William had come in from his long day's work, Peter had fallen asleep and Sarah left him to his night's rest while she went and talked to William and her Mother about what she had learned.

Emily had another problem on her hands but with resignation she took a deep breath and closed her eyes in prayer as the three of them sought help from their Heavenly Father.

The following morning Emily woke to rain beating on the roof and wind blowing in through the window openings. In those few moments between waking and rising from sleep, she prayed as she had never prayed before. It was almost more than she could bear.

This morning there was one more crisis to affect her, one that was ever with her. Her beloved daughter Mary, was this morning coughing up blood-spattered phlegm. Her little body doubled-up with pain as she tried to cope with her problems. Mary had been struggling more than ever over the last few days since she knew about the Court Order and its implications. She was worried stiff, she was not sleeping well and she had been sick on the preceding day. Now her phlegm had blood in it. They couldn't afford to see a doctor and even if they could there was nothing that they could do. Emily went out into the garden and collected some cabbage leaves and coriander. She boiled them and when the juice had cooled she gave it to Mary as a drink to calm her stomach and stop the bleeding. As with most treatments, it was part received wisdom and part superstition, sometimes these things worked at other times they didn't. This morning it seemed to work. Before long Mary had returned to her chores of collecting water and looking after her plants.

The garden was vital for survival, the vegetables were important for themselves and to provide a few extra to sell. Most of the villagers also had a pig and chicken in their back yard but the Tilly's had decided that it was more beneficial and made better sense if they grew the vegetables and herbs in their plot.

They still struggled to make ends meet but they did have income from the fishing business, an income from selling cod and other sea fish. The money earned, had to pay the men, interest on the loan for buying the boat, nets and other equipment. There was little left over. William made some money during the summer months from fresh-water fish that he caught and from ferry work with his boat. The market stall and the Summer Festival had all brought in a little cash but their income did not cover their essential expenses.

The whole family, but especially Emily, were therefore constantly aware of the scarcity of food. There was no spare capacity; there was no storage except for the potato clamp at the bottom of the garden. They had a small store of smoked fish from the last voyage together with the remnant of cheese from the Summer Festival. Each week, if there was any money flour was purchased from the local mill and a couple loaves of bread were baked. If there was any lard from local farms when they slaughtered livestock, then some pastry was made.

Washing was done at the riverside with a bucket and laundry-board. The clothes were soaked in the river and then rubbed on the rough laundry-board with 'lye' used as soap. If the clothes were particularly dirty or greasy, then goose-fat was rubbed into the cloth. Making clothes and repairing torn or worn-out clothes was done by patching and sewing. In the summer months clothes were not a problem, but keeping warm and dry in the winter was well-nigh impossible.

Over and above all of this was the ever present possibility of becoming pregnant. Whenever John, Emily's husband was home from a fishing trip he would expect his marriage right. He would be looking forward for weeks to spending time with his wife and having sexual relations with her. The result of this union would normally be a pregnancy, she had already conceived ten children but lost two, one was stillborn, and the other died after a few weeks.

She dreaded the possibility that she might have conceived again and this was a real possibility. She had missed her regular 'blood' and was desperate for the next 'month'. Emily was worried!

One positive thing in her world was the fact that young Richard was going to start work for the carpenter in Fordingbridge. William was going to collect timber from the dock in Christchurch, and together with Richard, transport it to Fordingbridge. Richard would then stay at the carpenter's shop for the rest of the week.

When they arrived it was late afternoon so Richard was told to sweep-up all the wood-shavings into a large hessian bag as this was invaluable as 'tinder' for lighting fires. He was to sleep in a corner of the workshop on a bag of sawdust. This he found to be much more comfortable than his own bed and he had an excellent night's sleep. At dawn the next day he was woken with a shout and told to 'look lively', he could find something to eat in the kitchen and should be in the workshop ready to start work as soon as possible.

The carpenter's name was Joe Witchell, he was married with five children under the age of seven years of age. They lived next door to the workshop. He had inherited the carpenter's shop from his Father who had unexpectedly died of consumption two years earlier. Joe was finding it difficult to complete the contracts his father had signed. He could not afford to pay for staff or feed his family. He hoped that by having young Richard Tilly as an unofficial apprentice he might gain some valuable assistance. He just hoped that the lad was bright and would quickly learn the skills of the trade.

On that morning, Joe was finishing a cupboard for a gentleman in Salisbury. It had a frame made from oak with simple joints fixing the sides together with the back tacked with small nails. The front of the cupboard had an inlaid pattern on a separate piece of thin timber which Joe had to fix to the cupboard with glue. This was the first time Joe had done this job. It was the new 'fashionable look' and his customer wanted to be the first in Salisbury to have inlaid furniture. Joe needed an extra pair of hands to fit the two pieces of wood together. He had kept this job for Richard to assist him. He applied a thin layer of glue to both surfaces and then instructed Richard; "You just take the piece of inlaid and carefully match it to the front of the cupboard, push it firmly in place while I hold the cupboard firm. Then keep the whole thing together while I get a large clamp and fit it around the cupboard and screw it tight."

They did that successfully. Richard stood back and admired the finished job. "I like that pattern," he said, "it looks like the waves of the sea and several boats sailing across them." "That's the graining in the timber and the knots where branches grew out from the main trunk of the tree." Explained Joe excitedly, this was going to be good, he thought, the lad has a real interest in timber and it sounds as if he has got imagination too.

"Let's get started on the next piece. We are going to make a set of bookshelves in a similar style to the cupboard with similar timber. First let's go and select the timber from my store. Then we can lay out the pieces ready for cutting and fixing," said Joe to his new assistant. Outside in the covered shed, they selected a series of planks, they laid them in the pattern that would fit together and decided which to use. Joe was looking for plain, straight timbers with no irregularities. He measured the lengths and marked them accordingly. He showed Richard how to cut them to size by using a bow-saw. Joe marked the simple housing joints on the pieces and demonstrated to his new assistant how to prepare the joints. These they cut carefully, so that the completed timbers fitted together neatly and accurately.

Joe was pleased with the morning's work. At last he had an assistant who could take instructions, do the job and work accurately. They were going to work together famously – a real partnership.

The good-will continued for the rest of the week. Richard really enjoyed himself, he realised that he was doing something useful. Something that had value. Instead of playing and getting into mischief he was being creative and constructive. Not only that, he really enjoyed working with wood. He loved the rich smell of the timber as it was cut and he often admired the beauty of the finished job. Equally, Joe was pleased. Here was a young lad who had ability who above all things had a natural liking for working with timber. He was a natural.

When William called back at the end of the week to take young Richard home, both Joe and Richard pleaded for him to stay. "Alright, stay until this time next week and then you must come home for service next Sunday." They were all thrilled with the arrangement.

At least for Emily and William, this was one problem less. They had both been worried about the lad for several months. He had been getting into quite serious escapades, stealing and lying to cover-up his activities. Now, his energies were being channelled into something productive, they breathed a sigh of relief.

Meanwhile, back in Ringwood, Mary's health had deteriorated over a period of a couple of days. She had developed a really bad cough. It was apparent that she had measles, a particularly violent case at that. She had her usual respiratory problems, a high fever and very bad diarrhoea. Emily was convinced Mary was going to die. She and Mary Watts prayed night and day for her recovery. Slowly she re-gained her strength but remained unable to do any work in the garden. This had to be done by the rest of the family.

However, it soon became apparent that the sickness had affected Mary in other ways; she was not as determined as before. She seemed to have lost her 'spark'. In fact, William wondered whether or not she had become 'a little ill in the head' as he described it. Slowly, almost imperceptibly, her mental condition deteriorated. She became depressed, obsessively so. At the same time she became aggressive and challenging to everyone else. Steadily she degenerated into a downward spiral of personal despair and an aggressive rejection of everyone else. The family feared that Mary 'had gone mad'.

At that time most people believed that within each person there were 'humours' or 'vital fluids'. These had to be kept in balance in order to maintain good health. The four were; blood – a red sweet humour. Phlegm – a cold, moist fluid. Yellow bile - a hot, bitter fluid. Finally; black bile - thick and sour.

With respect to mental illness, this was deemed to be a physical condition. Hence, Mary's symptoms were thought to be caused by an excess of black bile causing melancholy. Changes in diet, bleeding and the application of various substances to the head or other parts of the body were standard treatments. Generally, there was little compassion or pity shown to such patients. They were treated to a harsh regime of discipline and medications.

Which, if that didn't work, then the patient was locked up or dispatched to the colonies as 'servants '.

Mary continued in this state for a couple of weeks during the month of August. Emily, the rest of the family and her friend next door all provided love and care for her. They tried to ignore her outbursts and comforted her in her despair. She was no longer open to reason but they continued to show love and understanding whenever possible.

Emily was almost beside herself. She was determined not to allow Mary to be taken away from her and 'put away'. At least she had a possible reason for Mary not to stand trial. She would have to pay for a doctor to visit and sign that Mary was incapable of leaving home. However, she had to be careful in such cases or the doctor could easily 'commit her as being insane' and she could be shipped to far off lands.

At least some of the other problems of the family had not re-surfaced, Sir Richard had not pursued his threat regarding Ruth, Sarah had not heard anything form Nick since the Summer Festival weekend.

William had been able to share his plans about getting his new employment. Richard was doing well at the carpenter's shop and nothing more had been heard from the priest at the local church. Maybe her fears were ungrounded and as her friend had told her time and time again; "The Lord will provide."

One evening in late-August when the younger children were asleep and the others were talking quietly, Emily asked William, Ruth and Sarah to walk with her down to the river. When they were sitting down on 'The Stones', their favourite place for talking, she began the little speech she had prepared. "Firstly, I want to thank you for the support and hard work you three have shown over the past few weeks. I couldn't have coped without you. You are the most wonderful people to have as children.

However, I fear that life is going to get even more difficult. I believe that I am pregnant again, I am sorry that this has happened but it's the way it is. I also think that Mary is not going to recover, at least not quickly, that will make life difficult for all of us. I am determined not to allow her to be taken away from us. I want her to be here when Father returns; I want her to be able to welcome him and her big brother back home. Please support me and help all of us to weather the storm."

Ruth bent forward and putting her arm round her Mother's shoulders, expressed their shared feelings and love; "Of course, Mother, we will do what we can, don't worry. We shall support you and our sister Mary, we love her dearly as does the whole family."

William had a sudden thought; "What about if we ask Hetti Stott to come across and spend some time with Mary? I understand that she has done some research into these kinds of illness and has some interesting ideas about treatment. She is also a very calming person. She knows our circumstances and she definitely will **not** pass-on any comments about Mary to anyone else." He suggested carefully, trying to think of something that might help relieve his Mother of some of her worry. "Yes, that is a good suggestion. But I am afraid that she will think we are very poor, our cottage is not like her nice home. However we must do something," replied Emily.

The next morning, Sarah went across to the Stott's house, to explain about Mary and ask for help. Hetti listened carefully to Sarah's request for assistance. "I will come across with you to see your sister. I missed seeing her at service last Sunday but I thought it was just the measles." Said Mrs Stott, as she packed up her things, put a shawl around her shoulders and followed Sarah across the village.

Hetti Stott had not been into the Tilly's cottage before, although they all had similar beliefs, the social differences were enormous. The one, a successful farmer, owning his own house, farm and animals, renting a hundred acres of land. The other, a fisherman with quite a large family living in small rented cottage, barely able to feed themselves.

Hetti followed Sarah into the cottage and upstairs to where Mary was resting. She didn't say a word, she just went and sat by Mary, holding her hand firmly. She quietly asked the others to leave them alone. Mary didn't scream or try to fight her, she just looked at Hetti appealingly, her eyes full of self-pity and inner pain. They sat like this all morning, Hetti just quietly soothing the girl.

When lunch was ready, Hetti was invited to stay and was asked about Mary, "She is in need of a lot of love, she needs a friend. She needs a lot of attention in order for her self-confidence to grow. She is not a lunatic, she is severely depressed," reported Hetti to Mother and Sarah, when they had all sat down at the table. "Let her come and stay with me for a few days, I can spend some time with her and it will give her an opportunity to talk," suggested Hetti to the women. Emily was quite overcome, she looked to Hetti and said quietly, "I couldn't do that; it wouldn't be fair on you." "Yes, I insist," replied Hetti. "I will not take no, for an answer". "Thank you," responded Emily with real appreciation.

It was arranged that very afternoon. Sarah took Mary across to the farm house and settled her into her new environment. Whilst she was there she was able to have an attempt at the spinning wheel which she found quite challenging and different. She was so used to reading, writing and calculating, not being creative and industrious.

For Emily, this was the break that she so desperately needed. For the first time in weeks she was able to rest for an hour or so. Grandma was playing with little Susan. George was asleep and everyone else was out. She went outside the back door, sat on the bench in the afternoon sun and promptly fell fast asleep.

When she awoke, it was late afternoon, it was very quiet in the cottage and she could not think where everyone had gone. Then she remembered and smiled to herself as she thought how fortunate she was in having friends who could help her. She thought of the proverb, "Better a friend that is near than a brother afar off." Then she paused, it's very quiet, she thought, too quiet. I wonder where Susan is. She scrambled to her feet and called, "Susan, Susan, where are you?" There was no answer. Panic filled her mind as she remembered that she had left Grandma playing with her. Grandma had probably just dozed off, leaving Susan to go 'walk-about'.

Emily, like any mother thought the worst! She immediately jumped to the conclusion that Susan had wandered down to the river. That she had fallen in, that she had drowned. She then thought that she might have wandered off down the street and been crushed by the wheels of a hay cart or by the giant hooves of a cart horse. Then she thought about the enormous sow with her piglets three doors away; the sow could be very dangerous if Susan had wandered near to her who knows what might have happened.

She was not quite sure where to look first and just thinking about the possibilities when her next door neighbour called out, "You looking for Susan? She's in here, safe and sound playing with my two little ones."

Emily sighed, she must try to stop worrying, and it would do her no good and definitely do the new baby no good. She often worried about little Susan, she was at that age when everything was interesting, when everything had to be investigated. But the little girl had no sense of danger. It was alright when all the family where at home because someone would see what she was doing. When everyone was out, then problems arose! The difficulty was that Emily had always worried about everyone and everything. It was part of her nature and she thought that it was very hard to change what you had been born with.

She went back into the cottage. There was Grandma, fast asleep in her chair, not a care in the world except 'old age'. In an era when most people did not live beyond sixty, Grandma disproved the facts. She was in her seventies, in reasonable health, had had a large family and had outlived her husband by fifteen years. She now slept and ate most of the time, just making the occasional contribution to family discussion.

Joe and Richard had completed the bookshelves and both craftsmen were pleased with the result. "A fine piece of craftsmanship," declared Joe, "I think that our gentleman friend in Salisbury will be very pleased. Let's see if we can find a horse and cart to deliver it tomorrow." They were able to arrange with a neighbour for transport and after carefully loading the new piece of furniture they went jogging along the dusty road to Salisbury. They found the correct address, a large house backing onto the river with beautiful gardens inside a walled garden. Fortunately, the owner was at home and they were able to carefully carry the new bookshelves into the house and position them in the library. "I think that we now need a desk in this room to complement the bookshelves," said the owner. "Yes, I think we could make one in the same timber," replied Joe with considerable interest. "I am sure that we could make a really smart desk with a chair to match."

It was agreed. The gentleman paid Joe for the bookshelves and ordered the rest of the furniture which they had discussed. As they left Salisbury, Joe and his young assistant were really excited – business was starting to grow. As they rode home, they talked, it wasn't usually possible as they were just so busy working, but on this happy day they talked; a craftsman and his young apprentice.

"I wonder how your Father is getting on fishing the waters off New-Found-Land," commented Joe. "Do you think that they been able to fill their boat with fish?

"I don't know," said Richard. "I find it hard to become enthusiastic about fish and fishing, but since working with you I have become interested in trees and timber, In fact, I have thought several times about the trees on New-Found-Land and what sort of timber they produce. When Father returns, I shall ask him."

Over the next few days they sketched some suitable ideas for a desk, this time Richard contributed to the design. Joe explained how to measure the sizes and to calculate how much timber they would need. Richard had progressed in a few short weeks from being just a boy, doing the odd jobs to actually working on a real job. He was growing up fast.

However, Peter four years younger was getting very frustrated during this period. With Mary unwell and Richard away from home, all of the domestic tasks had fallen on Peter. He didn't like it!

From early in the morning until he went to bed, he was fetching and carrying. First of all it was the water from the village well for washing and cooking. Then it was water for the vegetables and Mary's herbs. Then it was weeding and pulling vegetables for lunch. In the afternoon, he was expected to help look after Susan because Mother needed her rest and Grandma couldn't be trusted. Susan was a pain, she was always exploring somewhere and Peter had to keep on eye on her. Life was difficult. He wanted to read, he wanted to find out about things, he wanted to explore the real world. Peter was frustrated, he was also becoming angry and difficult, argumentative and resentful.

One hot and dusty day in August, Peter had been working from dawn till lunchtime without a break. He was tired and fed-up. He wanted to curl-up in the sunshine and go to sleep but his Mother said to him; "This afternoon, I need you to dig some new potatoes for Sunday, I also need you to go the Johnson's farm towards Burley to see if they have any lard and scraps of meat left. I understand that they have been killing some of their cows. We may also be able to get some offal or other bits. When you come back, then I would like you to go and sit with your sister Mary while Mrs Stott is out."

Under his breath, Peter was muttering; "Do this and do that, and when you get back. I'm not coming back." But his mother didn't hear and even if she had, the words wouldn't have registered anyway. Peter had become very moody of late and Emily had learnt to ignore.

Anyway, Peter dug the new potatoes and carried them to the back door, he then secretly raided the family's little store of pennies, their only money left. A dry crust of bread in the cupboard and a small piece of cheese was all he could find. He put on his one pair of shoes and was gone.

He walked in the direction of the farm, but instead of going down the track to the farm, he continued walking. He walked for several hours towards the setting sun. When he felt that the air was getting a bit cooler, he started looking for some shelter where he could sleep for the night. At last he found some tall pine trees with bracken at their feet and some gorse bushes. He thought that he would be safe from wild animals and he would know if anyone approached him. Nearby, there was a small pool with clear water from which he could drink. He eat just part of his bread and cheese, keeping the rest for the following day. He made a bed of bracken and dried grass, curled-up and fell fast asleep.

Back home, everyone was frantic with worry. Emily had sent out the children of her neighbour to search and ask if anyone had seen Peter. When William came home, he was dispatched to walk to the farm to see if Peter had had an accident and was lying at the side of the track. Sarah went to the river and walked both river banks, but in vain.

By the time it got dark, Emily was convinced that Peter had been abducted by their enemies or that he had been killed, that she would not see him again. William, sensible as ever, observed; "We are not going to find him tonight, He is a sensible lad, if he's lost, he will find somewhere to sleep and will be home in the morning."

But the morning came and went with no sign of Peter. In fact, there was no sign of Peter for several days.

He just kept walking in the same direction the next day. He had eaten his bread and cheese but found some early blackberries and these kept him going till nightfall. Then he felt really hungry, his stomach started to ache and he felt a little worried.

He noticed that the area was inhabited by many rabbits; He knew how to catch rabbits so he studied the runs for a few minutes, blocked-up exits with earth and then waited by another. All of this was done very quietly so that the rabbits just kept sunning themselves and playing. He jumped as a rabbit emerged from its burrow. He caught it by its ears, immediately killed it with a stone - he had his supper! He was an expert in getting a small fire going and in no time at all he had skinned and gutted the rabbit and was roasting his supper. Parts of the rabbit he wrapped in leaves ready for the morrow. Again, he found a comfortable place in the bracken where he could rest and was quickly asleep.

In the morning he thought about his situation and thought that he was doing quite well, all things considered. He didn't know where he was going but he knew he wasn't going back. Again he walked for most of the day. By now the countryside was changing and he knew that he was almost out of the Forest and into farmland. The ground was wetter and not so easy to walk. But he kept walking, eating the rabbit with blackberries and drinking water from the various streams. He was enjoying himself, free of the irksome tasks that he had to complete at home, free of the village community which he so hated and free from rules and responsibilities.

After two full days walking, he found that it was more difficult to find shelter; he was frequently crossing streams. He wondered whether or not he was walking in the best direction to find a new life. But he kept going until he came to a much larger river which he could not cross. He decided to walk against the flow, towards its source, reasoning that there would soon be a crossing and a village. After a couple of hours walking along the river bank, he saw some cottages. Then further on, some people working in the fields and some boats on the river. Boats like his brother William's.

Suddenly, he heard a shout from behind him; "Hey, you, where do you think you are going?" Peter turned and saw a short, older man who was obviously a farmer walking towards him. He was well dressed, smart and spoke with a strange accent. "You're a stranger round here, you are not one of my workers' children, where have you come from?" questioned the farmer. Peter thought that he had better tell the truth. "I've walked through the Forest. I have left home and I am starting a new life."

"Oh, you are, are you? I think that you had better come home with me and we can find out where you have come from. Your parents will be worried about you." The farmer grabbed hold of Peter so that he could not escape. He propelled him in the direction of the farmhouse which Peter could now see quite clearly across the grass meadows.

The farmer didn't talk further until they had arrived at the house when he told Peter; "Don't try to run away again, just don't even think about it. My wife will clean you up and give you some food; I will talk to you later." With that he was gone, replaced by large women who seemed to fill the room. "Off with your clothes young man, you can't go in the house smelling like a pig-sty. There is a well in the yard, wash yourself and your clothes and then when you've dried yourself. You can come inside for something to eat."

For once, Peter did as he was told, the promise of food and being treated as a young adult appealed to him. He thought that he might be on the thresh-hold of a new life. Later, when washed and smelling clean, he was ushered by a maid into the dining room of the farm. It was a house similar to that which the Stott's owned back in Ringwood but with a little more furniture. The farmer sat on his chair in the corner of the room with his arms resting on the back of the chair, Peter stood, embarrassed, not knowing quite what to do or say. "So, what's your name young man?" asked the farmer, "and where do you come from?"

"My name is Peter and I live in Ringwood, my father is John Tilly, the fisherman, he is fishing in New-Found-Land at the moment and I er, er, miss him..." said Peter, ending in a flurry of words. "I didn't really want to run away but it all became too much, my sister is ill, my brother is working at a carpenter's shop in Fordingbridge, my other sister picks on me and I ... just couldn't take it anymore," finished Peter through his tears.

"So, you ran away, slept rough and walked for three days, that's not bad going," said the farmer. "How old did you say you were?" asked the farmer more gently. "Eight, nearly nine," said Peter. "I can write and read and do sums, at least a bit." said Peter, trying to regain his self-confidence. "Alright", said the farmer, "the maid will give you something to eat and then we are going to take you back home."

So ended the attempted escape, the farmer took Peter back on his horse later in the evening. The family, neighbours and everyone else in the village were ecstatic. They thought that he had been abducted or had met with a fatal accident. No-one thought that he had just run away and survived for two nights and three days on his own. Mother was just overjoyed, she could not stop talking about it and as for Sarah, she just hugged her brother.

William thought differently, he thought to himself that he would really have to have a long talk with Master Peter, this kind of behaviour just couldn't go on!

Life in the Tilly household, like every other large family, had its highs and lows. But there were still dark clouds looming on the horizon. There was still the threat of Sir Richard against Ruth, she was still working at Sopley Hall and although Sir Richard had returned to London, she still felt under threat.

Mary, although now almost fully recovered from her illness had the murder charge and the impending court case to face in October. She and the family knew that she was totally innocent but they had no hope against money, power and influence.

William was about to start on his new job but he felt that there were so many unknowns in the air that the marriage plans were still 'on hold'. Richard seemed to be very happy and progressing well in his new work at the carpenter's shop. But no-one knew whether or not Peter had learnt from his trip into the unknown. Then there was the absence of Father and John the less. They should be on their way home, but no-one would know until they actually arrived home as to whether or not they had been successful!

All of these things concerned Emily, in addition to her own 'personal condition' which her husband knew nothing about. She also had the daily concerns of the two younger children and her mother to think about. Yes, Emily had many, many problems. Even her faith, which for many other souls provided relief, gave her only worry and even despair. As she said to herself; 'if I have so many problems, then I must be a terrible person, unacceptable to God, a miserable sinner, a failure. In truth, a woman unworthy of his care and protection.' Yes, Emily had problems.

It was therefore, with fear and trepidation that Emily prepared for her Sunday worship. She fussed around everyone as they prepared to walk across to the Stott's house. As she made her own way, she felt a certain premonition that something dreadful was about to happen. It was therefore not a surprise to Emily when she heard the soldiers and the horses outside their meeting room. She knew that God's Judgement was about to be meted out upon her. She trembled within as the violent knocking and the commanding voice shook the room.

'Worlds Apart'

Seven – 'Arrest & Trial'

William moved quickly to the door and opened it. Outside there was a platoon of soldiers with muskets drawn, ready to storm the house. The captain, accompanied by two soldiers entered the room. The children screamed in fear as some of the soldiers moved into the room and others filled the doorway.

"We have a warrant for the arrest of the men leading the worship of God in this house. It is illegal to convene a religious meeting other than in a consecrated place of worship. It is illegal for non-ordained members of the Established Church of England to give communion. It is illegal to form a separate congregation and not worship according to the Book of Common Prayer as laid down by His Royal Highness, King Charles. As you are clearly breaking the law, we have no alternative but to arrest the perpetrators of these crimes and hold them in prison until they be summoned to appear in a court of law to answer for their crimes. In the meantime, this meeting must be disbanded and you will not meet in such circumstances again. You will attend your local parish church each first day of the week and take communion from this day forward," stated the captain of the soldiers with an authority that could not be challenged.

There was silence in the room except for the sobbing of the younger children. The women were stunned, Ruth looked like death, Sarah slumped on her bench and fell to the floor in a faint. Emily just couldn't take in what she had heard. Mary Watts recovered her nerve and was about to challenge the soldier, when John Stott stood to his feet and said in a measured tone; "Take me, I am leading the worship today and this is my house. I am responsible for everything that has taken place in this room and am prepared to go with you, but let everyone else go free; they are not guilty of any crimes."

"No, that is insufficient, I need to know that illegal activities will cease in this place," stated the captain as he instructed his soldiers to seize John Stott, William Tilly and the two other men. They were held fast by the soldiers. Marched out of the room and bundled onto an open cart. In minutes the platoon had surrounded the cart and the horses were commanded to move forward. The captain finally looked around the room and commented to the women; "Go home, do not meet together again. Next Sunday, you will be expected to attend your parish church to take communion."

Off to prison ...

The soldiers were heard to be moving off with the cart trundling forward over the rough ground. For a few moments, nobody moved, Sarah was just stirring on the floor, her mother stooped to help her. Then Hetti Stott stood up and through her tears spoke with authority to everyone. "We must be calm, we must trust in our heavenly Father that he will keep us in His care. Whatever happens to our men or to our families. Before we go, let us stay seated and Mary, will you pray for us?

Mary Watts stood trembling but clear in her voice as she repeated the words that her Master had spoken just before he was arrested, "Abba Father, all things are possible unto thee; take way this cup from us; nevertheless not what we will, but what thou wilt." As she finished these words, the realisation of what had happened penetrated their minds.

Slowly, they recovered their composure. The children needed attention as mothers picked the up and held them closely. The teenagers were still shattered and would be for several days. Ruth was particularly devastated as she thought that this was entirely her fault. She could not stop shaking and crying, she wished that she had volunteered to go with the soldiers instead of her wonderful brother. He was innocent and they had taken him. How would they cope without him? She couldn't go back to work, not now!

Meanwhile, the four men were being taken by cart to the barracks at Winchester. This was a long, thirty mile journey in a filthy cart used for transporting animals. At each village they passed through, the local children and many of the people shouted obscenities at them and threw their rubbish and animal waste at them. The soldiers made sure that they were not in the line of fire but ensured that the prisoners got the maximum coverage! This was terrible for the men, because they of course were dressed in their best clothes, their only decent clothes and these were now ruined.

By the time they got to Winchester, it was late afternoon; they were hungry, tired and filthy dirty. They were taken from the cart and escorted into the dungeon of the prison. It was pitch dark, wet with running water and it stunk of urine and faeces of past and present prisoners. They were fastened to the wall of their prison by iron chains to large iron rings. They were informed that they would have something to eat before nightfall.

The women and children dispersed to their respective homes, emotionally traumatised. They were shocked and extremely frightened that this could have happened in their village. These things happened in London but not in rural Hampshire! These things happened to other people, not to simple village folk like themselves.

They each blamed themselves for what had happened. Hetti Lott knew the risks when they had invited people to their house for worship on Sundays. She now realised that it had been foolhardy to invite others to share their worship. Mary Watts blamed herself for educating her next-door neighbours in such matters. Encouraging them to listen to and read the Bible for themselves. Emily thought it was all her fault; she shouldn't have let her faithful son William, go to prison, she should have gone herself.. Ruth knew in her heart she was the real culprit. If only she had ignored her principles and accepted Sir Richard's ultimatum, the others would have been spared. Sarah had a nagging doubt that she was to blame. That maybe it had been Nick who had passed on the information that she had so trustingly passed to him. Why had he never been in touch? Where was he? Mary was convinced that she was to blame as she had caused the death of a wealthy man by her herbs. She had been so ill that they had needed to arrest her brother instead of her. Peter was re-calling his conversation with the parish priest. He had forgotten it, but now he was re-living the nightmare in his active imagination.

All of them who had been present that fateful Sunday morning blamed themselves for the situation. Each believed that they were individually guilty for what had happened. They were each consumed with guilt.

When they returned home, Ruth was the first person to get to grips with the situation. She was now the eldest of the children at home. She believed that the crisis was probably her fault so she had better do something about it.

Firstly, she got some food organised, directing Sarah and Mary to collect vegetables and do some cooking. She sent Peter next door to see that they were alright and got Emily to sort out the younger children. Emily was in a mess! Her worries had now got the better of her and she was just sitting in the front room crying deeply whilst holding on to baby George and little Susan.

When they had had eaten something and Emily had calmed down a little, Ruth called a meeting of the family, saying;"I have got to decide whether or not I am going to return to work. I need to earn some money but I need to know that you will survive without me for the next few days. We also need to get news to Richard and ideally to William's new employer. William was due to start work tomorrow. What about the boat? What about ferrying people on the river? Finally, what are we going to do about William and the others in prison?"

Ruth's business-like manner focused their minds on reality. They all started talking about the problems and how to resolve them. It was agreed that Ruth should go back to Sopley Hall that afternoon. She hated the thought of this, but knew that there was no alternative. Sarah would take Peter in the boat immediately to Fordingbridge to tell Richard what had happened. They would attempt relay news to Salisbury to warn Eddie Otter about William. Finally, Emily would get the cottage sorted, plan some meals for the next few days and try to sort out a plan of campaign with Hetti and her next-door neighbour, Mary.

With something to do, the family members began to reassess their situation. Once Ruth had got matters sorted, she took a very deep breath, assured her mother that she would return home if there was any trouble at the Hall and left for Sopley. It would be good to get back to work. She couldn't do anything about her brother and it would be useful to find out if it really was Sir Richard behind the arrest.

Sarah and Peter made progress up the river. There was a good breeze blowing in from the sea and between them they were quite adept at 'reading the currents' on the river. When they arrived at Fordingbridge, they tied up the boat and ran to the carpenter's shop to find Richard. Breathlessly they poured-out their story of the morning's events. When they reported that William had been led away by the soldiers, Sarah was overcome with emotion and could not talk for several minutes. Eventually, when they had poured out the whole tale, Richard was dumbstruck. The three children just sat amongst the wood shavings and pieces of timber, in shock and silence for a time

Finally, Richard said, "I am going to find Joe, he is very sensible, he will know what to do, I trust him, he is a good man." Joe was with his children in the fields and came immediately, sat down with the others and heard their story. "I think that we need to get word to Salisbury as soon as possible. I am going to see if I can borrow a horse this evening. Ride to Salisbury and find Mr Otter, William's new employer, who I hear is quite an important man with friends in high places. Also our gentlemen-friend for whom we are making furniture. He might also be able to help," said Joe, taking the initiative to get something done.

Sarah, immediately jumped up and gave Joe a hug, "Thank you, that's very kind of you." she said with spontaneous enthusiasm. "Hey, don't get too excited, it will be a long, hard battle to get anything done," replied Joe. "If you go hugging me like that, you'll make my wife jealous," he added with a grin.

Sarah and Peter thought that they ought to get back to Ringwood while it was still light and before Mother got too worried. They returned home on the river whilst the other two went to borrow a horse to take them to Salisbury.

Back at Ringwood, there was a very subdued atmosphere. Not only in the Tilly household but throughout the village. There was no-one at the Inn, no-one out walking in the warmth of the summer Sunday evening. No-one chatting on the side of the street. The whole place was deserted with a tangible silence.

Although the majority of the inhabitants did not support the small group of dissident puritans, neither did they support the state when it interfered with their community. 'Let and let live' was the motto of most people, politics and religion were matters for the individual, not for coercion and military reinforcement.

Joe and Richard were able to borrow a fast red mare from a friend which took them rapidly to Salisbury. They went first to the Crown Inn where Joe thought that the wealthy developer would be staying. They were in luck, the said gentleman was just settling down to his evening meal of venison. At first he was not too keen to be interrupted but when he heard their story he ordered food and ale for them so that they could eat and talk together. Richard was amazed; he had never seen such food before in all his life, let alone be treated to eat some of it. For a moment, he forgot his older brother in prison, as he tucked into the best meal he had ever eaten.

Mr Otter liked Joe and young Richard; they were honest, hard-working folk. Eddie Otter had been hoping to get started the next day on surveying the river down at Christchurch, but that would have to wait. This was more important. Although he was not particularly religious, he did try to worship from time to time. He could take it or leave it. However, he did not agree with coercion. Although the law of the land stated that one had to worship in the Church of England according to certain rules and regulations, he personally thought that it was 'so much humbug'. People should be allowed to worship as their conscience dictated. As long they didn't do anything to overthrow the state, they should be left alone.

"You leave this matter with me; I need my boatman back as soon as possible, so I will look into this. Just don't you worry,"

.With this comment, he bade leave of Joe and Richard. Who, because it was now late, decided that they must return to Fordingbridge as soon as possible, leaving their other visit for another time.

After they had gone, Eddie Otter ordered another tankard of ale and sat thinking about the news he had received. One thought occurred to him, "I wonder whether those intent on stopping my development have used this 'religious thing' to get at me. If that is the case, I had better do something about it." With this in his mind he went to bed, mulling over possible strategies to solve the matter.

By the morning he had decided what to do. Leaving a note for his surveyor James Proudfoot, who was due to arrive by coach later in the morning. He left his lodging, crossing Cathedral Green Salisbury and down the main street of the town. He was going to call on his old school friend, John Heathcote-Jones, known to his friends as Old Jonesy. He was a High Court judge and would probably preside over the case of the 'puritan dissenters' when it came to court.

Old Jonsey had only just got up from his bed, having been out drinking the night before. Over a cup of coffee, which was a new experience for the gentry at that time, Eddie told his old friend about the villagers from Ringwood.

"Serve them right, they should abide by the law, all this conscience stuff, gets in the way of good discipline," said Old Jonsey. "It's time we cracked down on these puritans, they need to be taught a lesson", he concluded.

"Yes, I agree," said Eddie tactfully, "but what if their situation is being used as an excuse to stop commercial progress, economic development and better communications? If various interested parties have bribed the authorities to arrest these people so that new initiatives were stopped. Would that be right?" "No, of course not," replied Old Jonesy.

"I am sure that you would find an efficient postal system between London and Salisbury helpful to you wouldn't you?" suggested Eddie. "Be able to ride your carriage from Winchester to your own home on a good road? That would be good wouldn't it?" questioned Eddie of the judge carefully. "Yes, I suppose that would be quite good, I would enjoy that," replied the judge

"What about if you were included as a share holder in the project? You would have an income for life as this road I am planning will be the link between London and the West Country. There will be much money to be made in taxes etc." Suggested Eddie, laying the bait for the Judge to swallow.

"And what's this got to do with the Puritans and their crimes?" asked the Judge at last.

"Well, one young man, William Tilly, who was not the leader of the group but was arrested, is a key worker in my proposals. I need him to make the whole project work." stated Eddie.

"Alright, I will see what I can do, if this man Tilly is released, it will cost you, say £50.00 and a share of the profits of this venture. With no risk and no involvement," agreed the Judge, with a shake of the hand and a return to his hearty breakfast.

In the seventeenth century, judges were open to bribery and corruption. Justice was scant and arbitrary, very much determined by who you were and by whom you were known.

Back home in Ringwood, Monday morning brought a return to a form of normality. The daily duties had to be completed. Fortunately, Mary had now recovered sufficiently to tend to her plants in the garden with Peter helping her with the watering. Sarah had decided that between Peter and herself they could manage the boat. At least, they could run a ferry service from Ringwood to Fordingbridge and if all went well, they would extend their facilities. She was quite proud of the journey they had managed on the previous evening. She wanted to continue the good work. One task that she had to do that Monday morning was to go and see Miriam at the blacksmith's forge. To tell her about the arrest of William. She might be able to help the family see him in prison and because of her job at the forge and who she might meet, find out was going to happen to him.

Emily was still very upset by what had happened, the children seem to recover much quicker in a crisis, they were much more resourceful, she thought. She had not slept at all and was now feeling very tired and depressed. Mary from next door had been a tower of strength, she had been in to visit her several times the previous evening. She had got George and Susan off to sleep and was now organising Emily to do some baking. She had been given some flour and thought that a 'good bake' would take Emily's mind off her problems. Grandma just couldn't understand what had happened, She kept asking why had there been soldiers in Ringwood on a Sunday and why was everyone so upset and where was William?

However, once the children had been organised and fully occupied, with Emily busy preparing her dough for baking, it was a little more peaceful in the cottage.

But it was not quiet in gaol. The men had been locked-up overnight in a dark, damp prison. Breakfast was a bowl of watery soup and mouldy bread. Other prisoners were constantly shouting from the pain caused by their shackles or from the nightmares they were experiencing. At least our four friends were near to each other and could talk to each other. This was a great strength during that first night when fear was uppermost in their minds. You can imagine the thoughts that went through each of their minds. They had no idea what was happening back home, but they were very much aware of the possibility of the hangman's noose. They had no idea what was going to happen.

John Stott as the elder, educated man amongst them, took the lead in trying to provide a positive focus in their hour of need. After the warder had left them, he started to give them some help; "Let us remember Paul and Silas who when they were imprisoned for their faith, prayed and sang praises to God and God heard them. Let us remember Daniel and his friends when they were in prison; they believed that God would deliver them out of the fiery furnace. God will deliver us. We have been called by God to witness to his name and by his grace we will do that." With many other such thoughts they helped each other through the hours of despair. They prayed together, they chanted the psalms together, they cried and laughed together and were strengthened.

As light seeped through the prison corridors, they could see that there were probably fifty or sixty men in the prison. Most were in a very poor state of health, in filthy rags, unkempt and unwashed.

About midday on the Monday morning, a warder brought them some more soup which was cold but with some scraps of vegetable floating on its greasy surface. William asked him what was happening and when would they be released. "The only release from here is to the gallows," the warder said with a sneer on his face. "You will be seen in court sometime this week, I expect. But don't expect any mercy. It's Judge Heathcote-Jones on this week and he hates religious fanatics, so don't hold your hopes up," he added as he collected the empty bowls from the prisoners.

The next few days were all exactly the same, night and day, some scraps of food, dirty water and pervading everything - the stench of the place. A rank, damp smell of unwashed bodies, vomit and excrement, it was unbearable.

Life continued, almost as normal in Ringwood, it was as if Sunday had not occurred. Yet Emily and her neighbour Mary had been shocked and changed forever by the incidents. Life would never be the same for these women – they shared their grief, they shared their uncertainty.

On the other side of the village, Hetti Stott was also deeply affected by the arrest but she had to continue to manage the farm in her husband's absence. She also had the household staff and her children to manage. The thousand and one other things that her husband normally did as a businessman, these had to be completed. However, she was an educated woman, resourceful and competent in talking to people and making things happen. She was part of the new 'middle class' that was emerging at that time, self sufficient, not dependent upon wealthy land-owners.

On the Monday she had written to a family friend, a solicitor in Salisbury, explaining what had happened and asking for his support and advice. She had sent this letter by one of their farm workers by horse. By the afternoon, she had received a letter in return expressing her friend's sorrow and concern. He stated that he would go to Winchester Prison to see the men as soon as he was able and would represent them at any future trial. He also said that he would make a formal application for the prisoners to be bailed forthwith..

By Wednesday, Hetti had been able to make arrangements to go to Winchester and stay for a few days. She wanted to visit her husband, to take him some food, a change of clothes and to find out what was happening. She went to see the other wives to collect some things from them for their men and by Wednesday morning she was ready to travel.

In Fordingbridge, Miriam had received the news about the arrest with alarm and with a degree of annoyance. Although she was a devout 'dissenter' she was also a feisty young woman. I suppose working at the blacksmith's forge all day with farm workers and other tough tradesmen, she was used to standing up for herself. So when she heard about the arrest, she was annoyed, if not downright angry. However, upon reflection she became quite sad and desperate for news. She had to continue to work for the next few days before she could do anything about the arrest. The blacksmith was very busy, shoeing carthorses which were working hard hauling in the hay and the straw off the fields. But by Wednesday, she managed to arrange a lift into Winchester on the back of a trailer loaded with sacks of grain bound for the city.

Unbeknown to the prisoners, all of these activities were proceeding behind the scenes. During Wednesday several people were making their way to visit the prisoners, each hoping that they could gain an early release.

On Thursday morning the warder was joined by six other guards who unshackled the prisoners and marched them out of their cell and out into the fresh air. They were marched to the Prison Governor's Office. He told them that bail had been requested and refused on the grounds 'that they were a threat to the people of Hampshire, that their teaching was seditious and their heresies would lead to insurrection and treason.'

In those days, religious intolerance was widespread. Extremism, whether Catholic, Protestant or Puritan could lead to civil unrest and even war, hence the strong line taken by the authorities.

The Prison Governor also told the men that they would be allowed a visitor, but only for a brief visit. That any food or clothing that visitors brought would have to be used for all the prisoners. With this comment, they were marched back to their cell and chained up as they had been earlier.

Later that day, Hetti and Miriam from their respective backgrounds and circumstances, visited the prisoners. The food and clothing that Hetti brought, was confiscated at the prison gate and used most probably for the prison staff. The two women were forged together in their common task in providing support for the men and spent as long as they could, talking to them. When they left, Hetti thanked the younger woman for her help and hoped that William would realise that she would make an excellent God-fearing wife for him. Hetti went to find her friend's house whilst Miriam searched for some transport back to Fordingbridge.

Nothing more was heard about our friends for two weeks, Sarah had managed to organise a visit to Winchester for her Mother, via the boat to Fordingbridge and with Miriam to Winchester, She knew where to go and had been able to get transport via a grain wagon going up to Winchester, returning in the evening. For those who were poor, transport was difficult, time consuming and dependent upon arranging a deal with someone. When they arrived at the gaol, they were told that the men had left for court as they were to appear that morning. The women were both shocked and excited. On the one hand it could be that by the end of the day their men would be executed. On the other, it could be that they would be free and would be able to go home with them. Fortunately, Hetti had been staying at her friend's house in the city overnight so she knew about the court appearance and was eagerly waiting outside the court.

Earlier that morning the men had been unshackled, herded outside like animals and told to wash themselves using the well in the yard. This was so that they didn't smell too bad to appear in court before Judge Heathcoat-Jones, who was a bit fastidious about such things! They were escorted down the hill to the ancient court house at 'The Castle' and locked like animals in a cage-like contraption outside the back door to the court house.

The judicial system was anything but fair or just. This was particularly true in cases involving matters of religion. There was a certain acceptance of highway robbery as fair game, a certain notoriety and sympathy with cases of infidelity. But religion was a matter for the state and the church with little patience with those who had 'matters of conscience' about forms of worship or particular beliefs. This was very true with respect to the 'Congregational Puritans' who were judged to be 'non-conformists'. Most judges and their courts treated such people with contempt and wished to use any cases that came before them as 'public examples' to warn others about the consequences of such behaviour.

'The Court Rise. The Right Honourable Judge Heathcote-Jones, presiding over the case of the King versus persons who claim to be 'Congregational Puritans." The court usher intoned in his formal, court voice. The four men filed into the court room, there were no defence lawyers. In fact, no prosecution lawyers either. Just the Judge and a motley group of jurors who would do as they were told by the Judge! A crowd had pressed into the public gallery, this was entertainment! For most of them. Crushed at the back of the crowd were the three women who were so personally involved in this case.

The prisoners were shackled with iron chains to each other so they could only shuffle into the court, one behind the other. "What is the crime?" the judge intoned. To which the captain of the accompanying guard replied; "We arrested these men, who together with their respective women and children, were taking part in an illegal assembly in the village of Ringwood on Sunday August 31st, in the year of our Lord, 1625."

"How do you plead?" asked the judge of the four men in turn, each replied clearly,

"Guilty, my Lord". The Judge looked up and asked; "Do you have anything to say in your defence?" The court was silent, waiting for the men to condemn themselves.

John Stott moved forward and replied in a clear, confident voice. "We met together in my house to worship God as he commanded. We shared in reading of God's word, the Bible. We talked about its teaching, prayed together and shared in bread and wine. We have done that which God has commanded that 'we ought to obey God rather than men' as the Apostle Peter has said. If that is against the laws of this land, then the laws must be changed. Our conscience is clear, we have done what is right. It is you who are here this day that have done what is wrong. If I am guilty of obeying God rather than man, then I am guilty and stand judged of you this day. But when I stand before the Judgement Seat of Christ I shall be acquitted and you will be found guilty!"

This was more than Judge Heathcote-Jones could stand; "Away with this heretic". He did not even look to the jury for a judgement on the matter. He just commanded the soldiers to take the men to a place of execution and hang them before dusk. There was a scream from the public gallery. There was shouting mixed with crying from around the room as the significance of the judgement was realised.

The Judge marched out of his court room in anger, his face red and his knuckles white. However, waiting for him in his personal room with glasses of port ready poured, was our old friend, Eddie Otter. "That was a fine piece of acting, my friend", said Eddie. "Here, have a glass of port and regain your sense of priorities."

The Judge gratefully took the proffered glass and downed it in one gulp, reaching out for the other glass which he sipped more gently.

"Here are the papers for you to sign, releasing young William Tilly from the custody of the soldiers. Also, here are the documents giving you a part-share in my new company and finally here is the sum of £50.00 we agreed."

Judge Heathcote-Jones signed the forms, pocketed the money and bid 'farewell' to his old friend. Eddie immediately left and hurried out of the building to his waiting carriage. He quickly left the centre of town to where he had agreed a rendezvous with some of his men who took the 'document of release' and rode quickly to intercept the soldiers with the prisoners.

The crowd had grown enormously – execution was a major spectacle. The women followed the cart with the condemned prisoners inside, each overcome with grief, repeating prayer after prayer in the hope that something miraculous would happen.

Miriam for a moment looked up at the cart, 'where was William?' She couldn't see him at all. The other three with there with their heads bowed. They were covered with horrible stinking refuse, rotten vegetables and horse dung. But no William. "Where was he? Had he been killed already?" She whispered to Emily who struggled to even look up as she just could not comprehend what was happening, she just sobbed in total anguish.

They arrived at the place of execution, The cart stopped under the rope of execution. The men were given a last opportunity to make a speech, two of the men declined. But John Stott stood up straight and said in is usual clear voice; "Lord, lay not this sin to their charge." With those words ringing in the air, the executioner placed a noose around his neck and of the others as the cart moved forward and they were killed. The crowd shouted and threw their hats into the air, baying for even more blood.

With the act of execution, Hetti fainted straight into the arms of Miriam, who strong as an ox, picked her up and carried her. With Emily hanging on to her, they forced their way through the crowd. Miriam just kept going, up the hill, past 'The Castle' to the place where she knew she would find some friends with transport home. Her first thought was to get out of this horrible place; her second thought was about William – What had happened? Was he dead or alive? Had he been captured by someone else? Had he been already killed by the soldiers?

By the time she had reached the transport yard, she was out of breath and trembling. Somebody took care of Hetti and revived her whilst Emily was also given some water and seated on a bale of straw. A man spoke to her quietly, "I've arranged for us to leave in a few minutes in this load of hay, I think it's best if we hide ourselves carefully, at least till we are out of town." Miriam knew that voice, but she didn't believe it – it couldn't be. She opened her eyes and looked into his face and she knew that William was alive."

"I don't know how, but I'm free. I was released not an hour ago. As we were led out from the Court Room and bundled into a cart, these men came up to the soldiers, showed them a piece of paper and they released me. I just ran and ran' till I got here. I knew you would come. Let's get out of here." William explained as they climbed aboard the hay cart and buried themselves in the hay. Soon they were on their way home. Miriam and William held tight in each other's arms, Emily in a daze of unreality, comforting Hetti who was still only semi-conscious. The trauma of the day's events had just been too much to bear. Slowly, imperceptibly, the reality began to dawn on Miriam, that William was alive and safe.

She also realised that the other two women back in Ringwood did not even know of the trial, let alone the fact that their husbands had been executed. She whispered to William about her concerns. He held Miriam's hand tightly, telling her not to worry as in the morning he would go and tell them.

Eventually, they arrived home. They briefly stopped at Fordingbridge to collect an amazed Richard. The excitement of the Tilly family was tempered by the sadness of the deaths of the other three men. Hetti Stott was inconsolable. They all agreed that she would stay the night with Emily. That the morning would be early enough to go home and face her family and servants with the news.

Over the next few days, shock and horror at what had happened filled their minds. No-one had ever thought that arrest and execution would visit them in Ringwood. The children were frightened to go outside the cottage. The older ones scurried to and fro to complete their tasks without pausing. William had the difficult task of visiting the two women whose men had been hanged and trying to get the family back to normality. In the village and on the river he was treated as 'one who had come back from the dead.' Local people being somewhat in awe of him.

Miriam had stayed over at the cottage in Ringwood with William taking her to work each day by boat. They had decided that they would get married as soon as possible, as soon as the boat had returned from 'the voyage'. Miriam had started to make enquiries about accommodation – she just didn't want William to be out of her sight. On the Saturday, William sailed down the river to Sopley to collect his beloved sister Ruth from work. He explained that he did not know who had reported 'their worship' to the authorities. The other men in the prison had thought it had been a servant at the Stott's household who had been recently dismissed and had felt aggrieved. She was just so relieved to have her brother back home. She just cried all the way back home on Saturday evening, clinging tightly to him.

Sunday was going to be a difficult day. They talked about the difficulties in holding their normal service and also how to conduct a funeral service for their three friends. But it was thought just too dangerous and foolhardy to meet together, even to remember the dead.

William, as the elder member of their small group of believers worked out a simple service which he dictated to Sarah. She then wrote down the details, he distributed these notes to Hetti and to the other families. At the appointed time they could meet, but in their own homes, sharing in the same thoughts, readings and prayers as if they were together. If they were raided again, he instructed each family to destroy the notes. They each agreed that despite the instruction to worship at the local church, they could not do so. As William commented, 'that to go the altar rail and take communion from one who worships idols would be to 'share in their evil practises.'

The Sunday service was therefore held in each other's homes, with the exception of Hetti who had stayed with the Tilly's and therefore shared in their fellowship. It was an emotional service with much sadness. It was however, tinged with thankfulness that the Lord had saved William out of the 'jaws of death.'

Worlds Apart'

Eight – 'It could never be quite the same again'

On Monday morning, William was back at work, now assisted by Sarah, who having built up the business in William's absence, desperately wanted to continue. She quite enjoyed the open air and the challenge of managing the boat. When she had got into difficulties there was always someone on hand to help, or so it seemed. When they arrived at Fordingbridge, there was a message for William from James Proudfoot. William was to make arrangements to start work immediately so that they survey the lower reaches of the the river as soon as possible.

William was utterly dumbfounded that James and presumably his employer should know about his release. With William only just starting to recover from his ordeal, it was quite an effort for him to recall the arrangements which they had made several weeks ago. It seemed like a whole lifetime ago since they had talked about such matters.

That Monday morning was significant. William had so much on his mind; the death of his fellow believers, his own freedom, his relationship with Miriam and not least where were his Father and brother? Would they be back soon or would the family never see them again?

But a new set of questions were attacking his thoughts that morning, matters relating to work and its implications. Something which he had not considered since that fatal Sunday morning when they had been arrested, now he had to concentrate on a new subject. He also felt quite guilty, why was he alive when the others were dead? Why was he able to be back on his beloved river and they were dead? It should have been me, he thought, not them.

So, what about the boat and his business of ferrying and fishing? At lunchtime he happened to see an old fellow-boatman who greeted William as if he had come back from the dead. William explained that he had an offer to do some special 'charter work' and wondered if his friend would like to take on extra ferrying work. "Yes, I could do that but I need someone to work my boat. I have a terrible problem with my back, I can't row any longer." William had a brainwave, "If Sarah and young Peter look after your boat and take-on my ferry work. They can pay you a rental for the boat and earn some money for us as well." So it was agreed. Sarah and Peter would look after one boat, leaving William to use the other for his 'charter work' with James Proudfoot.

It was amazing, in just forty-eight hours. William had gone from being a condemned criminal to being a businessman with a job and a future. Was this the work of God or was this just a matter of chance? William had always believed that 'the angel of the Lord encampeth round about them that fear him'. That God guided and protected his followers but this was unbelievable. If this was true, then God had saved him from death and had blessed him exceedingly.

But what about poor Hetti and the other women? They had lost everything, their men-folk and their livelihood. As a result of which, at least two of the other women would become paupers, thrown out of their homes and have to beg in order to survive. Where was God in their lives? Why hadn't their men been saved as well? It just couldn't be explained. William just couldn't understand it.

These questions were mind-blowing, but for the time being, William had to shelve consideration of them. He had to get on with his life and show his gratitude to his God by serving Him to the uttermost. He now had an even greater responsibility - to provide for his family and also for the new ' love of his life,' Miriam. He had to show real care for his mother and also for those widows in their little community. A care that would enable them to cope with the grieving and make them able to provide for their families. Having made these decisions, William prepared for his new role in life with an intensity of purpose that no-one had seen in him before.

Ruth had been affected by the events in a different way. Initially, it was one of relief that her brother had been saved, that he had not been hanged but had walked free to return to them all. Then subsequently, one of curiosity tinged with deep sadness that three men had been hanged for no other reason than obeying their conscience. Her curiosity was heightened because she had heard nothing more from Sir Richard. He had returned to London. Rumour amongst the servants was, that he had a young mistress in the city with whom he consorted regularly. She wondered whether anything more would come of her encounter with him.

Lady Susan, of course, knew nothing of the situation which had arisen between Sir Richard and Ruth. She could see no reason why the conversations about religion couldn't continue. Ruth therefore, continued learning to read and discussing religion but from a more neutral stance. Ruth was a matter-of-fact girl, seeing reality as it was, not dreaming of either gloom or unrelieved happiness. She therefore continued with both her work and her studies with interest and enthusiasm. That was, until one particular Wednesday morning, about two weeks after William had been released.

Lady Susan and Ruth were talking in her Ladyship's bedroom, they had just opened the Bible and Lady Susan asked a question which had obviously been bothering her; "If your God looks after his followers in 'the way' that you believe, why did he allow three of your friends to die in such a dreadful manner?"

Ruth was silenced. This was something she had also thought about but had not come to any satisfactory conclusion. After a few moments thought, she replied; "Firstly, although it's the law of the land to worship in a certain manner, the laws of God are more important. As the Apostle Peter said in similar circumstances; 'We ought to obey God rather than men.' Secondly, everything happens according to cause and effect. We worship God in a way which is against the law of the land. The men were arrested, were declared guilty and hung. That's a matter of fact and I think I accept it in that way. The challenge for me is how I respond to what has happened. I believe that they will be raised from the dead at Judgement Day. I therefore have to show my faith by trusting in God that he knows best. 'That all things work together for good to those who love God'. This is a very hard teaching and I am finding it very difficult to accept, but I must try."

"Wow, that was a bit of a speech, young lady," said Lady Susan, "Yes, I can understand your response to this situation, but why should it have happened in the first place? Surely, if you had all obeyed the laws of the land, then this would not have happened. Your friends would not have died."

"I know that what you have said may be true," replied Ruth, "but I have to take the rough with the smooth. I believe that God gives me everything for this life and also the promise of eternal life in the future. Equally, I must also accept that the problems of life are according to the will of God. In fact the Bible teaches me that the suffering of this life is part of God's chastening. Just as a father punishes a child so that a child is not spoilt but matures into a responsible adult, so we suffer at God's hand in order for us to be 'chastened as sons'.

"I think that sounds all right in theory but it's a little more difficult to accept in practice," answered Lady Susan carefully, "I don't think that I could actually accept pain and suffering in that way. If I was attacked or someone I loved was killed. I would be angry and would want revenge. Justice meted out to the guilty. I just wouldn't accept it like a dog rolling over onto its back and taking the kicks of a violent man."

"But that's the whole point of being a disciple of Jesus. That's the challenge that the Bible lays down for us. As Jesus said; 'If any man will come after me, let him deny himself and take up his cross and follow me'. That is really difficult to achieve. However, he did give us some very helpful guidelines. Such as; 'Therefore all things whatsoever ye would that men should do to you, do ye even so to them.' That means that, we need to treat other people the way in which we would like them to treat us. Jesus never said that it would be easy. In fact, he said that disciples would be like 'sheep in the midst of wolves.'"

"Thank you for that," said Lady Susan with a smile on her face, "I think that is enough lecturing for one day."

"I am sorry, I didn't mean it like that ...", stuttered Ruth, realising that she had talked to her employer as if she was voicing her opinions at home. "That's alright," replied Lady Susan, "I asked the questions and you have given me the answers. Now, you had better go and get on with your tasks." "Yes, your ladyship," said Ruth with a curtsey.

Both women spent the rest of the day thinking about what had been said. Lady Susan, in particular was thinking about the implications of this new teaching. She thought about ways in which the Established Church of the day, did not practice what it preached, whether Protestant, Catholic. This was quite a shock for Lady Susan, she had just not thought about such matters before. She had never heard the idea that to be a Christian was in reality, to be selfless and consequently a difficult way of life. That it was a denial of self with little to do with religious ritual, even less about heaven and hell.

Later in the day, she turned to the words of Jesus, and read for herself the Sermon on the Mount. She also read on into the next chapter about the leper who came to Jesus seeking to be healed. Suddenly, she got up from her couch and fell to her knees repeating the words of the leper; "Lord, if thou wilt, thou canst make me clean."

Lady Susan had no idea that her brief act of prayer would have such an effect upon her thoughts and actions! But we have to remember that in the 'Year of Our Lord 1625'; religion affected every aspect of life. One lived or died depending upon one's faith and allegiance to a particular religious creed.

Two days later, a lone horseman galloped into the stable yard at Sopley Hall. He jumped down from his horse, commanded a stable lad to look after the horse and demanded to see Lady Susan immediately. When he had been ushered into her presence, he delivered a letter from her husband. The letter requested her to accompany him at a special service of dedication at Westminster Abbey in London.

Apparently, a number of leading churchmen and others had recently been appointed to the House of Lords by King Charles and they were to be 'sworn into office'. The letter stated that she was to take her maid and that they were to travel by coach during the next week to arrive in London by the following Sunday. She knew that she could not refuse. It was more of an order than a request for both of them and thought crossed her mind as to whether this was a trap. But if she refused to attend, it would be snub of monumental proportions which she could not risk. So over the next few days, Lady Susan and her maid made their arrangements to travel to London. For both of them the trip was both exciting and frightening

They just did not know what to expect .The journey was reasonably comfortable. They stopped for two night's en-route, one at Winchester and the other at Windsor at 'Wayside Inns'. When they arrived in London, they went straight to Sir Richard's London house which was situated near Hatton Garden. This was a newly built town-house in one of the fashionable suburbs of the city. Everything went well for the rest of the week. The two women were able to do some sightseeing. Ruth had never been to London before, she was amazed at the sights and the sounds of a busy city. Its traffic, its people and above all, the splendid houses of the rich and famous.

The service to which Lady Susan had been commanded to attend was to be on the following Sunday. She did not have any problems of conscience about taking part in the service and taking communion. But Ruth was troubled in her heart and worried in her mind about the consequences of taking part or not taking part. Although she desperately wanted to be included in the pageantry, to see the king and witness at first-hand the pomp and ceremony of a royal occasion, yet she was troubled. She knew that the religious service would demand that she participate, ultimately to go up to the altar rail to take communion. We might think that these matters were unimportant but to a young woman who had been taught that these things were evil, for Ruth this was heresy and the work of the devil. It was a matter of life or death, it would be tantamount to denying everything she and her family had lived and almost died for.

However, by Sunday morning she was so worried that she was violently sick with a terrible headache; she therefore asked if she could stay at home. Lady Susan reluctantly agreed. She knew that Sir Richard would ask where Ruth was, she would have to defend her maid. A matter which could easily compromise herself as well and have both of them thrown into prison!

The service was amazing. All the pomp and ceremony. All the rich colours, the sounds and the sights were just unbelievable. However, Lady Susan was, for the first time in her life, made uncomfortable by the outward show, particularly by the activities of the clergy. As a result of her recent discussions with Ruth, she sensed the decree of hypocrisy in their ritual. She squirmed in her inner being when some of the prayers were intoned. When it came to taking the communion, she nearly 'lost it'.

From their position, about half-way down the abbey, all eyes were on her, as first Sir Richard and then she rose to walk down to the altar rail to receive the wafer of bread. She could barely walk as she shuffled in the line of dignitaries proceeding towards the altar. Her husband noticed her reluctance, her seeming inability to do something which should have been second nature.

Sir Richard realised what he had suspected for some time was in fact, true. His wife had been converted to 'Congregational Puritanism'. That was unforgivable! Any affection which he had for his wife now evaporated and he could barely wait until the service was ended before challenging his wife with her crime.

"You have been brainwashed by that numb skull of a maid, you've become one of them, and you're an evil witch, you …." He thundered at Lady Susan as soon as they were back in his house near Hatton Garden. "I knew that she was one of them, I have had her watched for several months. She and her family are evil. Somehow her brother escaped the death penalty a few weeks ago. How I don't know, but he did. At least his three friends were hanged. She will hang as well if I have anything to do with it. Mark my words. If you continue in her evil ways, I will have you arrested as well and tried for sedition and treason."

Sir Richard gradually calmed down but he was still annoyed. Lady Susan knew that she would have to be very careful about what she said. However, the immediate question was how to extradite her beloved maid, from his clutches? After careful thought, she replied,

"Yes dear, it was a little difficult today; I really enjoyed the pomp and the ceremony. I thought that you looked very handsome, a really important knight of the realm. It was obvious that King Charles sees you as one of his most trusted and important subjects. However, when it came to the religious part. I did find it a little hypocritical, some of the rituals practised by the clergy seem to have more to do with church tradition than Bible teaching," said Lady Susan tactfully. "But I wouldn't want to do anything to rock the boat, I am very much aware of how important your position in Parliament is to you. I realise that your position requires both of us to accept the official Church of England stance on religious worship. However, it would be helpful if you could allow young Ruth to continue as my maid. She is very good at her job and I am sure that she would have been at the service today, if she had been well enough."

Sir Richard, having now calmed down appreciated what she had said. It was useful to have a wife to give him status and a good standing in the country. She had also brought with her, many lands and much property which he now owned. So maybe, he could overlook her qualms about religion, as long as she kept it to herself. It also might be quite useful to keep the young maid on a piece of string, get her a little worried about her future. As long as she didn't convert his wife or anyone else to her strange notions. After he had mulled over these thoughts, he commented to Lady Susan; "Yes, alright, I agree to what you have requested. But if there is any indication that she has affected you beyond what is acceptable, I will have her arrested and imprisoned."

The next day, he arranged to take the two women on a tour of London by coach, showing them the sights a little further a field, They went to the Inns of Court and on to The Tower. At lunchtime, they stopped at a well-known Inn adjacent to the river. Sir Richard ordered some beef and Madeira wine as a special treat for the women. When Lady Susan went to find a toilet place, Sir Richard had a few minutes to comment confidentially to Ruth; "I haven't forgotten our little conversation back in the summer. In fact you have now grown into a more mature young woman with a pleasant personality. I wouldn't mind showing you the sights on your own, if you get my meaning. But if you continue to subvert your mistress with your religious nonsense, undermining my authority, you are dead. Do you understand?"

Ruth cast her eyes to the ground and managed to stammer a reply; "Yes, I understand, Sir Richard. I will not forget what you have said." "Good", replied Sir Richard, "That's settled then, no more fancy religious ideas, alright?"

In the afternoon, they visited St Paul's Cathedral and had a look at the bookshops which were a feature of that area, finally the goldsmiths and the market traders around Covent Garden. But for Ruth, the excitement had gone,

She was just a maid, following her master and mistress, to do their bidding and obey their command.

The rest of the trip to London passed without further incident and the two women were soon travelling back to their rural outback in Southern Hampshire. On the way home, Ruth explained that she was no longer able to learn to read and talk about the Bible. That it would be wiser not to even talk about such matters. Lady Susan studied Ruth's face and said no more, realising that Ruth had probably been warned off by her husband. She realised that for the time being, it was probably wiser to accept the situation.

On the River Avon, back in Hampshire, members of the Tilly family had been very busy. Sarah had been ferrying passengers and transporting cargo up and down the river. She had developed muscles where she didn't think she had any. Her broken arm had not only healed but had been fully exercised. Peter had grown-up overnight; he had not only had his ninth birthday during August but had become quite adept at handling the oar on the boat. In fact, he was almost an equal partner. He took the fares and looked after the money. He kept a record of the goods being transported and was rapidly learning how to write out 'a bill of payment' for the business customers. The month of September passed rapidly for both of them and they were thinking about winter as the days grew shorter and the mornings colder.

Meanwhile, William was also working the river but in a totally different manner. Right from the first day, he liked his new colleague, James Proudfoot. He was nearly ten years older than William and had trained as a river surveyor in Bristol for the city docks authority. He had been involved in keeping a record of the changing position of the mud banks, in order for the larger vessels using Bristol harbour not to be grounded. He was therefore, an excellent choice to survey the Hampshire Avon in readiness for commercial use.

He brought with him a range of equipment; leaded lines and marker-boys, chains for measuring, pieces of white cloth, miles of rope and sketch pads with pens for the first part of the river-survey. They made a base in the Christchurch area, staying with a fishing family at Mudeford. They began their work with James completing a series of sketches of the harbour from different perspectives. They used the boat to traverse the harbour with James dropping his weighted line every couple of yards. All the measurements were recorded on the sketches to provide them with an indication of depth and current. They also studied the existing harbour walls, again drawing the scene from different viewpoints. All the time, James was making notes and talking through his observations with his assistant, William.

After a week studying the harbour, they moved onto the river. Again with James sketching the scene every five hundred yards and in-filling the sketches with detailed measurements. These measurements illustrated the width and depth of the river showing obstructions, sandbanks or other items of interest which might endanger the barges. Finally, William was asked to row carefully over each section, providing a 'running commentary' regarding river currents and the speed of flow. William found the work fascinating. After a week or two he was beginning to learn some basic methods of calculation and being able to write down some of the notes for James.

There were two things that William missed, however, firstly it was the opportunity to talk about life and religion. As his work was so demanding there was just no time to stand and talk. Secondly, he particularly missed his time with Miriam. At the very period of his life when he wanted to spend all his waking moments with her, he couldn't spend any.

Young Richard was equally busy; you will no doubt remember that he had obtained for himself an apprenticeship in carpentry with Joe Witchell. When we left him, he was working on a special desk and chair for a gentleman in Salisbury. They had completed the desk and were busy carving the legs and arms for the chair. They also had other orders to finish.

Again, Richard missed home and the opportunity for talking. On reflection, he had liked listening to the animated discussion which had been a feature of family life at the Tilly household for as long as he could remember. Now that he couldn't easily ask questions, he had lots of them. Although it was fun working with wood and he enjoyed the smell of the timber, the creation of a beautiful product, however, it was at times quite boring! He missed the stories of travel and adventure. He missed the animated discussion at home on all manner of topics. He found himself looking forward to Sundays. Not just to see his family, but also to be able to listen to the Bible stories. To be able to dream about the past and the future.

Back home in Ringwood, Emily was still desperately depressed. She felt guilty that the other men and been killed and her William was alive and well. She felt very alone. Her friend, Hetti Stott had been shattered by the hanging of her husband and had left the village to go and stay with her sister in the West Country.

Emily's beloved husband was somewhere on the high seas. In her heart she even doubted whether he would return. Her older children were all working hard and away from home during the week. Only Mary, Susan and George remained homebound. With of course, Grandma, who seemed to sleep more and more and Emily hoped that that's the way she would die. But the real thing that caused Emily's depression was the baby inside her. She knew that the baby was there and growing as she could now feel it from time to time. But she worried whether it would survive. If it did, would it be normal. Because of the traumatic events of the recent past, she just thought that the baby might be born deformed or mad. If only her beloved John would return, he would reassure her.

Just as Emily was mulling over these matters, Sarah and Peter burst into the cottage. "The boat has been sighted off Hengistbury Head and it should be near Mudeford by now. If we go immediately we could make it to Christchurch by the time they dock. Come on, hurry," cried Peter. They scrambled for the door, ran down to the boat and Sarah quickly cast off.

As they sailed down the river, Emily wondered what they would find when the boat docked. Would everyone be safe? Would her men be alive or had something dreadful happened to them? She prayed for them all;

"Please God, may they all be safe and if not, help us to accept what has happened with grace and fortitude."

'Worlds Apart'

Nine – 'The Homecoming'

As they sailed over the sand bar at the entrance to Mudeford and Christchurch Harbour, all on-board heaved a sigh of relief. At least, they were back in familiar territory, they were back home. The captain, John Tilly, breathed a prayer of thanks to God that although they had been to the end of the world, they had returned home safe and sound.

The wind had almost died as they brought in the canvas sails for the last time. They had about an hour to dock before the tide ebbed fully. Hopefully, the wind would just keep them going until they were able to tie up at the quay side. As they moved slowly across the harbour they could see a crowd growing in numbers on the quay, people were waving and cheering. Dogs were barking, children crying and the crew on board equally full of excitement. Homecoming was something special, something that they had longed for, dreamed about and now it was happening.

As they got nearer, shouts were heard: "Is everyone well? Have you lost anyone?" And they could answer; "We are all here, everyone is well." Great shouts of joy from the quay side welcomed everyone home; "Thank God, they have all returned safely," muttered the wives and children of the fishermen as they prepared to welcome home their loved ones.

At last, the boat was alongside the harbour wall and the ropes were fixed around the bollards. The boards linking the boat to the quay side were put down and the crew scrambled on to dry ground. The family-members of each man, crowded around their loved ones. Everybody was there. The news of the homecoming had spread like wildfire and almost everyone had managed to get to the quay-side. There were tears of joy and thankfulness that all had safely returned.

Slowly, the emotion subsided and the crew members drifted back on board to collect their personal belongings and wend their way homeward. William went on board with John the less to off-load the perishable items – fresh fish that had been caught in the last few days. This had to be immediately eaten or sold. The rest was salted or kept in ice in the hold of the boat and could be offloaded over the next day or so.

William started to ferry his family members up-river home, he sent Peter to collect Ruth from Sopley Hall, Sarah to collect Richard from Fordingbridge and Miriam from Ellingham. Everybody must be home that night for a special meal to celebrate the homecoming. As soon as Emily and Mary reached home, they started preparing the food. This was going to be a special celebration. For the present, Emily's worries were forgotten, she had her family home.

That evening they all sat down for a meal of thanksgiving. They filled the whole of the ground floor of the cottage, on benches and on the floor. Each person was excited and full of expectation. Each bursting with news to tell, but each waiting for the right moment.

Father began the meal with a deeply moving prayer, "Father thank you for bringing us safely home. Thank you for keeping my whole family safe in your care. Thank you for everything. May we give glory and honour to your name. We express this prayer in the name of Jesus Christ our Lord and Master, Amen." He could barely finish his prayer through the emotion he felt in his inner being. But when he sat down he felt a wonderful warm glow. He was home again with his beloved family. His dear wife had whispered to him on the way from Christchurch that she was expecting another baby, for this he was deeply thankful.

Ruth and Sarah served everyone their first course, a fish soup with fresh crisp bread. As they ate, the younger children started with their news. This was a family tradition at a homecoming. They would tell their news, beginning at the youngest to the oldest. So little Susan started with saying; "I walk, I walk everywhere, to market, to river, to trees." To this everyone collapsed in laughter – this was a good start to what would be a long night, a night of shared experiences. Family members listening to each other in sadness and in joy.

By the time they reached the main course of fresh cod with new potatoes, peas, beans and other vegetables, they had heard about Peter and his new responsibilities on the boat. Mary talked about her herbs, her illness and recovery. Richard described his new work in the carpenter's shop and the pieces of furniture he had made. Sarah spoke of her mastery of the boat and egged-on by the others described 'her first love' who had just disappeared! By this time, the two youngest children were asleep as Ruth described her work at Sopley Hall. She was able to describe the Ball and her visit to London, avoiding any mention of her discussions with Lady Susan until she could talk alone with her father.

William described in broad terms, his arrest, trial and release. He looked to his Father in a way which suggested he would also talk to him later about the details. He described to great effect, his work for Eddie Otter and James Proudfoot. Finally he grabbed hold of Miriam's hand and looking directly at Father said; "We would like to get married as soon as possible. We have waited until your return so that we may gain your blessing and ask you to bless us and if you are willing, to marry us?"

"That's really something to come home for," said Father, wiping a tear from his eye, "Of course, I would love to do the honour, and we will make the arrangements as soon as possible." Then came the moment they had all been waiting for. With mugs full of ale and stomachs full of food, with cake and plum pudding being slowly eaten, father and John the less, began their story.

"When we left the harbour, we began to realise the immensity of the voyage and the smallness of our vessel", started Father. "So we busied ourselves by coiling the various halyards on the deck and setting the sails. We started to pick up the south-westerly which swept around the Needles and through the Solent. We set a course which would take us east away from the sand spits and into the channel. With the Isle of Wight on our starboard side and Southampton Water on the port side we began our momentous voyage.

As we sailed into the lee of the Isle of Wight, the wind reduced dramatically, the boat became almost stationary. The wind which had taken us down the Solent was obscured by the bulk of the island and we were reduced in speed to almost a standstill. A situation which lasted for several days and nights until one morning we detected a change in conditions. The wind started to rattle the jib sail and the sea started to rise and fall, we were on our way. The wind did not fail for the next two weeks!

Several of the men began to suffer from serious seasickness. But this was normal when we got onto the high seas, we all knew that before many days, we would all be suffering as well. The boat began to toss and turn as we started to sail down the Channel leaving the Isle of Wight on our starboard side. Before long, with a steady wind blowing in the main sail we were out into the deeper water of the Southern Channel.

By now, we were all sea-sick. Sleep was beginning to be really difficult as everything was constantly wet. We were eternally grateful for our new boots which proved to be invaluable. John the less has managed to keep his feet completely dry throughout the voyage, even when a gigantic wave broke over the boat and nearly swamped us. Life was getting tough; the shriek of the wind in the rigging and the grinding of the ropes around the boat, was unnerving. The water washing over the boat was devastating, and the wind, it threatened to break the boat apart.

Each night, we wondered whether we would see the light of a new day. Whether or not we would go down into the deep and never come up again. But at the end of the second week at sea, we really hit rough seas."

John the less now took up the story; "The day had dawned as normal but by mid-morning you could not tell where the sea finished and the sky began. The seas became wilder, the waves towering above the boat and then crashing down upon us threatening to crush everything under its mighty power. The boat was being tossed like a cork. At times almost vertical, at others almost swamped. We were all roped individually to structural parts of the boat. Although Jo Watts was fixed to quite a long rope, one enormous wave took him overboard." Everyone gasped at this news, as they all knew that once overboard in a storm, it was often fatal.

John continued; "Two of us grabbed his rope and held on for all we were worth. It seemed like hours but it was probably only a few minutes before we could pull him back. Yard by yard. It was very difficult but we succeeded. We thought that we had lost him or at least he would be seriously injured. But no, apart from minor cuts and bruises he was unharmed. Of course, Jo being Jo will joke about the incident. But for a time, we thought that he was a goner. The storm lasted for three days, there was barely any difference between day and night. However, gradually the winds abated and the sea calmed. The sun was seen and we gained a feeling of survival. If we can survive that storm, by God's grace we can do anything. I remembered the Psalm which talks about storms and I quoted it to Father;

'They that go down to the sea in ships, that do business in great waters; that see the works of the Lord and his wonders in the deep. For he commanded and raiseth the stormy wind, which lifteth up the waves thereof. They mount up to the heavens, they go down again to the depths; their soul is melted because of trouble. They reel to and fro like a drunken man, and are at their wits end. Then they cry unto the Lord in their trouble, and he bringeth them out of their distresses. He maketh the storm a calm, so that the waves thereof are still. Then they are glad because they be quiet, so he bringeth them unto their desired haven'.

With those thoughts in our minds we thanked God for our safe passage through the storm and we sailed on. John Hayter could now take a fix on our location by reading the stars, he reckoned that the storm had blown us further north than we had planned to travel. This was confirmed in another week or so, when the air started to become noticeably colder and the water seemed like liquid ice. Then, an amazing event happened; five weeks from England we woke one morning to see an iceberg!" Richard interrupted with a question; "What's an iceberg?"

Father answered, "An iceberg is a floating island of ice which can be as big as mountain, although normally they are no more than several hundred yards in length,. The ice had been broken off from a glacier and as it floats south it melts in the warmer seas. The important thing to realise is that what you see above the water is only a fraction of what is below the water." "That's amazing!" cried Richard. "I would love to see an iceberg, that would be awesome!"

At this point, Sarah and Ruth took a platter of cakes and a pitcher of ale to top up everyone's mugs, providing a necessary break in the story-telling.

Father continued; "The iceberg was amazing, the mass of ice was a brilliant icy blue as it reflected the sun. It moved like a giant lady dressed for the ball, slowly and gracefully across the sea. We took great care to keep our distance. We just watched in awed silence as it drifted across the vast expanse of ocean. All around us there were smaller pieces of ice, the sea itself seemed to have a 'skin of frazil ice', a layer of milky, ice water. The surface of the sea was beginning to freeze over, congealing silently and quickly as we moved through it. We didn't sleep much during the next few days as we steered though that strange ocean.

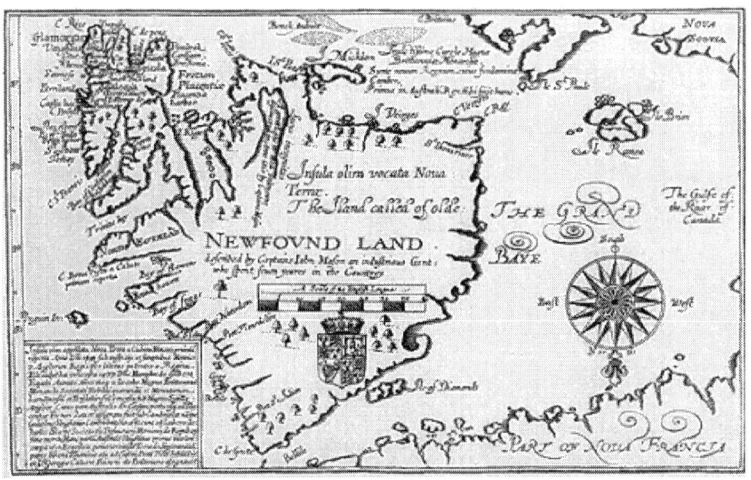

New-Found-Land

As shown by John Mason's map of c. 1617

(N.B. Old maps like this were often inverted in their orientation and drawn with the North at the bottom of the map.)

At least we knew that we had crossed most of the ocean because the icebergs only travel down the eastern coastline of the 'New World'. We had now travelled into that region by John's calculations, so sooner or later we would sight land.

We did. It was a wonderfully clear and sharp day. One of the men who was on watch, suddenly called; 'Land Ahoy'. Everyone rushed to have sight of land.

After six weeks of sailing we were all desperate for land, for the feel of solid ground under our feet, to be able to make a fire to get warm and dry.

We raised as much sail as we could carry, forcing our faithful boat to move as fast as was possible toward land. We did not know what land it would be. We just hoped that it would be New-Found-Land. Gradually, the land-mass grew larger as we drew nearer until we could make out cliffs and the sea pounding on the shore. John had a cross-staff with him with which he was able to accurately determine our north/south position. He decided that we were several hundred miles north of where we needed to be but not far from the best fishing area.

We decided that we could not land on that coastline, it was just too rocky. We decided to sail south along the coast to find a more friendly kind of harbour. The next day we were able to make an exact location on our map, the one drawn last year by John Mason, a copy of which we had taken with us. After sailing for another day or so, the coastline became gentler and a bay opened before us.

We had found Bonavista! This is the place that John Cabot discovered many years ago. It's an easily accessible place with relatively flat ground and plenty of space where we could smoke fish. It didn't have much protection from the sea and storms but for a summer base it was excellent. We liked Bonavista, it seemed like home to us Hampshire men.

We slowly inched our way along the coast until we could drop anchor and row ashore in our small shallop (dingy). Oh, to be on land once more, to be able to run and jump and walk on dry ground. The first thing to do was to find some timber and light a fire. Then we could have a hot stew of salted pork left over from our voyage.

We were, however, not alone in this area. There were several other fishing boats and their crews. Each of which having made an area of the shore-line their own with fires and racks of drying fish ready to be shipped back to Europe. It was an exciting place with different languages being spoken with men from various parts of Europe.

We brought our beds ashore to have a night on dry ground before we started work on the morrow. We didn't have time for exploring. As this was now late in the season, we had to catch our boat-load of fish as soon as possible and be back on the high seas in a matter of days.

We divided the team into catchers and curers. The curers or smokers were our shore crew, they went in search of timber to make a small landing stage for the shallop. They built platforms of timber covered in brushwood on which the fish would be cured. The catchers meanwhile, put the two shallops to work, we were a much smaller crew than most of the fishing boats, but we managed. We were able to use the lines to catch the fish and sometimes we were even able to scoop them up with our buckets! There were just millions of them. Half-a-mile or so off shore, we found shoals of lovely fat fish just waiting to be caught and we caught them. As the fish were emptied into the boat, at least one of the team gutted the fish, rubbing salt into the flesh and stacking them, ready for smoking and curing on shore.

We worked hard for two weeks, almost non-stop except for eating and sleeping. Of course, we had a break on the Lord's Day when those of us who are religious had our simple service on the shore with the gulls for company. We could do as we wished, other fishing crews practised their worship, Catholics and Protestants, each respecting the other. It was just wonderful to behold.

We filled all our barrels and containers with fish and after two weeks we were ready to return. Before setting sail however, we just allowed ourselves one day to explore the area. Most of the bay at Bonavista is relatively flat with a rocky headland at the one end. There didn't seem to be any native dwellers. Just the various boats and their crews although there were some buildings a few miles away but we did not have time to walk that far. The place seemed warm and friendly, although I am sure that it's wild with the winter wind and very cold with snow and ice.

On the first day of September we left New-Found-Land for home. We have had a good journey home with no major problems. I think that it has been quicker coming home than when we went. It must be that the boat wanted to get home quickly!"

Everyone burst into applause. It was wonderful to have them back home. The family was together again. Sarah took the pitcher of ale around again and filled everyone's mugs to the brim. This was time for celebration.

Father struggled to his feet and raised his tankard; "May the Lord be praised who has given us of his bountiful hand, who has given us life and peace. May the Lord be praised." With this they all raised their mugs and echoed father's words; "May the Lord be praised."

After a moment's quiet, William stood and said carefully; "May the Lord have mercy on those who have caused pain and suffering in the past few months. May the Lord be with those who suffer this night. The widows and orphans in this place. May the Lord give them life and peace. May the Lord have mercy." They all echoed these words, remembering the loss of their friends; "May the Lord have mercy."

In the morning they all had work to do. Sarah in her role as boatman took the men down to Christchurch. They had left a night watchman on board, but now they had to unload the fish. They had to sort out the catch, wash the boat and get everything clean and tidy. John the less had to make contact with a fish wholesaler so that they could unload and sell the bulk of the fish to one man, if possible. John walked across to Mudeford and discussed terms with a fisherman who had contacts in Southampton and Salisbury. As he was doing this, he was thinking that it would be a great advantage to be able to unload direct into a barge and transfer the catch immediately to Salisbury. The project that William had become involved in, would be a wonderful opportunity for trade. It would really put Christchurch on the map

A deal was struck. He could return with the wholesaler together with his wagon and horses to unload the catch. On the quay side, Emily and Mary had set up a stall to sell some of the poorer quality fish to local people. The men were hauling out the baskets and barrels of fish from the hold of the boat on to the quay side and they were able to load the fish directly onto the wagon. Some went into William's boat for sale locally and for their own family. John Tilly paid the crew their wages and shared the balance of money, from the fish sales, with his partners. All of these transactions were recorded by Mary Watts who had come down to Christchurch specifically to do this job. She would then be able to draw up a detailed statement of the accounts for the voyage. All of the proceedings were watched-over carefully by the Customs and Excise man who recorded the weight of the catch, the price paid, the cost of wages and the expenses of the trip. Before any of them could go home they would have to pay quite a hefty tax to the Government.

At the end of the day, they were not left with that much money. Definitely not enough to see them through the winter. John had already decided that they would have to go out fishing again in November or December into the Bay of Biscay. This would be in direct competition with the French and Spanish boats which were larger and more efficient than his own. However, that was something to be talked about in the next few weeks. For now, there were more pressing concerns that he needed to give his attention to.

He needed to spend time with each member of his family. He needed to visit each of the widows and think about what they were going to do about their services of worship. All matters needing his attention.

First of all, John needed to spend time with his wife. Her self-esteem was at low-ebb and she needed him to re-assure her and take his share of the burden of family worries.

Over the next few days, John spent time with each of his children, finding out what they had been doing and some of the problems they had had to deal with while he had been away. One major item on the immediate horizon was the court summons for Mary, regarding the supposed murder of Lady Elizabeth Varney, due for October 10th which was in a few days time. This was causing considerable worry for both Emily and Mary. Nobody had had the time or inclination to do anything about it but now that Father was home, it was time for ACTION.

After considerable discussion, it was decided that father should take Sarah and go to Winchester to make tactful enquiries about the case. Sarah was chosen because she could read all of the official papers easily without arousing suspicion. They borrowed a horse and rode one October morning across the countryside to Winchester. They found their way to the courthouse and made some enquiries. To their relief they discovered that the charges had been dropped. Sir Randolf Varney himself had been arrested and had been charged with embezzlement and fraud. He was himself a prisoner in the Tower of London awaiting trial. They were overjoyed, no-one had thought to send a message to them, they were just poor fisher-folk not worthy of such information. With that good news ringing in the ears, they hurried back to Ringwood to share the information with the rest of the family.

Another problem which faced John was the arrangement for their religious services. He knew that the authorities would be watching for any sign of a 'gathering together' of the puritan believers, now that they had returned from the high seas. However, John also knew that the widows and illiterate families desperately needed a congregation in which to share worship. Most people in the villages could not read and John knew that he had a responsibility to share the Bible's teaching with others. Somehow, he had to form a 'Congregation of Worship' without endangering the lives of his family and others in the area. He talked over the possibilities with his older children, Ruth had a suggestion. "I wonder whether Lady Susan would be able to help us? I am sure that she is quite convinced of the rightness of what we believe. I just sense that she would be glad to do something practical. When there is a suitable opportunity I will ask her."

John the less had now taken charge of the boat to ferry people and goods on the river relieving Sarah of the work. Her job was to teach everyone in the family to read, write and do some basic sums. John and Emily were now convinced that it was vitally important that everyone should be able to read, not least to be able to read God's Word for themselves. If persecution was to increase, they would not be allowed to worship together at all. Each individual must be able to read for themselves. She set about preparing some simple exercises.

William was progressing with his work on the River. He and James had completed the survey work up to Ringwood. It was now getting cold and dark in the afternoons. One afternoon, Eddie called them to a meeting in his hotel room in Salisbury. "You have done an excellent job this summer on surveying the river. I now have detailed plans, drawings and considerable information from Christchurch to Fordingbridge. We need to organise this into a schedule of work with an indication of items to be done and their respective costs. Next year we can complete the task of surveying the river all the way to Salisbury. In the meantime I have rented a room at this hotel for you two to work and prepare detailed schedules for submission to Parliament and our financial backers. Is that alright?"

James spoke for both of them; "We will be only too pleased to work on the submission here in Salisbury. William can sleep here in the office and I can get lodgings nearby." Eddie nodded appreciatively and commented; "That's good then, let's have a look at how far you have developed the project." They then spent several hours perusing the sketches and measurements that they had already completed.

A week after the 'homecoming'. The various crisis in the family seemed to be slipping into history. Emily was visibly calming down, able to take a rest each afternoon, Mary had relaxed, back into her old routines. The other children were all in their respective jobs, reasonably satisfied and happy.

However, John had only just got his 'feet under the table' or so it seemed, before a real crisis occurred. They were all involved in their normal early morning tasks when an anguished cry caused everyone to stop whatever they were doing. "Mary is ill again," cried mother. "She has a high fever and looks terrible." During the rest of the day, Mary grew worse, her face was running with sweat. She oscillated between being icy cold and boiling hot with a violent headache. For the next three days, she was reasonably stable, with Mother trying a series of herbal remedies; Chamomile and Common Rue, but all to none effect.

On the morning of the fourth day, the fever seemed to subside but during the day a rash appeared all over her body. They all knew what this meant. The family became very subdued as they realised it was smallpox, a disease that was often fatal and usually spread quite quickly. The rash developed over several days, growing into blister-like pustules which would leave pot-marks all over her body. Emily was beside herself, worried about her frail little girl, the other children and also her own baby. By the second week, Mary was obviously weaker; she had become listless and weary of life.

With no doctors as such and no hospitals, most diseases were treated by herbal remedies which did not provide a cure. The wealthy paid for 'doctors' to prescribe various treatments but most were based on guesswork and superstition.

By the thirteenth day, Mary was beginning to be delirious and all the family were worried that she might not survive. Two days later she was drifting in and out of consciousness. The various family members spent time with her to say their own prayers at her bedside.

During the next night, Mary breathed her last. Father prayed at her bedside. "Father into thy hands we commend her spirit. You have given, you have taken away. Blessed be the name of the Lord." Life was often brief in those days, cut short by disease, poverty and poor food. The death of a child was always tragic, however it was almost taken for granted that in a large family only a few children would reach adult life.

A few days later, they buried their beloved Mary. They carried her small body into the woods and buried her at the foot of a giant beech tree. John the less, gave the eulogy reminding them all of Mary's exemplary character. Whether in getting up early in the morning, in the cultivation of her herbs or in the growing and preparing of vegetables for them all. Mary was the embodiment of a commitment to hard work and family life. William quoted words which he had learnt from childhood;

"We shall not all sleep, but we shall be changed. In a moment, in the twinkling of an eye, at the last trump; for the trumpet shall sound, and the dead shall be raised incorruptible, and we shall be changed."

Then Father gave a final prayer before they filled-in the soil onto the coffin; "Father, we long for the day when you will wipe away all tears, when there shall be no more death, neither sorrow, nor crying, neither shall be any more pain, for the former things will be passed away. We long for that time when our Saviour will return to the earth to raise the dead and give eternal life to your children. Accept the life of our beloved Mary as we commend her body into your care. In the name of our Lord Jesus Christ. Amen."

For several days after these tragic events, there was a numbness felt by the members of the family. Life had to continue, but there was no spark, no excitement, just a routine completion of tasks.

William was particularly affected because he had thought deeply about his sister's illness and knew that she probably had contracted smallpox from himself. He must have brought it home with him from prison. Because Mary was so frail, she had caught it and had died. It was his fault! He felt this guilt keenly, wondering whether or not it was God's way of telling him that he may have escaped death, but he was now being judged for his release.

William had a very acute sense of conscience. As the eldest son of the family it was his responsibility to set the standard for the rest. With the transfer of work from the river to an office in Salisbury, he was thrown into the midst of people of which he didn't always approve. Although his colleague, James Proudfoot, seemed to be a God-fearing man and they got on extremely well. Relations were only acceptable to William out on the river.

However, when they were in town, a different side to his personality emerged. William came face to face with this when on one October evening when they had finished their work. James suggested that they visit as many taverns as possible during the evening. They started at one which was next to the room they used as an office and proceeded to visit one after another. After an hour or two of heavy drinking they were both 'dead drunk'. William was vaguely aware that they were in a part of the town with which he was not familiar. A rougher and wilder place than he would have visited on his own. The next thing he knew was stirring from sleep in a strange room and in a strange house with a young woman gently waking him and presenting him with breakfast on a plate.

William jumped up, suddenly realising that he was not fully dressed, totally embarrassed and utterly humiliated. He grabbed his shirt and ran from the building. Back at his place of work, he found James, sober and laughing at him for his naivety and innocence. From that moment on, William started to question whether or not he was in the right place, Whether or not he would be better off working for himself on the river. A place where he could be closer to his God with less temptation of the world around him. Where he could live with his wife, bring up a family in simplicity and truth. He realised that it was time to make some arrangements to get married.

As soon as the opportunity presented itself. He raised the matter with his parents, with Miriam and her mother. One Saturday evening they all met at Ellingham to make suitable arrangements. It was agreed that on the Sunday afternoon of the following week, they would all meet at the 'Old Oak', a large and venerated spot in the Forest. John Tilly would officiate at the religious service with the two families acting as witnesses together with the Watts family, Sarah and Mary would draft a letter to the local minister at the church, stating what had happened and requesting that the wedding be recorded in the parish records. They hoped that this would avoid them having to participate in an official ceremony in the church. Whether or not this would help or make matters a lot worse, they did not know.

The following Sunday, everything was in place. After their usual family service and lunch, they all walked quietly from their respective homes to the appointed place. Miriam was dressed in a new gown which had been made by her mother, in cream with several underskirts. A bright blue new apron with a grey cloak and blue bonnet completed her ensemble. William was dressed in a close-fitting doublet in grey, buttoned down the front over new cream breeches and smart buckled shoes. He wore a new black coat which had been donated by Miriam's employer. Sarah and Ruth acted as maids of honour and they wore their best blue skirts, white blouses and grey capes. This was a special day. They were all laughing and teasing each other as they made their way through the trees on this cool autumnal day.

When they arrived at the 'Old Oak', they grouped around the happy couple in front of the respected tree. John Tilly opened their Bible and Mary Watts read from the beautiful chapter on love which concludes with these words; "And now abideth faith, hope and charity, these three, but the greatest of these is charity." John then drew the couple in front of him and asked each in turn whether they loved each other completely. He asked them to simply reply whether each wished to marry and live together as husband and wife for the rest of their days. When they replied; "Yes, we do," he continued; "With this promise made to each other in the presence of these witnesses and before God, I declare that you are husband and wife."

John took the hands of the couple and bound them together with a golden thread and stated; "What God hath joined, let not man put asunder." William and Miriam kissed each other, everyone cheered and clapped in excitement and happiness.

A simple ceremony conducted in the open air before their friends and family was a wonderful start to their marriage. They all walked back to the Tilly home where drink and food had been prepared for everyone. The letter which Sarah and Mary had written was duly read and signed by William and Miriam with the relevant parents as witnesses. The couple finally left the family home to be rowed up river to Ellingham. They were to live in a room in Miriam's family home. This gave them a little independence but where she could also continue to help her mother with the family.

When Ruth returned to Sopley Hall that night, she was thinking about how to ask her mistress regarding a possible place for meeting on a Sunday. Now that Father and John the less were back home she felt emboldened. She had almost forgotten Sir Richard's threats to her. He had not been home for a month or so and rumour had it that he had a new woman in London. A lady who was a high society celebrity, in close contact with the court of King Charles.

An occasion arose one afternoon, Lady Susan was having her hair washed and trying to set it in ringlets, a practice that took ages. Ruth broached the topic; "I wonder whether your Ladyship knows of a suitable room which would accommodate twenty people for worship on a Sunday? It would need to be easily accessible but in a location which would be secret from the authorities. Please forgive my audacity but with Sir Richard away in London, I thought that you might be reasonably sympathetic to us." She had briefly paused at her reference to Sir Richard and London, hoping that her mistress would pick up the inference and respond to her suggestion positively.

"Thank you for raising the subject of your religious worship." Lady Susan replied. "I have been missing our discussions over the past few weeks. I was wondering what you were managing to do without your friend John Stott's house in which to worship."

"We have been meeting in family groups since the death of our men. But now that Father has returned, he feels that we need to meet together again.

Many of our members are not able to read, without Mary Watts and Sarah, they are not able to hear the Word of God." explained Ruth. With her heart in her mouth, she realised that she could be jeopardising the freedom, even the lives, of her family and friends.

"Don't worry," said Lady Susan, "I will not betray you. In fact, I have much sympathy with your cause and I too would like to share in your worship. I believe that there is much hypocrisy in our religion in England. People attend church services because they are expected to attend. It's a kind of 'badge of membership of a particular political faction. I don't like it."

I will have a think about your request and see what I can find. There might be something on the estate which people have forgotten about," concluded Lady Susan.

A few days later, Lady Susan spoke again with Ruth. "I think that I have found a place which may be suitable for us to worship, a place without prying eyes or wagging tongues. If you like we can go and see if we can find it today?"

Ruth became excited at her employer's comments; "You really mean this don't you? You have decided to become one of us haven't you?" she exclaimed. Lady Susan laughed and said; "I am not so sure about that, but I am really interested to hear what you have to say about lots and lots of subjects. I miss our conversations. I am really intrigued by what I have heard about your services."

They donned suitable boots and outer cloaks, as if going for an autumnal walk. They walked for about a mile until they reached some disused farm buildings. Lady Susan explained; "This used to be Ripley with two farms which provided food for Christchurch Priory. King Henry VIII destroyed the Priory and the farms fell into disuse. The farms are part of the property I inherited from my uncle. I don't think Sir Richard even knows of their existence, let alone where they are. I think we could make them habitable, ideal for a meeting place, even suitable accommodation for somebody to live."

They went into the broken-down buildings, both could see that with a little work, they would have a very useful meeting place. There were also several rooms where people could live, if required. Ruth was thrilled with all that she saw and asked if she could bring her father and brothers to visit the farm. They could then do some work on the buildings to make them weatherproof and habitable. Lady Susan was pleased to be able to assist with 'The Congregation' as she termed it as they wended their way back to Sopley Hall.

Back in Christchurch harbour, the boat had been emptied of cargo, personal possessions and everything else was spread out on the quay side to be scrubbed clean and to be packed away for the next trip. This had been delayed because of the illness of Mary but now, winter was beginning to close in. The nights were shortening by the day and the temperature was dropping by the night. Fishing was difficult and dangerous in good weather, but in the winter it was purgatory. The boat was therefore prepared and if there was a mild period of weather, they would set out to sea and hope for a quick catch.

Even on the small boat on the River Avon, it was getting more and more uncomfortable with less and less trade. John the less had little to do, but fish and row the occasional passenger on the River Avon.

Richard, however, was working hard in the carpenter's shop at Fordingbridge. They had several pieces of furniture to construct. They had now finished the desk and chair for the gentleman in Salisbury. The chair had been very difficult to make with the rudimentary tools at their disposal. However, they had finally finished the legs and fitted them to the seat and back. They were now involved in two sets of bookcases. It would seem that all the aspiring gentlemen of Salisbury wanted to have bookcases in their houses. Then they could display their newly bought books and mementoes of their travels. Everything was going well for Richard. He had an employer who he liked and he was learning new skills every day.

Sarah missed her younger sister, partly because she did not have her to do all the menial tasks around the house and without her she was lonely. She had prepared lesson notes for the rest of the family but they were not excited by learning to read. Now that John was back, he was doing the ferry work and therefore Sarah was out of a job. There was also little going on in the village. The summer had given way to autumn and life was quiet and boring. She also missed her young love of the summer. 'Why had Nick not contacted her? Why had he been so wonderful, only to disappear into the mist?'

Emily was blooming in more ways than one. With her husband home, problems seemed to disappear, although she had been desperately upset by the illness and subsequent death of her beloved Mary. Yet even that, could be accepted with John at her side. With the baby growing inside her, she knew that everything was going to be alright. The wedding had been very exciting and she was now looking forward to a baby from the newly married couple. Her own earlier fears had evaporated and now she was much more relaxed. She was confident that everything would be alright. The homecoming had been wonderful – everything was going to be good.

However, just around the corner was an event that was to affect them all in one way or another, something that would determine their future in Ringwood.

One day, while several of the family were eating their lunch, John Watts, their next door neighbour burst in; "There's been a terrible accident near Burley, his Lordship has been thrown from his mare and is fighting for his life". There was a stunned silence. The Lord of the Ringwood Manor was not only the most important man in town but he was also their landlord. If he died, as he had no heir, the estate would be sold and they could be homeless. Immediately, John went with his neighbour to find out what had happened and if they could do anything to help. However, by the time they had walked to nearby Burley, they were met by a sad group of servants walking back to Ringwood with a body draped over a horse. Several of the injured people were walking slowly, in a state of shock. Apparently, his Lordship's horse had suddenly shied, reared-up and thrown His Lordship who had hit his head on a small heap of flint-stones. He had been knocked unconscious and had not recovered.

The town went immediately into mourning; Thomas Braithwaite had been Lord of the Manor of Ringwood since 1594. He had been much loved and respected. He was a gentleman, respecting individual views of life and religion. He had been a very fair and just landlord. He had been lenient on bad debtors and had assisted everyone in the town in their difficulties. Unfortunately, he was not a very good businessman, he had allowed his own debts to rise. He and his wife had had no children and therefore they had no heir to either wreck the estate further or manage it more efficiently.

In a week, the funeral had been held, the whole town had turned out to show their respects. Within two weeks, a high court had served a writ ordering the estate to be sold, its assets used to pay the creditors. By the third week of November, the house and estate had been sold to a city banker, a well-known royalist with strong religious convictions.

The ink was barely dry on the sale agreement when the new owner arrived in Ringwood to inspect his new purchase. He intended to plan and build a new country mansion in the area. He had that air of the 'new rich'. An air which says; 'I have arrived on the scene and I demand to be respected and obeyed.' He stayed for a few days, walking the estate and getting the 'feel of the country'. For most of this time he was accompanied by the Estate Manager who was of the 'old school'. A man who had looked after the estate for His Lordship and cared for the well-being of the community. Unfortunately, the new owner immediately took a dislike to him and told him to pack his bags and go.

In his place a much younger businessman was appointed who soon had proposals for re-development. The scene was set for massive changes in the Ringwood area during the winter of 1625.

John and his son, John the less, had returned home from an amazing trip to New-Found-Land. However, on arrival back home they found that frightening events had taken place in their absence. Within a matter of days of their return, their beloved Mary had died, a few weeks later, William had married. Now there was the very real prospect of being made homeless. John had not yet met his new landlord or the new Estate Manager, but he did not like what he had heard. It didn't sound too good and he was very concerned.

'Worlds Apart'

Ten – 'A Winter of Difficulty'

They waited with baited breath to discover their future at the hands of the new owner of the manor. The Estate was now owned by a forward-thinking economist who saw matters in terms of a balance sheet, not in terms of humanity. He wanted to ensure that the estate was a financial success. That each farm was managed efficiently and that all of the properties on the estate yielded a satisfactory income. In other words, rents would rise and in return he would renovate and rebuild. To that end he had commissioned an 'estate review' of all holdings; buildings and personnel to be able to plan effectively for the future. All of this sounded impressive. But its impact on the people in the Ringwood area in 1625 would be catastrophic.

Almost all of the townsfolk lived in rented cottages. The most significant local yeoman farmer in the area had been executed. His widow had not returned to Ringwood. The farm that the Stott's had loved, was already starting to show signs of neglect. Most of the villagers lived in 'tied cottages'. In other words they worked in some capacity or other for the Lord of the Manor and therefore paid a token rent. Whereas, the Tilly's and their next door neighbours, were in a different category, they were fishermen. They had lived in Ringwood for generations and paid a rent as tenants. Because of this, John knew that they would be the first targets in a rationalisation of property and land in the area.

They therefore waited with some trepidation for the Estate Manager to complete his review. The resultant news came in the form of a formal notice to Mr & Mrs Tilly. It stated that; 'As a result of the estate review on behalf of Mr Sowerbut, the new owner. The annual rental for No 3 Waterside Cottages, Ringwood will be eight pounds and ten shillings per annum, to be paid weekly. This rent to be paid from the first day of January in the year of our Lord, sixteen twenty six. Failure to pay will result in immediate eviction from the property.' Signed, Will Smith, Estate Manager.

When Sarah read the letter aloud, there was a silence in the room. This was three times what they were paying at present. It had been very difficult last winter to pay the rent. This year it would be totally impossible. John, reflective and hopeful, as always, commented; "The Lord will provide, just don't worry." Inwardly, he was sick with worry but outwardly, he showed confidence and resolve.

Other practical matters were also crowding upon their lives on a daily basis. Winter was the most difficult time of the year. At the end of October, the temperature plummeted with three nights of really sharp frosts. Although it looked beautiful it was a real problem on the river. There were patches of ice and it was really cold trying to row the boat up-river with three passengers on-board.

It was quite hard for Ruth in the cold of winter. Sopley Hall had great fires in each of the main rooms but they were only lit at the weekends and for special occasions. There were fires in the main bedrooms and living areas but they had to be lit each morning. They did not provide much heat. In fact, it was often colder in the big house than it was at home. However, in her little room in the attic it was quite warm as was also the great kitchen.

Her daily routine did not change very much but during that autumn and winter a new member of staff came into her life. Sir Richard had decided that it would be good for several of his horses from London to spend some time in the country. One mare, which was his favourite, had gone lame and was very much in need of some care and attention. This mare and two other horses were brought to Sopley Hall by a stable-hand by the name of Andrew. His job was to work in the stables, exercise the horses and get them back to good health. This meant that he was working alongside Bess, the permanent stable hand.

As soon as Andrew arrived in the yard, Bess was infatuated by him. She thought he was quite sophisticated, a city boy who could really enliven the scene at Sopley. He, conversely, thought that Bess although quite good looking, was in reality, a country girl with no personality or knowledge of life at all.

Ruth didn't meet him for several days, although she had heard all about him from Bess! When she met him it was in the corridor leading from the back door to the servants' room, just past the door into the kitchen. Ruth came one way with her arms full of washing. They had to squeeze past each other. She was aware of someone different near to her. He took advantage of the situation to tickle her in the ribs, commenting; "Take care not to drop them!" Ruth went scarlet and nearly dropped the bundle of clothes. Instead, she scurried on to the laundry room, closing the door behind herself to give her a moment to recover, before venturing out again.

A couple of days later, she saw him properly. He wasn't bad looking either as he rubbed down one of the horses. She plucked-up courage and spoke to him as she passed; "Not bad work for a city boy!" He turned and caught her hand as she passed; "Meet me after supper tonight at the back door to the stables," he whispered to her. He immediately returned to his work without a further glance. Ruth was in turmoil, she had never flirted with anyone before, she was part excited and part afraid. She did not have much idea about sex or even about kissing. She just knew that to some people like her sister Sarah, it seemed to be a natural thing. Others didn't seem to be bothered, being much more concerned about friendship and having a family like her brother, William.

Later that night, she made her way to the stable-block to meet Andrew not knowing what to expect. As she crept round the corner, strong arms enveloped her and almost lifted her of her feet. "Shush, don't say anything, just come. Follow me, I know a good spot where no-one will find us." said Andrew, in a commanding tone. A tone which didn't allow Ruth to challenge, she just followed like a lamb to the slaughter! He led the way into the hay store to a wooden ladder which he indicated she should climb. With her heart thumping, her skirts held tight in her one hand, she climbed holding-on with the other.

When they had both crawled into the hay loft, he came close to her so that they could talk easily or so she thought!

They spent a couple of hours just talking, nothing more! When Ruth thought it was about time to go. Andrew just kissed her on the cheek and said; "It's been good talking, it's a bit boring in this forgotten corner of the world. Tonight has been good, let's meet again." Without really thinking of the consequences or of the reaction of her parents, Ruth agreed to meet him again the following evening at the same time and place.

These arrangements continued for several days. Andrew took the relationship carefully and slowly. There wasn't any passion, just friendship or so she thought. Each night, Andrew showed a little more tenderness and become a little more passionate until at the end of the week he made love to her. He showed tenderness and care, teaching her slowly and carefully what to do. She didn't really understand what was happening and by the time she did it was too late. He finally gave her a long kiss and quite an emotional hug before saying quite casually; "I enjoyed that, thanks. By the way, I shall be leaving to go back to London tomorrow. I shall probably be back in the spring, look after yourself."

With that he was gone, cleverly slipping away down the steps and out of the hay store. Ruth started to cry and couldn't stop. She knew in her heart that she would never see Andrew again, that he had just used her as a plaything, leaving her distraught and destroyed. Her honour in tatters, her reputation destroyed.

After an hour or so, Ruth heard some movement below, she tried to stop trembling but she could not. Then she heard someone on the stable steps and a voice speaking gently; "Ruth, are you up there?" It was Bess looking for her room-mate. "I was cleaning-up in the stable and I saw young Andrew slipping out of the hay store. I thought that he had been up to no-good. When you didn't come to bed, I just wondered whether or not you were the object of his desire," explained Bess as she climbed up into the hay store and shone the light of the oil lamp in the direction of Ruth. When she saw how distraught Ruth was, she went across to her, put her arm round her and held her tight. "We have got to stick together," she said. "Men, they think that they have a God-given right to do to us just what they like – it's shameful. It's disgusting, it shouldn't be allowed. Come on, let's go and make a drink in the kitchen. We need to get to bed because it will soon be morning and we shall have work to do tomorrow."

In the light of day, things didn't seem quite so bad for Ruth and her future. But, things were never quite the same again. She found it very difficult to concentrate that morning. Her thoughts kept drifting back to the events of the previous night. Oh, what a fool she had been! What a silly, naive fool she had been. The very things that she despised in her fellow women. She had herself fallen for – the charms of a man, the praise of a man, the brief pleasure of being thought – special. Oh, what a fool.

As the morning progressed, instead of being filled with pity, she became angry. Angry at the duplicity of men and the naivety of women. Angry at the situation which gave men power and women became powerless. The inequality of it all, the injustice of it all.

During the next few days, Ruth oscillated in her thinking between anger and despair. On the one hand she was angry at being duped and trapped by a man. On the other hand she felt very, very guilty. She had failed her parents, her family and her faith. She had been taught that she must keep herself pure for her husband. She believed that to have sexual relations outside marriage was wrong. But no-one had told her what 'having a sexual relationship was all about. However, she now realised what it was and despised herself for bring such a simple fool. She just hoped that the events of the night before did not result in a baby. That would be disastrous!

Meanwhile, John the less, was bored and lonely. He found rowing and sailing the little boat on the River Avon a bit tame after the high seas. With Father involved in the illness and death of Mary, with the wedding of William and Miriam and in the care of Mother and the rest of the family. A fishing trip in October or November with Father had just not been possible. John the less therefore, talked to the members of the other fishing families in the area. They discussed a possible three week trip at the end of November. It was finally agreed that they would use the Tilly fishing boat but with John Hayter from

Sopley as skipper and a crew drawn from the same team as had previously gone to New-Found-Land.

This time John the less was really in charge of the provisioning of the boat and the preparation for the fishing. They would sail across the English Channel to try their luck in the fishing grounds off the Bay of Biscay. Here the weather would be rough and wild. However, if it was too bad, they could run for shelter near the French coast. While they were preparing, John contemplated his 'love-life' and realised that there was something drastically wrong with his life. On the one hand, he loved the adventure of the sea but on the other hand, it was not a job which allowed an on-going romance! He decided that he would do this trip and then seriously think about finding a wife. Thus resolved, he gave his mind totally to the planning of the fishing trip.

They left in the third week of November and almost immediately wished that they hadn't! They were able to sail out of harbour and into the Solent, then the wind died and the fog came down. A cold, damp fog which obliterated everything. They could barely see one end of the boat from the other. At one point they very nearly ran into another boat that was returning to harbour. They just drifted with the tides until the wind was felt by the sails.

Slowly the fog lifted and so did their spirits. They raised the main sail as the wind started to freshen and slowly but surely the boat started to move. As they rounded the Isle of Wight, the wind became stronger, the air became warmer and it started to rain. It rained for two days without stopping. By now the wind had changed direction and they were being driven south west by an easterly wind that steadily became colder and colder. The rain turned to snow. This they hadn't expected. It snowed all night, covering the boat in a layer a couple of inches deep by dawn. They had had to reduce their sail down to a small 'jib' during the night for fear of being capsized by the weight of snow. In the morning they cleared the snow from the deck, sails and ropes and decided that maybe they would set some lines out to see if the fish would bite.

They baited their lines and let them trail behind the boat as they sailed further south. They caught mackerel and whiting, not in significant numbers but sufficient. They settled into a steady rhythm each day; hauling the lines in, removing the fish, gutting and laying them in salt, re-baiting the lines and dropping them overboard again. All went well for several days and then disaster.

The seas had been getting rougher during the night. They had taken-in most of the sail. It was just breaking dawn when a freak wave hit the boat broadside. The boat shook from stem to stern as if a giant hand had shaken it. The main mast bent, the mizzen mast with the small sail broke in two as the wind caught the boat sideways. As it hadn't been storm weather only those on deck were tied to safety ropes. Those below deck where thrown across the cabin. John the less and John Hayter both hit timber of the boat and were knocked unconscious. One of the crew was cut badly by the sharp knives they used for gutting.

Water was pouring through the open hatch into the cabin. The water mixed with fish and their personal belongings was swirling around the cabin. On the deck, the cry went up 'man overboard' as one of the crew was swept by the turbulent seas over the stern of the boat, never to be seen again.

As John the less gained consciousness, he realised that they were in trouble. He shouted to everyone; "Get roped quickly. Get on deck and batten-down the hatches. Someone grab the tiller and get this boat back into the wind. Fasten the sails but leave a storm jib and for goodness sake, hang on." At this moment he did not know that they had lost one of the crew. His first concern was to get the boat back into the wind. His next thought was for the men as he shouted to each man in turn. Then he realised that they were a man short. One of the men from Mudeford whom he had known since childhood, was missing.

"Please God help us, save us from drowning, keep us in your care," he prayed as he struggled to batten down the hatches. Gradually, order returned as they began to bale out the cabin and sort out the chaos. They were subdued. Each with their own thoughts, each with their memories of the man they had lost. There was nothing that they could do for him. They could not turn round. They were totally dependent upon the wind which was driving them away from their fellow fisherman.

They continued fishing for another three days, but their heart was not in it anymore. As soon as they had caught a reasonable amount of fish. They turned back to port. Slowly but carefully they tacked against the north easterly wind and made their way back up the English Channel. The two Johns recovered and were none the worse for their injuries. However, the crew member who had cut himself was not recovering very well. In the damp and cold his cuts were not healing. The main one had gone septic, causing him considerable pain and anguish. The sooner they arrived home the better, thought John as he cared for the injured man. If they were becalmed, the injury would become gangrenous and someone would have to amputate the arm, This was a difficult task at home, let alone at sea in a small boat with no facilities.

The wind was reasonably kind to them. It kept blowing in the right direction. They were able to make good time back to the calmer waters as they passed Durleston Head and Old Harry Rocks. Finally they could see Hengitsbury Head and they knew that they were almost home. However, this was no happy and excited return. People sensed that they had bad news as they saw the fishing boat easing into Christchurch harbour. The boat came alongside the harbour wall. John the less was the first to jump ashore and greet the wife of the lost crewman with the bad news.

The man with the injuries was carefully assisted ashore and taken by his wife to their cottage so that he could be treated. However, John the less knew that he would need an amputation to save the rest of his body from gangrene. It was a sad end to a voyage. A voyage which had gained them quite a reasonable catch of fish ready to be sold yet at what a cost? As he rowed up the river Avon back home, he thought; 'fishing is a dangerous business, this trip was doomed before we began.'

William, by contrast, had had a quiet few weeks after his wedding to Miriam. He had settled down to life in a new village. Ellingham was really only a hamlet, a few cottages surrounding the blacksmith's forge. For the first few days, he and Miriam were entertained by each family in turn as they celebrated the wedding and he got to know his new neighbours. Their room at Miriam's home was very small, barely a room but it did give them a little privacy.

You will remember that Miriam's father had died in a fishing accident and that she was the eldest of nine children. There were therefore, many domestic tasks to be done each day to assist Miriam's mother. Each of the children had a job to do, the older ones supervising the younger. But the family were poorer than the Tilly's, so William felt that he ought to contribute to the family income as well as to his own family back in Ringwood.

Although life was quiet, there were several moral dilemmas which he had to face during this period. To what extent was he going to get involved with the politics of his world? It was obvious to William that his new employer was a moderate man, willing to 'let sleeping dogs lie' as they say. But many of the people with whom he was now working were much more outspoken. These were investors and business men, men who were strong royalist supporters of both a catholic and protestant persuasion. The challenge of Parliament to the power and authority of King Charles was a 'talking point'. Several times he had been asked his opinion and had decided that it was wise to keep quiet. But one morning, he couldn't escape the specific question fired at him; "Tilly, what do you think? Is it right to fight against the Scots to save us from popery?"

William thought for a moment and then carefully answered; "I do not accept that it's right to fight at all, whether for king or country. My king is Jesus Christ and he taught us not fight and kill but to show compassion and mercy."

"So you would let the Scots bring the religion of popery back to England? If you did that, then you wouldn't be able to say what you have just said. You would be arrested and burnt at the stake for your views," said one of the group of men who were in the office that morning. "We believe that in supporting the king is the surest way of maintaining peace and stability in this country. We need a strong king with strong support to ensure freedom of speech and religion," commented another, with some feeling.

"It's the likes of you young Tilly, that encourages subversion and insurrection. Soon you will be backing parliament against the king. That will be the slippery slope to anarchy and the end of England." retorted the first speaker, leaving William floundering. Back home it had been quite simple. You read the Bible, practised what it taught and kept out of harm's way. Now it was different. He had to think for himself and defend his views. He began to realise that he was 'out of his depth'.

Another issue which he found difficult to challenge was the idea that a married man could and should have more than one woman. At least, to be married and have another woman 'on the side'. He had been brought up to believe that when you married, you stayed for life with ' the wife of your youth'.

He had been taught that you made an oath before God to keep 'your marriage bed undefiled'. But in Salisbury, he found that most men seemed to have a wife and at least one mistress besides. What William found particularly distressing was the fact that many leading figures of the city and even some members of the clergy did not seem to keep their marriage vows. They expected their wives to do so but had a different view of their own morality. He tried to discuss this with James, but all he got was a grunt and the observation; "When your wife is pregnant you will want another woman, you mark my words." It was clear to William that in this matter, he was 'worlds apart' from those about him.

Honesty was another issue over which William was concerned. He had always believed that; 'His word had to be his bond'. But as he became more involved in the business world, fewer and fewer people seemed to speak honestly. Their words appeared to be honest but in reality, there was a hidden message. They said one thing but actually meant something quite different. People would lie and cheat so that they were never caught out. A practice he saw clearly when it involved money.

In the past, it had been a simple case of taking a penny as a fare, sometimes people pleaded poverty or they didn't have any cash and that was alright. William just gave them the benefit of the doubt. But now he was hearing about all sorts of deals, he called them bribes. 'If you vote in Parliament for the opening-up of the River Avon for freight traffic, then you will personally get a slice of the trade.' And more precisely, 'If you build a wharf at Salisbury, you will be able to charge a tax on everybody using it'. They seemed to be fairly straight forward business deals but he also heard of quite substantial bribes to leading officials.

One day, he asked Eddie Otter about these business deals. William did not understand the reply which he received; "Just be careful young man who you go accusing of bribery and fraud. It might seem wrong to you just now. But you don't know who might benefit from such activities. The recipient might be grateful in the future, of deals made on their behalf." With that comment, he left the office to return to his hotel room.

William was left totally unaware of what Eddie meant. He knew nothing about the deal made to release him from hanging. He didn't make the connection until several months later.

Sarah like John the less, was bored with life. After all the excitement of the summer, the homecoming, the death of Mary and the wedding of William. Nothing seemed to be happening in Ringwood. She also found it well-nigh impossible to teach members of the family how to read. They just didn't see the point.

She kept the financial records up to date, it was obvious that they were going to be in real difficulties in the forthcoming winter. The news about the increase in rent had worried her for a time but she could not see any way of solving their problems. She couldn't solve their problems on her own, so eventually she stopped worrying about them. When all was said and done she was bored. She had nothing to stimulate her mind, nor her emotions.

Her mother realised that her brightest child was becoming listless but she couldn't think of anything to distract her. Talking to her neighbour, they came up with a plan which Emily shared with Sarah later that day. "What about learning to play a musical instrument and writing some music to accompany our Psalms? You will probably need to travel to Salisbury or even Winchester to get an introduction to a musician. But it could lead to higher things, to a wider scene. You ought to try, you would enjoy it."

Initially, Sarah thought it was a silly idea. But later that night she thought about it and realised that it could be her passport out of Ringwood. Even a passage to University, if she played her cards right. It could be an exciting opportunity.

It was therefore agreed that Sarah would travel to Salisbury by walking to Ellingham, get a lift with William to make some enquiries at the cathedral. The next day, in an excited frame of mind she went as planned. By mid-morning she found herself outside the house of the Director of Music at the Cathedral. Her stomach was churning. She did not know quite what to say when the doorman opened the door in response to her timid knock.

"Err, is the gentleman of the house available?" she asked hesitantly. "I would like five minutes of his time, if that is possible?"

He has choir practice in fifteen minutes, I will see if he can see you before he goes across to the cathedral." The man was gone for just a moment before he returned and asked Sarah to follow him. This was a smart town house with wood panelling on the walls, a woven rug on the tiled floor with pictures on the walls. Sarah was ushered into a small study which was lined with books. On the table was a large piece of musical manuscript with pen marks scribbled all over it.

"My name is Marcus Theodore Wallace, what can I do for you?" said the gentleman holding out his hand to Sarah who shook it and replied; "My name is Sarah Tilly, I come from Ringwood and would like to learn how to play and write music to accompany Psalms in worship." In her nervousness, the words came out in a rush, they all ran together and piled one on top of the other in her rural burr.

Mr Wallace smiled and said; "Just a minute Missy. It's not quite as simple as that. I am really thrilled that a country girl should want to learn to play an instrument but it needs money and time to learn. Do you know anything about music?"

"No, but I can read and write. I think that I am quite bright. At least everyone is always telling me that I am the brightest girl in Ringwood." Sarah replied with a degree of self-confidence and boldness.

Alright, come with me to choir practice and let's see if you have an ear for music. Let's see what you can do."

Without more ado, they walked across the Cathedral Green and entered a wooden door into a an interesting building. It was larger than a cottage but smaller than a church. Inside, a group of about thirty boys, all much younger than Sarah, were playing games around the room.

Mr Wallace called them to order and introduced Sarah. There was a little giggling and chatter which soon stopped when Mr Wallace sat at the harpsichord and began to play. He played several tunes before settling on one. He asked one boy to sing a solo part followed with everyone else joining in as a chorus. They sang the song twice, he turned to Sarah and said, "Have a go at the solo part with this young lad, I guess that your voice will match his. Sing with him and let's see whether you have a musical pitch or not."

Sarah was petrified. She had never sung before, let alone in front of others. However, because they were there watching her and she was not going to be beaten by them. She cleared her throat and at the right moment – sang! She enjoyed it. It was amazing. She lifted her voice as the Psalm progressed and just let go. When they had finished, the choir clapped and cheered. Sarah went scarlet with embarrassment. They had never had a girl singing with them before. This was something novel and interesting.

Mr Wallace got up from the harpsichord, went across to Sarah, put his arm on her shoulder and said; "Welcome to Salisbury Cathedral Choir. You may join and I will teach you how to play. You are a natural musician. Thank you for coming today."

After the choir practice, Mr Wallace discussed with Sarah about studying how to play and sing. As a musician he was thrilled to have someone with natural ability come to him. He wasn't concerned about tradition and custom which would not allow a female to take part in the choir. He would have to face that problem later. For the present, he was far more concerned about getting his new prodigy into the school.

Sarah walked from the house in a dream. She had a new challenge. She had the possibility of breaking free. She walked quickly up the main street to the hotel where William worked, bursting into his office. "I have been asked to join the choir. To learn music and to play the harpsichord," she shouted as she flung her arms around William's neck.

James looked up from his work at this interruption and laughed at Sarah's enthusiasm He took a second look at Sarah. "Wow, what a beauty! You didn't tell me about this wonderful vision." exclaimed James Proudfoot to his friend. "Let me introduce my sister, Sarah," said William, "Sarah, this is James Proudfoot, my learned surveyor and colleague." They all laughed and James shouted; "Let's go and celebrate, It's time for lunch. Let's go next door and have something to eat and drink – I'm paying."

After this introduction to music, Sarah started her new career with commitment and enthusiasm. She went up to Salisbury three days a week. She stayed with her brother and was able to attend regular classes for music theory and practice. Once a week she joined the choir experiencing considerable fun practicing scales and joining in the canticles. She learned quite quickly. Mr Wallace was really pleased at her obvious progress. By the end of November, they were learning the various Christmas carols to sing at the usual range of Christmas services. Mr Wallace was so pleased with her rapid progress that he asked her to play the harpsichord at the Christmas Mass in the Cathedral. He wanted to show off his new prodigy.

She asked for time to consider the invitation, to be discuss with her parents about it. She was worried. To learn and practice in secret was one thing, but to play in public in an alien church was another. But more than that, she had been taught that Christmas was a pagan festival and to take part in it was to approve of the pagan festivities. This provided Sarah with a real dilemma, a matter of conscience.

That night she asked her Father for his advice. He replied "When you went in search of music lessons I said that sooner or later this kind of problem would arise. However, you are learning to play and to sing praise to God. That is good. You are meeting people in the city who can challenge your thinking. That is good. You now have a problem and you are trying to sort out what you should do. That is good. My advice is that you take time to talk to this Mr Wallace about your problem. He seems a sensible sort of fellow. If he is, he will understand and help you with your conscience."

The next time she was alone with Mr Wallace. She outlined her problem and asked for his guidance. He thought for a few moments and then replied; "Thank you for being so honest, I already knew that your family are separatists. I am impressed that although they have fundamentalist views about religion. they have, however, allowed their intelligent daughter to study here in the midst of Anglican worship. They must trust you a lot and now I know why. You have risked everything because you trust me and I will reciprocate that trust. I would like you to continue as a student for as long as you are able. But you will not need to perform in public in the Cathedral."

Sarah was really thrilled at his response. She concentrated her effort in her studies, practising whenever she could at the music school. One day, while she was practising. An older man entered the room and stood listening to her for quite a time. He asked her; "You are very good, but who gave you permission to play and sing here and what are you doing here anyway?"

"I asked, was given permission and I am receiving lessons." She replied nervously as this man seemed to have some authority. She wondered whether he was the bishop or some other senior person in the church. The man continued; "Yes, I had heard there was a girl attending choir school. However, I didn't realise it was a young woman of some ability. You will have to come and entertain us at the Bishop's Palace. I will arrange it with Mr Wallace. You may continue." With that, the man left the room, closing the door behind him.

Sarah's heart was thudding. She just couldn't do that! She would just have to leave Salisbury and return home. She couldn't play before the Bishop and his friends. If they discovered her background, she and her family would be imprisoned immediately. Oh, this was terrible, why did she have to be so clever? If she was plain and unintelligent she could just be a village girl.

Again, she presented her dilemma to parents, pleading with her whole being for some simple answer. But her Father had no simple answer, "Life's problems have to be faced. There is no simple solution. You have an opportunity to demonstrate your musical ability. You can show your faith in the way you conduct yourself. You will be an ambassador for Puritan values in the midst of evil. Remember the Apostle Paul said that 'A great door and an effectual is opened unto me, and there are many adversaries.' If you go, you will have to be very careful and discrete. There may be an opportunity for you to witness to that which you believe. I can't say that I am not worried but if this is God's Will, then you must accept it. You must use the opportunity that God has provided."

Sarah was relieved. On one hand she did not want to give up something in which she had found success. But on the other hand, she was nervous of what might happen as a result of this opportunity.

In due course, Mr Wallace told her that the man who had visited her was in fact the Bishop. He told her that the Bishop had reprimanded him for teaching a girl with the choir. He also stated that his own future was dependent upon her. It was therefore with some trepidation that they both prepared for the performance. This was to follow dinner one evening. It would consist of a series of madrigals, recently composed by Orlando Gibbons, a well-known composer of the day. They practised until Sarah was note perfect and ready to perform at the evening function.

At last, they were ushered in to a large room with about fifteen ladies and gentlemen seated at a long table with the debris of a substantial meal on the table. Sarah sat at the harpsichord and began to play, everyone listened with careful attention until she had finished. They applauded her performance and she carefully curtsied to the Bishop and his guests. The Bishop addressed Sarah; "That was a wonderful performance. You are very gifted. Tell us, where do you come from and why haven't we seen and heard you before in Salisbury?"

Sarah replied; "My name is Sarah Tilly and I come from Ringwood. I have been studying music with Mr Wallace since October and would like to continue if it pleases your lordship."

But the Bishop was not listening to her, he was whispering to one of his guests. He then spoke to Sarah again; "You say that you come from Ringwood and that your name is Tilly. Wasn't that where that evil Puritan scoundrel William Tilly came from, who escaped from the hangman's noose back in the summer? Are you any relative of him?"

Sarah gasped and just managed to say; "Yes, he is my brother. He is a good man who worships God according to his conscience and not according to your rules." She did not think of the implications of her comments, merely to support her beloved brother. The Bishop and those with him had become very agitated and ordered Sarah and Mr Wallace to leave the room. The next day, Mr Wallace was dismissed from office at the Cathedral and told to leave his job and his house as quickly as possible.

Sarah was mortified by what she had done to her beloved Mr Wallace. She knew that he would never get another job, all because of her few words. She was desperately worried for him but couldn't think of anything that she could do to save him.

It was therefore, with deep concern that they welcomed Sarah home. She had tried to make the break and had failed. Her parents commiserated with her, but there was little that they could do to help her.

They had other problems on their mind. They had just received a letter from their local rector stating, that the wedding of William and Miriam was illegal. He was therefore not able to register the marriage. He also stated that as John Tilly had acknowledged that he had committed the crime, he should expect to hear further about this matter from the church authorities.

Surely, in the light of these two scenarios, the church authorities in Salisbury, would sooner or later act against the Tilly family? Only time would tell.

John Tilly had not been to sea since the return from New-Found-Land. Somehow, there just seemed too much to do at home. To go back to sea, risking life and limb for very little in return, seemed crazy. Since the illness and death of Mary, he had been very busy clearing the garden of the summer's crop of herbs. He had cut back the plants, dug over the ground and prepared it for the winter. He had also spent some time with the widows of the past summer, the two members of their tiny 'congregation' and the family of the fishing boat crew. They needed much support, both moral and financial in order to survive.

He had also made a long trip, by boat up-river, by walking and riding to find Hetti Stott. She had gone to stay with her sister near Bristol. After many enquiries and much searching, he found her. She was a shadow of her former self. Three months after the death of her husband she was a frightened old lady, whereas before, she had been a determined middle aged woman. He spent a day with her, comforting and talking to her about her husband and the difficult times in which they were now living. Before he left, he shared a simple communion service with her.

The winter began in earnest in December that year, with a significant fall of snow followed by several nights of hard frost. This made travel really difficult. It was almost impossible to use the boat on the river. William was marooned in Salisbury, Ruth at Sopley Hall and Richard at Fordingbridge The rest of the family were stuck in the cottage in Ringwood. It was not easy being cooped-up in a small cottage in the cold weather. But it did give them a roof over their heads. A home in a pleasant, small town with friends nearby.

John was now becoming increasingly worried about the proposed increase in rent. They were only a matter of weeks away from the threatened escalation of expenses. He sat down one afternoon with John the less and Sarah to sort out their finances. To speculate as to what they could do. As matters stood, they were insolvent.

Sarah reported that there was temporary work at Ringwood Mill which she was prepared to try. John the less, reported that the fishing crew would return to fishing off the coast as soon as the weather improved. But even with increased work they would still be insolvent by February. If the weather was really cold, they would be unable to pay their expenses long before then.

When Ruth returned home the next Sunday, she had two pieces of news for her family, one good, one bad. As she explained; "The good news is that Lady Susan has found us a place where we can worship together, without fear of being found and arrested. She has offered to allow Father and John the less to have a look at the property which is at Ripley. They can then complete any repairs that need doing and we can use it for our meetings." She then took a deep breath and with eyes cast down to the ground, she said, "The bad news is that I think I am expecting a baby."

There were gasps around the room and everyone looked at Ruth in amazement. John the less and Sarah looked at each other and said, almost as one voice, "How do you know? You couldn't be. You haven't slept with anyone, have you?" they asked incredulously. Mother spoke out, "Hush you two, you don't know what Ruth has had to put up with at the Hall. I knew that something was up last week. Has Sir Richard been near you, has he forced himself upon you?" Looking to Ruth for confirmation as to whether her daughter had been raped or whether this was a genuine love affair.

Ruth, wishing that she could be anywhere else other than subject to this inquisition, nervously fidgeted with her hair. With her eyes still cast down to the ground, she spoke in a muffled voice, "I am sorry, so sorry but there was this young stable lad who took my heart away. We talked and talked, I spent some time with him, he took advantage of me and now I have missed 'my blood' for the second month and I am sure that I am carrying his baby. I am so sorry, I have failed all of you, especially you my dear parents. I am so sorry. Please forgive me and help me?"

Father recovered the quickest as he beckoned his eldest daughter across to him. When she was seated at his side, he put his arm around her and said; "Whatever's happened has happened. Let's cope with this together. Let's not judge who is guilty or innocent but let us provide for your child with love and care just as we are for Mother's." Ruth looked up to him with tears in her eyes and kissed him. Thanking him so much for his love and kindness to her.

The others were aghast at the news but also grateful that Father had said what he had said. They were grateful that Father had shown such grace in the face of such foolishness.

On Sunday morning as they sat down for their regular Communion Service, Ruth and Sarah sat together, holding hands. They both had had a rude awakening to the ways of the world in the recent past. They were now joined together in a shared friendship. Neither had been lectured by their parents, both had been given love and support in their hour of need. The one who tried to use her talents to sing and play, had learnt that life wasn't as simple as she had thought. The other, who had naively trusted in a man she did not know, had been used as a plaything, but who had to suffer the consequences of her actions.

John Tilly in his prayer asked for guidance to make the right decisions, that God might help each member of the family in their particular circumstances. Above all, that they might be true to their conscience which might in turn, be instructed from God's Word.

The next few weeks were cold and bleak in more ways than one. They each tried not to moan about the cold or the lack of food. Sarah worked in the mill, moving bags of flour around for a pittance of a wage. Struggling to do the work of a man without complaining that she was just a girl. John the less was struggling to keep the small boat sailing, fishing when possible, ferrying passengers when not. Ruth went back at Sopley Hall, trying to keep her condition a secret from Lady Susan, trying to cope with her impending crisis. John and Emily were not talking about that which they knew was inevitable. Whilst all of the younger children found that being cooped-up in a small cottage in the bitterly cold weather was so difficult.

Then, one morning towards the end of January, there was a knock on the door of the cottage. John knew that this was the beginning of the end. The estate manager delivered a letter giving them one week's notice to vacate the cottage. He delivered a similar letter next door and to several other cottages around the village.

John went upstairs and knelt at one of the beds. "Please Father, help us. Show us the way to live, that we might serve you in freedom according to our conscience." He prayed desperately for help. Emily also joined him in his devotions and together they prayed fervently for help.

Meanwhile, unbeknown to Father, John the less, was visiting Sopley Hall to see if he could make contact with Bess. He walked through the melting snow via Ripley farm to investigate the outbuildings a little more closely than he had viewed them before. He soon realised that if they were all evicted from the cottage in Ringwood, they might be allowed to live in secret at Ripley. When he arrived at Sopley Hall, he went to the kitchen and asked if he could see his sister. When she arrived he explained his plan. "I don't know," she replied, "It's asking Lady Susan a lot, I don't know whether I dare risk everything by asking."

At that point, Lady Susan came into the kitchen looking for the cook and exclaimed; "Who is this handsome young man, then?" Ruth replied; "This is my older brother John, he was just asking about Ripley Farm." "Shush, let's go outside for a moment," commented Lady Susan.

As they crossed the yard, she seemed to anticipate their request by saying; "Yes, I am sure a family could live there. It would need some work done on it but if you needed to move in suddenly, go ahead. Of course, it could not be long-term, but it might provide a home for the next few months."

When John the less returned home that night, he had some good news to offset the bad news of the morning. Over supper, Father commented to everyone; "You see, 'all things do work together for good to those who fear God.' We shall not be homeless and our new babies will have a roof over their heads. Everything will be alright. We must learn to trust in God and not in our own abilities."

The following day, John the less took his father across the fields to the broken-down farm buildings. They walked around the farm, identifying what needed to be done and how they could all fit into the buildings. They would also have space to hold a service on a Sunday. "We will just tell those whom we trust, about this place. If we move the day before the eviction order is carried out, we shall all have flown the nest. They won't be able to catch us." observed father, looking wistfully around the buildings. "All this place needs is money and hard work. It could then be a productive farm once again."

"Yes, I know, but we would still not be allowed to stay here, we can't stay in England." stated John the less; "Wherever we live we shall be hounded, arrested and killed. The authorities do not want men and women of conscience. They only want people who obey their rules, so that they can live in plenty and the rest live in poverty. We shall never be free as long as we stay here in England."

"What are you saying?" asked Father; "Are you suggesting that we need to emigrate to the New World, to America?" "No, not America, but New-Found-Land," said John, "I believe that's where we need to go – a fisherman's paradise, a place of freedom, a place to make a new home."

For the next few weeks, these ideas were forgotten in the battle to survive. They moved to Ripley on a cold, wet day using a horse and cart from Ringwood.

At least with it being wet and cold, nobody was bothered to know where they were going except their next door neighbours. They would join them in a few days time. They took their few possessions and the food that they had managed to store. Ruth had the day off work and Lady Susan provided a store of vegetables to help them all settle in. William also helped for part of the day. He didn't want to make too much fuss at work, as he did not want anyone else to know about his parents' move.

You might wonder why the family had not been able to save more money from the summer fishing trip and from their work during the summer. It wasn't quite as simple as that. There were no banks in those days, at least not for rural folk. Much of the food was obtained by growing the crops and exchanging the surplus. There was no margin for changed circumstances. If the rent for the cottage had not been so drastically increased then they would have managed to eke out a living. Yes, they did have a good catch of fish in the summer and that provided them with money during the autumn but not for the winter. They had needed several fishing trips during the autumn but with the trauma of Mary's death and with everything else, they had been robbed of the will to earn and provide food for the winter.

They also tended to think much more short term than we are used to, as do all people in poorer societies. There was no possibility of saving for tomorrow and beyond, they had to react to circumstances as they unfolded. Hence, when the notice of eviction was actually delivered, they had no option but to move out and trust that something would happen to save them.

We now find the family, trying to survive in a broken-down farm in the middle of winter, with young children and a mother expecting a baby in a few weeks. The older teenagers were at work but any wishing to return home had a walk of several miles across the fields. Ruth was the nearest at Sopley Hall. John the less was not near his boat and had to cross several fields to reach the river. William was working many miles away in Salisbury and supporting his wife's family as well as his parents. Sarah was working unhappily at the flour mill back in Ringwood. Richard was working hard at Fordingbridge in the carpenter's workshop.

We could say that this was now a fragmented family living in very difficult circumstances, a family struggling to survive. John Tilly was very much aware that in a few months they had gone from being financially viable to poverty and possible disaster. But he was also very fatalistic about such matters. He had an attitude of mind which we find hard to understand, but which was commonplace in the seventeenth century amongst similar families.

His faith was summarised by the attitude which said that 'everything in his life was according to God's will', that suffering and death was the normal lot of mankind. Life was a blessing, to be accepted gratefully. Suffering and death were inevitable. All things would be made perfect in a future life in God's Kingdom. Bible texts were always at the forefront of his thinking; "The sufferings of this present time are not worthy to be compared with the glory which shall be revealed in us." And; "Who shall separate us from the love of Christ? Shall tribulation, or distress, or persecution, or famine, or nakedness, or sword? ... Nay, in all these things we are more than conquerors, through him that loved us."

He did not for one moment ask why this had happened to him. His task was to accept the problems of life as a test of his character." For whom the Lord loveth he chasteneth, and scourgeth every son whom he receiveth. If ye endure chastening, God dealeth with you as with sons."

Having considered a little of John's philosophy of life, let's spend a few moments looking around their new home and thinking about their lives in this new environment.

The farm had once been quite large and successful. There were therefore quite a few buildings scattered around a central cobble stone yard. A track from the road led across the fields to the farm which was hidden by many trees. There was a main barn which would have housed hay, straw and several wagons and a series of stables with associated accommodation. Two cattle sheds and three cottages completed the buildings. Each building had lost its roof but one of the cottages had some protection from the weather and this one they decided to make their home. The men cut and dragged tree branches to make a roof which could be covered with reed to make it reasonably watertight.

The grate in the hearth could still be used and so a fire was quickly lit. In the centre of the yard was an old well which was also brought back into use. They had brought a few items of furniture and food which were quickly stored in the dry areas and within two days, they had brought order out of chaos. They had water, warmth and shelter.

Fortunately, they had had a break in the weather so that they could get themselves organised, but then snow and ice hit them.

It was a particularly cold February and they suffered considerably. No-one could leave the farm after their little service on their second Sunday. Everyone had returned home from their respective places of work to give support to the family. But once they had arrived, they all had to stay there because of the weather.

John Tilly used the opportunity to have a family conference about their future. He recalled his son's comments made a few days ago and asked him to explain his thoughts to everyone else;

"We are in a crisis," he began, "we have lost our family home. We cannot afford to rent a place for the family. We are starving and without enough food. We cannot stay here next summer. We cannot worship as we would like to. We are in constant fear of arrest and imprisonment. William was nearly executed last summer, Sarah lost her opportunity to study music and be educated. Ruth is expecting a baby in the summer, in the near future she will not be able to work at the Hall, Father and I cannot earn enough money from fishing off the English coast to keep the family fed. We cannot continue as we are. We have to do something. We are in crisis."

"So what do you suggest that we do?" said Father.

"I believe that we ought to emigrate." replied John the less. "I believe we need to seek entitlement to land from the 'Merchant Venturers' and book passage by ship to New-Found-Land. We could then start afresh with a new home, new freedom and new opportunities."

Immediately everyone started talking, the children were excited and started to talk about the trip. The older teenagers thought of the opportunities of such a move but almost immediately thought about leaving their home and their friends.

Emily and John looked at each other with a mixture of doubt and hope. It could solve all their problems. Equally it could create many more problems. For Emily, the imminent birth of her child was her prime concern. She also realised that this was not far from an ideal place to bring up a child. This suggestion could answer so many problems.

John Tilly was thinking about the wider scene. Into his thoughts sprung quotations which he would recall many times in the forthcoming weeks;

"For here we have no continuing city, but we seek one to come." and, "Come out from among them and be ye separate, saith the Lord."

After a little while, the conversation quietened and William spoke for them all when he said; "It sounds an interesting idea. It needs looking into and in a few weeks time we need to talk again when we have obtained some facts. We will need to think carefully about the practicalities and implications of such a move."

The idea had been conceived, whether or not it would or could be delivered was another matter!

Worlds Apart

Eleven - 'Is new life possible?'

No sooner had they talked about the possibility of a 'new life' when suddenly they had one. That very night, Emily went into her labour pains, marooned as they were in their makeshift home in the middle of fields and trees cut off by snow and ice. By morning, she had delivered a baby boy. Both Mother and baby were fit and well. The birth was uncomplicated and the pains of childbirth were the least that Emily had known.

Maybe, the Lord was looking after them after all, that he would protect them, giving them new life out of the old. "Maybe, this is what resurrection is all about", mused William as he gazed on the new bundle of life. "God giveth it a body, as it hath pleased him, and to every seed his own body." They called the new baby, 'Seth' remembering that God had given such a son to Adam 'as a new beginning'.

John Tilly was enthusiastic and excited about the possibility of moving overseas. A place where there would be freedom of belief and freedom for his family to gain a spiritual purity. Unlike some of the Puritans, he did not support exclusivity, nor a judgemental attitude to those who did not agree with him. He was a pragmatist. He had no formal sense of a group of believers who were perfect. Rather he saw himself and his family demonstrating love and tolerance in the midst of bigoted intolerance.

As soon as the weather improved, the two Johns determined to travel to Bristol to find out more about immigration and passage to New-Found-Land. Bristol was the focus of travel between England and New-Found-Land. All of the larger fishing fleets and all of the export/import of goods from England were made via Bristol.

With some food in their bags, they made their way across country. Their first stop was in Salisbury and then to visit Hetti Stott to give her their latest news. She was still far from well and had not been back to her old home since the death of her husband.

From there they made their way through Bradford-on-Avon to Bristol. They negotiated their way to the docks by asking folk. Eventually they arrived at the dockside and walked between the stores and the warehouses alongside the different wharfs. They marvelled at the size of the ships and multitude of the boats. At the many warehouses and at the industries around the docks. They had never been to a large city before and they were just mesmerised. There were hundreds of workers, unloading ships, moving stores and loading myriads of stores on to horse carts ready for transport.

As they rounded the corner of one street, John the less stopped and stared at the sign above one of the warehouses. It said in bold letters; 'John Tilly, Sail and Cloth Merchant'. "Wasn't that the name of your uncle, Father? Weren't you named after him? Didn't you say, that he had come to Bristol to make his fortune?"

John Tilly stopped in his tracks and also studied the sign carefully. He looked beyond to the large warehouse beyond; "Well, I suppose there is only one way to find out." With that, they both walked into the warehouse. Pausing as they did so to wonder at the size of the place, the bales of cloth racked down one wall and the sail cloth being spread out on the floor by several workmen.

"Is Mr Tilly available? Could we see him?" asked John the less. "One moment," replied one of the men who seemed to be in charge; "I will see if he is in the office. Who shall I say wishes to speak with Mr Tilly?" asked the man. "Just say, it's two visitors from the past, will you?" replied John the less.

The man disappeared and returned a few moments later; "Come this way please." He invited the two men to follow him to the back of the warehouse into an inner office where several clerks were working at ledgers. At the far end, he knocked on a door, opened it, walked into a spacious office with a large desk and chairs. On the wall were maps of Europe, Ireland and New-Found-Land. The man seated at the desk was well-dressed, with a cape thrown over his shoulder and a large hat hung on the wall above his head. He was obviously a successful business man; employing many people. He undeniably had wealth, power and influence.

The man got up from his chair and came to the side of his desk holding out his hand to greet his visitors. "Welcome to my office. To whom do I have the honour?" He asked, looking quizzically at the two men in front of him who were very poorly dressed, rather dirty and unkempt. Then he looked closer at them and exclaimed; "I don't believe it, it's my nephew, it's John Tilly. Welcome to Bristol my friend, welcome to my establishment." He gave each of them an emotional embrace.

"Who's this fine young man?" He asked as he held John the less by the shoulders whilst scrutinising him carefully. "This is John the less, my eldest son but one. He works with me on the fishing boat. He's a good lad, a tribute to our family name." replied his father.

"We need to talk," said the business man, "I want to find out what has been happening to the family in Ringwood. How is your wife, how many children do you have? What are you doing here in Bristol?" Looking a little more carefully at the two men he said quietly to them; "You look as if you need a good meal and a beer. Go out to the yard at the back, have a good wash and shave. Meanwhile I will send for food and drink. We can then eat and talk."

The two men did as they were bidden, not quite understanding what was happening to them but nevertheless, grateful for their good fortune.

After a wash and a shave, they returned to the office to find steaming dishes of beef stew and a tankard of beer waiting for each of them. This was more food than they had seen in weeks and it didn't take them long to consume everything. John Tilly, the business man, watched then with a wry smile on his face. He realised that these men were starving and judging by their appearances, they had been sleeping rough and were in dire straights. He let them finish their meal and when they all had a tankard of ale in front of them, he asked; "What brings you to Bristol? Tell me everything that has happened."

For the next couple of hours the two Johns poured out their story. Glad to be able to talk freely about their problems, their hopes and their fears.

Eventually, they came to a full-stop, exhausted and deflated. Realising that in the face of this obvious wealth and success, they were miserable, incompetent failures. John particularly felt that he had totally destroyed his family. Somehow, he had allowed the situation to deteriorate to an irredeemable situation, his religious convictions had clouded his judgement to the point of destruction. He would like the ground to have opened up in front of him and to have swallowed him up.

He looked up and saw not pity as he had expected, but pride and respect.

After a few moments of thought, John Tilly, the successful, wealthy businessman responded; "In the face of such great oppression and real hardship you have maintained your faith. You have taught your children to stand up for what is right and true. I am proud of what you have done. You give honour to the family name and I will do everything I can to assist you to achieve a new life."

The two Johns looked at each other with tears in their eyes and hope in their hearts, this was more than they had ever expected. This was beyond their wildest dreams. If this was true, then a new life was a possibility. They might be able to emigrate and begin a new life away from all the fears of arrest and trial, away from poverty and hardship.

"You must come home and meet Elizabeth and the children. You can stay with us while we think out the practical issues involved. We can show you Bristol, then you can return home to plan for your new life." said John the businessman, with enthusiasm.

It was an exciting few days for the two Johns. They discovered that the business was large and successful. John's Uncle owned several wharves, three or four warehouses, several ships and employed a hundred or more men. He had business contacts throughout Europe and in several ports in America. But his main business was in materials, particularly in linen - yarn and linen clothes. He had retail shops in Bath and London where he sold clothes to the rich and famous. One of the warehouses was devoted entirely to the manufacturer of sails which interested John the less considerably. The family lived in a large, rambling mansion on the slopes above the city in Clifton, from where they could look down on the busy streets and docks of Bristol.

During the next two days the three men prepared a plan of action for the two Johns to take back to Ringwood and discuss with the rest of the family. They discovered to their amazement, that their relative was not only a member of the 'Merchant Venturers' but was in fact, its chairman. He would therefore, on their behalf, make an application to his fellow-board members. He agreed to stand as guarantor for their proposal.

The two Johns would need to list the goods they would take with them and an indication of the skills that they would require to start a new life. They would also have to discuss with their neighbours and friends as to whether or not they were going to be involved in the venture as well as the immediate family. The big issue was how to get from England to New-Found-Land. If they could use their fishing boat to transport some of the goods needed it would be invaluable in their new life. However, it was too small for all the proposed party members. They would therefore need to book a passage on one of the ships travelling from Bristol, John the businessman, said that he would pay any fares required and assist in any way that he could.

It was an emotional parting, the two Johns had found a way of escape from penury and fear. They were now men with a mission, fired with zeal and enthusiasm to begin a new life. They were lent a horse so that they could make their journey home quickly, which together with food and a change of clothing, enabled them to return home, refreshed and invigorated.

While the two Johns had been away in Bristol, the rest of the family had got on with their lives. Lives which were beset with worry. Worries about food and shelter, worries about work and travel but above all about discovery. If Sir Richard returned home unexpectedly and discovered that the Tilly family and others were living on his land, they would be in dire straights. However, apart from these obvious concerns, life was even more focused than in Ringwood. There was work to be done in making several of the buildings weather-proof.

Firewood had to be gathered for their fires. Fire had to be maintained with care. Each day had to be considered individually. Anyone travelling into Ringwood had strict instructions to collect items of food from friends or old neighbours. At least, any money earned, could be used to buy flour or meat from people around the area rather than in paying rent for their accommodation. .

The baby was growing fast and the children enjoyed being able to play around the barn and the other buildings. The two widows of their little congregation and their children had joined them at Ripley together with their old neighbours from Ringwood who had also been evicted from their home. They had stayed a little longer, hoping to put-off the evil day with Mary Watts challenging the increase of rents, appealing directly to the new owner of the manor, Mr Sowerbut. But to no avail. In a few days, the estate manager accompanied by several farm workers armed with an array of frightening weapons, arrived at the cottage and proceeded to evict the family. As a result, there were quite a number of young children and others at Ripley Farm, steadily making it more habitable.

Ruth had found it much easier now that she had told the family about her possible pregnancy. Her immediate family were quite supportive of her but others in their little community were highly critical and shunned her. It was also much easier to walk to work, Sopley Hall was just across the fields.

Ruth found that Lady Susan was being very kind-hearted towards her family. It was as if Lady Susan had discovered 'personal guilt' that while she had plenty, others had nothing. Each day, Peter had been instructed to report to the kitchens at Sopley Hall where he could collect any spare vegetables or left-over meat or fish, taking it back to the others. Ruth and Lady Susan had talked several times about where to worship and it was agreed that as soon as father had returned from Bristol, they would make a suitable place for worship within the farm complex.

William was working hard in Salisbury. He and James were now preparing their first submission for the creation of a 'Commercial Waterway from Christchurch to Salisbury'. They had compiled detailed drawings of the proposed harbour at Christchurch and the work that needed to be done on the river. This required identifying the dredging, clearing of weed and preparation of a proper towpath throughout its length. Written agreements from the various owners en-route had been drawn-up and were included. They had produced detailed schedules of cost for the work and an indication of possible investors in the project. They were nearly ready to re-start on the river, sketching and planning the second part from Fordingbridge to Salisbury.

Sarah had continued her work at Ringwood Mill which she hated, but on occasion had gone with William up to Salisbury. This was ostensibly to assist William with the preparation of the submission. But she was also quite interested in James Proudfoot and he was very interested in her! You will remember that they had met after her disastrous encounter with the Bishop of Salisbury and her rapid exit from the Cathedral Choir. In the days that followed, James asked William several times about his sister and after one such question and answer session, suggested that Sarah be asked to assist them in the work!

Sarah was excellent at writing up the notes, James could dictate to her and she would write down the notes as quickly as he could speak the words. On her first day at such work she had combed her hair carefully and wore her best Sunday dress to impress. She thought that James was rather nice and flirted continuously with him. Equally, he became infatuated by her and decided to talk to Eddie Otter about employing her full-time!

Richard had really settled into his work as a carpenter's apprentice. He enjoyed the work working with Joe. They were a good team. So good that their work was being noted by gentlemen in Salisbury who wanted to commission pieces of furniture from Joe. He had also received a request for making church furniture, a pulpit for one church and an altar rail for another. Richard was not quite sure about these and determined to ask his father about it when he returned from Bristol. Richard was aware that these items were used in a form of worship with which his family did not agree. But he did not really understand the implications of how 'an altar rail' could be used to coerce everyone to conform to a particular religious practice.

We have not mentioned Peter for some time in our story. He had been kept fully occupied throughout the autumn and winter in the various domestic tasks and he had assisted John the less on the river, but since moving out of the cottage, he was fully occupied with collecting wood, keeping the fires burning and the other sundry tasks that were necessary for their existence.

Everything had settled down to a routine until the two Johns returned from Bristol and threw everything into turmoil. As news spread through the encampment, there was considerable excitement generated. Several members of the family just could not believe their story. Emily was just overcome with pent-up emotion when she heard about the kind offer from Uncle John.

At Ripley Farm there were now quite a few people living in the various buildings. They had managed to make roofs reasonably watertight and rooms serviceable. In each family group, discussion proceeded apace; what would it be like in New-Found-Land? Was it possible to live there? What would the sea crossing be like? Could they survive there during the severe winter? Who would emigrate and who would stay behind?

John and Emily, William and Miriam were of one mind, the circumstances had been an answer to their prayers. This was nothing short of miraculous. To turn down the offer of a new life was blasphemy against the Holy Spirit. A denial of the possibility of God working in their lives. Equally, the Watts family had a similar viewpoint; their children were younger and would all do what their parents wished. The discussion centred on the teenagers in the Tilly family and they had strong opinions.

Let's begin with Ruth; at three months pregnant, she would find the journey very difficult indeed. But she desperately wanted to start a new life. She had no husband to help her and always the threat of Sir Richard was in the back of her mind. She desperately wanted to leave England. However, Ruth also felt responsible to Lady Susan for the care she had shown to the family and felt quite guilty at even thinking of leaving. She decided to be frank with Lady Susan and see what she said.

One morning they were sitting in Lady Susan's room and looking out over the grounds of the Hall on a bright February morning. Ruth decided to broach the subject of New-Found-Land. She carefully explained what had happened on her father's visit to Bristol and the possibility of emigration. Although at this time, she did not tell her about her pregnancy for fear of being immediately dismissed.

Lady Susan interjected; "That's just wonderful, you could all go to New-Found-Land and start afresh. Your Father could start a new fishing business which could develop into an substantial enterprise You could build a new home and start a new life. In fact, I wish I could come with you." Ruth was taken aback by the excitement in her employer's voice. It took a moment or two for the last comment to sink in. When it did, she exclaimed; "But you couldn't come, you're married, you're wealthy. You have a beautiful home and your place is here, not in squalor and having to work to survive!" Lady Susan laughed at her young maid's vehement response.

"We shall just have to see, but I am not as incapable as you think I am. It would give me a real challenge, a reason for living. Whereas at present I just act as 'a lady' and await his Lordship's pleasure as and when he deems to come home. Which is not often." she added ruefully. "It's something that I am going to think about, although I do not want you to mention this to anyone, is that agreed?"

"Yes, my Lady." accepted Ruth with reluctance as she would dearly have liked to talk about this new idea with her family, but that would have to wait!

"Now, I want you to tell more about this Uncle of your Father's. He sounds an interesting man to know. His business could be quite exciting. I would like to hear more of his fashion shops. They would be fun to visit. I wonder whether he imports French and Italian clothes. If he does, then several of my friends would also be interested in his shops." Mused Lady Susan aloud, before turning to Ruth and asking specifically; "Ask your Father for details of his shop in Bath? It could be an excuse for a few days away for both us in the next week or so. I would like to visit Bath before it gets too busy with the summer visitors. We could have a little holiday, just you and me".

"Of course my Lady, I will ask tonight and report back to you tomorrow." replied Ruth as she realised that she ought to get down to work. Time was moving rapidly onwards and she had much to do. At night she asked her father about his uncle's business and gained a little more information. However, everyone else only wanted to talk about Bristol and New-Found-Land.

The next morning, Ruth reported back to her mistress and was totally amazed by her Ladyship's comments; "I have been thinking. In fact I have been thinking all night! I have carefully considered your comments about emigration and my involvement.

When I did get to sleep I had a dream, a dream which was very vivid and frightening. A dream which I can still remember this morning, I will describe it to you.

It was about a strange people, almost naked, dressed in furs, painted red and brandishing clutches of arrows. We were living in a makeshift timber house eating a meal and then sharing a prayer together as these strange people attacked. However, when they saw that we were praying they stopped, laid down their weapons and joined us in prayer. Yes, I was there with your family and friends. Then we went outside, it was very cold and icy. The strange people brought furs and wrapped them around us. It was a bewildering dream, but I believe that it had a message for me.

On Sunday, I would like to come across to Ripley Farm and share in your worship, do not tell anyone about this as I do not want your family to worry. I will just come quietly on my own. Sit at the back of your meeting in order to observe what goes on. I believe that this may be the beginning of a new life for me, I do not know where it will lead, but I know I must respond. It's as if God is calling me to respond to his invitation; 'Come and I will show you.' I cannot resist it."

Ruth was completely bewildered by what she had heard. Her head was just reeling from the comments of her employer. She just wondered whether or not her employer had gone mad. However, she seemed to be normal and in control. Surely, Lady Susan would not leave all her wealth and luxury to live in poverty. She just wouldn't survive in such terrible conditions. Let alone in the even harsher environment of New-Found-Land! Ah well, thought Ruth, if it's God's will, then it will happen, if not, it won't.

Lady Susan continued to confess her thoughts to her only friend, her maid. "You see, I have been thinking for quite a long time that my life here is a false one. My marriage was for political expedience. My dowry gave Sir Richard land, houses and money. Now that he is married, he is free to enjoy life with his female friends in the city. Whereas I am left in the country to manage the houses, farms and staff. According to my doctor I cannot have any children. I am barren and unable to conceive. I am therefore destined to a life of childlessness and nonentity. A life of wealth but worthlessness! Now, I have been given a new opportunity. I intend to take it and use it. May God be praised."

Ruth was humbled and chastened to realise that her employer had treated her as her equal and friend. Lady Susan had confided in her to such an extent that Ruth was quite overcome.

In her heart she prayed to God that he might give her strength and courage to do and say what was right. When she had collected her thoughts, she replied; "I am honoured Lady Susan to be your friend. To be able to share my beliefs with you. If it is God's will that you are able to share in our worship, then God's name be praised. If we decide to emigrate to New-Found-Land and you come with us. We shall be honoured by your presence."

When Ruth had finished this little speech she was blushing. Realising that she had spoken with some authority as if she represented her family and congregation, yet she knew that what she had said, was right.

Work was difficult after this momentous conversation. But routine is a help at such time. This is what Ruth did, she just worked away at her routine tasks until it was time to go home and back to normality.

William had had a different response from his employer and colleague. You will remember that they had spent the winter months in an office in Salisbury, preparing a report for Parliament and potential sponsors. They were now planning their Spring programme to survey the rest of the river up to Salisbury. When William mentioned tactfully to James the possibility of emigration, James was not best pleased. "What do you mean, you may be leaving, you can't leave. You have a contract to complete. We have work to be done. We shall be starting in a few weeks out on the river and you are vital to the work. We need you, here."

"Well I didn't imagine that I would leave you without a boatman. There are many others who could do my job, I am sure," replied William. But James wasn't to be put off that easily; "You are vital to our work. The report we are producing needs a consistency of information that only you can provide. Eddie has paid dearly for your services and he won't accept your excuses," stated James, realising that he had said more than he should have done. He wished that he had kept quiet. But it had been said, he just hoped that William had not realised that something else had been implied.

William decided that he should keep quiet, for the time being, about the possibility of emigrating. When plans where further developed he could raise the matter again. In the meantime he just kept his head down and worked even harder. But within days, his erstwhile supporter and employer was in Salisbury. He sent word that William was to present himself before Eddie Otter as soon as possible. William knew in his heart that this was to be the moment of truth. Although he did not know the extent of his employer's involvement in his life, he was nevertheless worried. He went quickly to his employer's room in the hotel and knocked on the door. "Come", said the voice within, William responded by carefully opening the door and walking in to the room.

"What I am going to say will no doubt come as a surprise to you," said Eddie looking William in the eye. "Last Summer, when you nearly lost your head because of your religious beliefs, I paid good money for your release. Your freedom was paid for in hard cash. Now I understand that you're thinking of emigrating. Leaving me without a good boatman to complete the essential survey work. I am not best pleased with your intentions. However, as you are a man of principle. I am going to leave you to make your own decision. I have given you the facts so that you can make an informed choice. I will give you one week to give me an answer. Either you stay and complete the work or leave, knowing that you owe a debt which has not been paid."

William was shocked beyond belief. He had no idea that his employer had obtained his freedom by paying money to the authorities. He stuttered his thanks to his employer and hastily exited, stumbling down the stairs and into the open-air where he was violently sick. He made his way carefully back to the room they used as an office in a haze, not fully comprehending what he had just heard. He returned to his work. But found it very difficult to concentrate. His mind was in turmoil. No wonder his escape from death had been so secret. No wonder no-one could understand what had happened.

He now realised that his release had all been planned and paid for, so that the River Project could proceed without hindrance. By comparison, his dreams of freedom and a new life across the seas seemed insignificant and unimportant. Yet such plans did give him the opportunity for a new start, away from the fears of re-arrest and possible death by hanging. He did not know what to think or do – his mind was in turmoil. Whatever else, he had to acknowledge that his employer was an extremely shrewd and clever man. If crossed it could be a man's downfall. It was wise to keep such men on one's own side. William had a lot to think about and even more to discuss with his wife and the rest of his family.

While all of this was unfolding in Salisbury, other events were happening in Ringwood and beyond. Sarah, you will remember after her abortive attempt to learn music, had obtained employment at the Ringwood Mill. This was heavy work, moving sacks of grain and flour around the mill. Her beautiful hands were now calloused and scarred; she had developed muscles and strength and was now able to move heavy loads. She also had to walk long distances to and from work each day, yet she only earned a small pittance of a wage. Her dream of pursuing an intellectual career at university was now out of the question, just to survive each day was as much as she could manage. However, whilst she was working, she could dream, dream of Nick and wonder where he was and what he was doing. She could also dream of a new life in New-Found-Land with new opportunities and new challenges.

One frosty February morning, she had to take some messages to Will Smith, the Estate Manager for the Lord of the Manor in Ringwood. She was just crossing the village when a lone horse and rider galloped down the street accompanied by a long-legged hound. The horse was reigned-in just near to where she had stopped. The rider jumped off and bowed to her, the dog bounded up to her, almost knocking her to the ground.

"Mistress Sarah, I your humble servant present myself to you with deepest apologies for my long absence from your life."

"Oh Nick, where have you been? I have so missed you, why did you leave without as much as a 'goodbye?" Sarah cried as she hugged him for all she was worth. He kissed her with real affection. Kisses which she returned in like manner. "Listen", she exclaimed, "I just cannot stop, I have to deliver these letters, I shall lose my job if I am late." As she tried reluctantly, to extradite herself from his embrace, Nick interjected; "Wait a minute, what job is there which is more important than spending a few moments with the man you love? A man who has been absent for months, pining and fretting about his beloved from afar."

"I just cannot stop at this moment, I must deliver these letters and get back to the Mill as fast as possible. But I will meet you this evening, then you can explain everything to me." stated Sarah in a sad, yet excited voice.

"All right, I see I am not going to persuade you otherwise. At the place where we used to meet, we will meet again." With a quick hug and a kiss she was gone like a feather flying away. But both young hearts were aflame, the one to work, the other to dream, as he walked and waited for the evening.

It was quite a cold day and Nick found it hard to find anything to do. He visited the cottage where the Tilly family used to live and found it empty except for some workmen who were repairing the roof. In answer to his questions he just drew non-committal replies and blank stares. He walked to the local Inn and again asked many questions but nobody would tell him anything except that Sarah worked at the Mill and that William Tilly worked in Salisbury. The rest of the family seemed to have vanished overnight. Although he did get the sense that several knew more but were afraid to say anything. In the end, he just went for a long walk with his hound until it grew dark, leaving his horse tethered by the river. He then made his way to 'The Rocks' on the bank of the river. At last, when he had almost given up hope. Sarah came running along the river bank and flung herself into his arms.

After quite a long time of hugging and kisses, they paused, Sarah asked again; "Why did you leave so suddenly and where have you been these long months?"

"I have been in prison," he said quietly. "After the summer festival, the group I played with decided to leave immediately. I had to go that evening otherwise I would not have had any transport. I fully intended to return after a few weeks. But only a week later, we were drinking and talking in a hostelry in St Albans. My tongue became loosened through drink and I boasted that I had attended a 'Puritan Service'. I even said that I had taken part in the service and shared in the Communion. Unknown to me, there was in the Inn, a high ranking soldier who was in the Royal Household Guard. He reported me to King Charles who issued a warrant for my arrest. I have been in prison ever since. If it wasn't for the fact that my father knows King Charles personally, pleading on my behalf, I would still be there."

"Oh Nick!" exclaimed Sarah, "If only I hadn't persuaded you to come to our service then you would never have been arrested and imprisoned. It's all my fault. Now you have returned to me. This time you are not going to go away from me. I need you and so does our family." Sarah proceeded to explain the dreadful things that had happened in Ringwood since the summer. As she talked, they began to walk to the family hideaway at Ripley Farm accompanied by horse and dog.

Nick also explained that whilst in prison, he had done a lot of hard thinking about religion and politics. He had been kept in a cell with an Anabaptist with whom he had debated for many long hours about religion. This fellow convict had explained the importance of adult immersion in water as a symbol of death and resurrection to a new life of discipleship. As a result of these long discussions, Nick stated that he had decided to renounce his family's Catholicism and become a Congregational Puritan. Sarah was dumfounded, "You mean that you would denounce all of your inheritance for what we believe. That you would be prepared to leave everything behind and come with us to New-Found-Land?"

"Just take it one step at a time!" retorted Nick with a huge grin, "For the moment, let's just take it that I wish to share in the life of your family and see where that leads me."

Before they reached the farm, they stopped for a short while to hug and kiss until Sarah drew back and said that they ought to be getting home. Otherwise the family would became worried about her and send out a search party.

As they walked into the yard hand in hand with the dog jumping at their side, there was a shout from Peter who was pulling up the bucket from the well. "It's Nick, he's come back, he's come back to marry Sarah." At this, everyone came running outside to see what the commotion was all about. Sarah was holding Nick's hand and grinning from ear to ear as she said; "Yes, this is Nick and he's come home to stay with us. He's decided to be one of us."

The family were excited beyond measure. The questions just kept coming from anyone and everyone until Nick and Sarah just spoke as if they were but one person; "Enough, we will explain over dinner."

That evening, they had a special meal in celebration of Nick's return. All of the adults and the children living at the farm all came together to hear about the 'Wanderer's Return'. They had made a bonfire in the yard and cooked some scraps of pork that Ruth had brought back from the Hall. They roasted their potatoes and cooked all sorts of vegetables in the hot ashes, whilst Nick held them all spell-bound by his story.

John the less had also been busy. He had been working hard on the river with their friend's boat, ferrying passengers and goods up and down river from Christchurch to Fordingbridge. It was doubly hard in the winter, some mornings he had to break away the ice from the boat before he could row it into mid-stream. On other days he would get soaked from the incessant rain that beat upon him. However, it wasn't all doom and gloom. He had managed to make friends with Bess at Sopley Hall. He had at first, sent messages via his sister Ruth, saying that he would like to meet her. Then one morning he spotted her walking across the fields to the ferry. She called to him and said, "Could you give me a boat ride to Christchurch? I have an errand to complete for her Ladyship?"

Fortunately, that morning he had no other passengers or bookings to complete. He could give his whole attention to the attractive Bess as she carefully stepped onto his boat and settled her skirts around her. He wasn't quite sure how to begin the conversation. But after one or two false starts they seemed to find some common ground and talked about fishing! Apparently, although Bess was good with horses and was therefore a stable hand at the Hall, she had grown up with her grandparents who were fishermen at Poole. In fact her grandfather had also been to the Grand Banks off New-Found-Land. They were soon chatting, as if they had known each other for years; about fish and fishing, about sailing a boat and managing a crew. Although Bess had never been to sea, she knew a lot about fishing and the sea. John the less liked what he heard. He dropped Bess off just before Christchurch harbour saying that he would wait for her while she completed her tasks.

John the less found himself day-dreaming while he waited. He had found a girl who understood about fishing, who was not only intelligent but also attractive. He just thought that it might be possible – she might even come to New-Found-Land with them. She just might even consent to be his wife.

A friendship was born which had all the possibility of blossoming into much more. John the less at least thought so and judging from the comments which his sister made about Bess, she also had thoughts in the same direction. John the less and Bess saw each other as often as possible, she was introduced to the family at Ripley Farm and whenever she could, rode there to exercise the horses from Sopley Hall.

The extended family of John Tilly had grown since they had moved to the farm. He was able to talk to every one individually about whether or not they would be prepared to emigrate. He was keen to establish what skills the various people had and how they could contribute to a fledgling community. He was realistic about the dangerous nature of the sea crossing, about the ice and snow they would encounter in New-Found-Land with the subsequent difficulties of survival. But he also spelt out the possibility of a new beginning, a freedom to worship according to their conscience. He was carefully preparing everyone for the decision that they would soon need to make.

'Worlds Apart'

Twelve – 'Decisions, Decisions'

At the beginning of March, a messenger arrived at Sopley Hall looking for one John Tilly. Ruth was able to leave her work for a moment and talk to him. She understood that the messenger had come from Bristol. He carried documents for John Tilly and his family to sign regarding emigration to New-Found-Land. She escorted the messenger across the fields to Ripley Farm to meet her father. She was so excited, yet not daring to think what the messenger would say.

"Your Uncle, John Tilly, businessman of the Port of Bristol has been able to secure passage aboard the ship 'Bonaventure' for twenty-five souls, departing Monday April 3rd 1626 for the port of Saint Johns, New-Found-Land. My employer suggests that you collect together such persons that wish to travel with you. That you all remove to Bristol and stay in one of his warehouses prior to sailing. He also suggests that you sail your own fishing boat from Christchurch to New-Found-Land with all your fishing equipment, small boats, any furniture and food you may be able to gather for your new life. You will need to sign these documents so that your uncle can obtain the various 'Rights of Land' for when you arrive in your new country."

John was dumbfounded, he had dreamt but not really thought that his uncle would be able to provide the passage. Let alone obtain the necessary 'Rights of Land'. It wasn't just going to be his immediate family either, who would benefit. The offer meant that his neighbours and partners together with his family could also travel and start afresh. What an opportunity. What a challenge, God surely worked in mysterious ways. John expressed his thanks to the messenger and invited him to stay with the family overnight so that the message could be explained to the families living at the farm.

Everyone was invited to attend a family get-together that evening at Ripley Farm to hear for themselves the offer of John Tilly's uncle regarding emigration to New-Found-Land. It was with some trepidation that they met together that night. For some it could be the start of something new and exciting. For others; the end of life as they knew it, with parents, brothers and sisters sailing to the end of the earth.

When they were all assembled, they shared the food which had been prepared. The messenger from Bristol was asked to repeat his information for everyone to hear. There were gasps of amazement and disbelief. However, he reassured them all that the offer was real. Finally, he gave them the ultimatum that his Master needed to know, whether or not the offer was acceptable so that he could proceed with negotiations.

Everyone began talking at once and John allowed this to continue for a short while so that they could express their excitement and talk about the implications of the offer. Everyone continued eating and talking until John raised his hand, requesting quiet.

"I am asking for a show of hands of everyone over the age of ten years as to whether we go ahead and accept the offer of a passage to New-Found-Land. However, before we make that decision, I want to outline the reasons for emigrating to New-Found-Land. The move would give us a new opportunity for life. We cannot continue to live here for more than a few months. We have no other home. We have no money and no food. Our families are in need of new opportunities and a new life. Above all, we need the freedom to worship as our conscience dictates without fear of arrest and punishment. However, we do not know what we will find on the other side of the world. We shall have to build new homes from the materials we find. We shall have to survive on what we can grow and fish. We do not know anything about the present inhabitants of the country. Above all, the weather will be much colder in New-Found-Land than we are used to here. In fact, it will be almost impossible to survive in such hostile conditions."

William stood up, he had been collected by John the less that afternoon for this important meeting. He spoke carefully and deliberately; "Although, my wife and I are desperate to leave England, I have a problem with my employer and in good conscience we shall not be able to leave and come with you. We shall hope that by next year we shall be able to get passage and sail across the Atlantic. But for the present time, we cannot come, although our hearts will be with you." There were gasps from around the group. They had all expected William to be a key member of the group.

Mary Watts spoke for many when she observed; "For those of us with no work, no money and no home, I do not think that we have any alternative. This offer has come from our Father in Heaven. His good hand has given us the hope of life. We cannot refuse it. If we do, we shall be denying the power of God to save us. For as many as can go, they must go or suffer the consequences." There were several murmurs of approval of these words around the group. She continued; This would give us the opportunity to practise First Century Christianity. We would have 'everything in common', we would be able to educate our children in the fear of the Lord without any man forbidding us. We would be able to keep ourselves pure from the evils of this present world."

John the less, ever the practical man, then addressed the group; "By taking the fishing boat across the Atlantic we would be able to transport everything we own and be able to transport some timber for making our first homes. It would also mean that we could provide for ourselves for the first few months with a means of fishing in the deeper waters off the coast."

"That would be true if we had anything to take." said Joe Watts, in his usual sceptical words.

Nick volunteered his thoughts, as an outsider who was nevertheless committed to the project and had been accepted by everyone and was respected by all. "It would seem to me that sooner or later everyone in this little community will be arrested and many will be killed. There is a conflict coming to this fair land of ours between King and Parliament, mark my words. We are caught in the middle. If we stay we will be destroyed. Neither faction has any time for 'men of conscience'. Even if Parliament destroys the King, everyone will have to obey their rules. I vote that we take up this wonderful offer and leave for New-Found-Land while there is opportunity."

On this note of wisdom, John held up his hand; "Those in favour of emigration, please show?" Almost everyone raised their hand, Only William and his wife with their heads bowed and their hands held tightly, refrained.

Just as they had taken their vote, there was a small disturbance at the edge of the group. Lady Susan crept in and sat quietly by Ruth. She was dressed in a long dark brown cloak with a hood which almost hid her face. John knew of her interest in their worship and she had visited their services on one or two occasions but even he was frightened and awed by her presence. Nick recovered first and spoke for all of them; "We are honoured by your presence Lady Susan. To what reason have you come this evening to share in our humble fare and discussion?"

Lady Susan looked up and gently spoke with tears in her eyes; "Please, I am just Susan to all of you. I admire all of you for your stand against false religious worship. I believe that your faith is right and true. I would like to become a member of your congregation. I am here tonight to ask if I can come with you to New-Found-Land? To begin a new life as a disciple of Jesus Christ and as member of your congregation. I hereby denounce my former life, my religion and my wealth. Please can I come with you?"

There were gasps around the company. Even Ruth who knew her mistress very well, had never thought that she would actually hear what she had just heard. Ruth was thrilled by these words, as she held Susan's hand tightly.

John looked round at everyone's amazement and excitement and quietly said; "Let us pray. 'Father, thank you for this wonderful opportunity. Thank you for this offer of new life. Thank you for the conversion of Susan to our faith. May we be blessed in our new venture to serve you as our conscience dictates according to your Holy Word. The grace of the Lord Jesus Christ, and the love of God, and the communion of the Holy Ghost, be with you all. Amen."

With this, the meeting broke up and everyone moved away from the fire, some to sleep, others to talk and yet others to plan. All excited, all uncertain as to what the future held for them. All had been taken aback by Susan's intervention and her promise of commitment. Some accepted this in good faith, others were very sceptical and uncertain.

John and Sarah worked out a message to send back to Bristol telling his uncle of their acceptance of his kind offer and his planning for the venture.

In the morning, they started to plan in detail for the transfer to Bristol. Not least was the exact make-up of the party to sail by the ship 'Bonaventure'. They created two lists, one for the passenger ship, the other for the fishing boat. Between the two, everyone who wished to go was able to be included. It meant the Tilly and the Watts families from Ringwood with the Hayward family from Ellingham could all go to New-Found-Land. This excluded William, his wife and young Richard who was to continue in employment. Hopefully they would travel the following summer to North America.

In addition to the families mentioned above, there were also Nick and Lady Susan. There was some disquiet in the company about these two as several saw them as interlopers, as being potential traitors to the cause. Both were from wealthy, aristocratic families and this was seen as making it impossible for them to fully share in the hard life they envisaged for the future. However, John insisted that these needed to be accepted and the others reluctantly agreed.

William was sick in heart and mind but he knew that he would not be able to live with himself if he did not complete the task he had started with Eddie. Once he had an inkling that he was in debt to Eddie for his life, he could not go with the others. He could not leave him in the lurch. If that meant that he would continue to be in danger of his life, then so be it. That was a risk he had to take. Further, it also meant that he could keep an eye on young Richard working at Fordingbridge. It would allow Richard to complete his training in carpentry and maybe they could all emigrate in the future. Richard would then be of real value in the new community as a fully fledged carpenter.

Lady Susan had cautioned everyone that no-one could talk about her decision. She just hoped that it could be kept a secret for a couple of weeks. She planned to go on a shopping expedition to Bath taking Ruth with her. They would stay at John Tilly's in Bristol until they sailed. This would enable her to have her last taste of luxury before she departed for her new life. She hoped that this subterfuge would not arouse any suspicion as to her long-term plans. Her other secret was that she intended to pay for the provisioning of the passenger ship and the cost of passage for some of the others. But that she had to negotiate the exact details with John Tilly, the businessman,

Meanwhile, at Ripley Farm, there was mayhem. Much excitement amongst the children and concern amongst the adults. With their sudden move from Ringwood, it had meant that all of their friends who normally helped them to provision their fishing expeditions, were now inaccessible. To make matters worse, they had little recourse or opportunity to prepare food and equipment. After much discussion, it was decided that John the less, Jo Watts and Thomas Hayward would take the fishing boat with several of the men and one or two women as crew. It was felt that John Tilly should lead the main party which would travel on the ship 'Bonaventure'. This was a precaution in case something happened to the fishing boat on its way across the Atlantic. They would still have leadership and experience to guide them all.

In Bristol, there was much work going on behind the scenes. John Tilly the businessman, had made formal application to the Merchant Venturer's for 'Rights of Land'. This would enable the settlers to legally occupy a piece of land in New-Found-Land. It would enable them to cultivate and build houses on the land, to build a community with their own fishing base. He had to buy these rights on behalf of the Ringwood fishermen, by applying to the Venturer's and to Parliament in London.

A warehouse was set aside for the Tilly goods. It was planned that they would sleep in the warehouse until they boarded the ship. Clothes and blankets were put aside for the families. It was well-known and understood in Bristol, that the travellers would need many warm clothes to survive the winter. Various seaman had returned to Bristol with tales of ice-burgs and freezing fog. John Tilly, the businessman, also consulted some of the captains who had taken passengers to the New World and he carefully noted their advice as to what was required to start life afresh.

Further to his discussions, he decided that if he collected a much wider range of goods, they could be stored and transferred to Christchurch and shipped to New-Found-Land aboard their fishing boat. Thus he set about collecting some of the following ; iron pots and copper kettles, cooking items like a 'spit', a gridiron and skillets for the kitchen. He collected tools for farming such as; pitchforks, a plough and metal shares for ploughing. Important tools like axes and handsaws, hammers, shovels and spades, pickaxes, hatchets and many other such items. A pair of bellows, a scoop and stones for grinding flour. Buckets and a wheelbarrow for transporting water, fish and other goods. He collected several wooden wheels, even the flat-bed of a cart and an axle. The most precious items were two lanterns and a supply of wicks and oil. All of these items he stored in his warehouse to await the arrival of the families from Hampshire.

Meanwhile, Lady Susan had managed to keep her plans secret from her husband and most of the staff at Sopley Hall. Bess, her stable girl had also decided to join the expedition. She had fallen in love with John the less and would accompany the men aboard the fishing boat. Lady Susan and Ruth made plans for a shopping spree to Bath. The plan was to buy as much clothing as they could find, items which would be suitable for life in a much colder climate. Neither woman had much idea about what would be necessary, they therefore decided to journey to Bristol, find John and Elisabeth Tilly, discuss with them their requirements and then shop in Bristol and Bath.

At Ripley Farm, the families were trying to gather as much food as possible. Some of their old friends in Ringwood area helped them to prepare. It was like cooking for a fishing voyage but without the advantages of a proper kitchen and facilities. Considering that they had little in the way of stores and no money, they managed to collect a significant store of food. All of this was carefully transferred down to Christchurch and stored in the boat.

Richard's employer gave them a table and chairs to take with them, these also were transported to Christchurch. John was concerned that they had no small boat of their own. They would need this in New-Found-Land to transport everything to the shore and to use for fishing off-shore. He decided to ask an old fishing friend if they could use an old disused boat. The man agreed.

It's probably helpful at this stage to stop and think about the reactions of the various members of the family to the planned voyage.

William was preoccupied with his work in Salisbury, after the initial shock of having to stay in England, he was largely forgotten in the planning operation.

Ruth was at the Hall and in due course moved to Bristol with Lady Susan, to await the rest of the family. She was apprehensive and quite worried. Firstly, regarding her employer who would soon become just one of the 'family' so to speak. Ruth worried that Susan would find it all too difficult and would end-up blaming her for a difficult, even impossible life. Ruth worried that Susan's conversion to their faith was only 'skin-deep and that it would crumble when they left England. Ruth was also worried about herself, she was now visibly pregnant. Lady Susan had accepted the situation without comment. There was however, very real opposition amongst other members of the party. Ruth had decided that she just had to keep a low profile and accept people's criticism without reaction. All she really knew was that the voyage would be really hard for her. But it couldn't be helped, she had always wanted to be given the opportunity to travel and this was it.

John the less was the one member of the family who knew something about their new environment and the probable reality of their new life. He was able to analyse the dangers and difficulties of the voyage. He was both excited and concerned at the same time. He did not quite share his Father's belief that this was God's Will and all they had to do was to 'accept in faith'. He was worried about his sister's pregnancy and the ability of the women to survive, both on board the ship and when they arrived.

Sarah was ecstatic, she had 'her man' and he was coming with them. She and Nick spent hours together with his dog bounding at their heels. They were responsible for the detailed planning of the trip, the marshalling of all the stores. They made lists of everything and had it all planned as to what was going to Bristol and what was to go to Christchurch. The only thing that they did not know about was the vast pile of stores being amassed in the warehouse in Bristol.

Richard, like William, was not directly involved in the planning, although he had a mix of thoughts about being left in Fordingbridge. He desperately wanted to continue his carpentry work but he was very keen to go with the rest of the family. If he stopped to think about it, he was easily upset by such thoughts.

Peter was one of the busiest people during this period. At the beck and call of his parents, of Sarah and Nick, he did not have two minutes to himself.

The younger children were all aware that major events were afoot but were too young to understand the implications of the plans.

Finally we come to John and Emily. They believed that they had no alternative but to emigrate. They both saw the opportunity as an answer to their prayers. To refuse to emigrate would be disobedience to their God. They believed therefore, that God would protect them and bring them to their 'Promised Land.' John saw the situation as the way in which God was testing him as a leader of the community. Just as Moses had led the children of Israel out of Egypt through the wilderness. In the same way he had been given the task of leading his family and others to a new life. Emily saw her role as a supportive one, looking after her brood of children which together with her neighbours, they would establish a new spiritual home in a far-off land for the Children of God.

The great day arrived. They had borrowed two wagons with horses to transport everyone and their baggage to Bristol. The carts had been loaded the day before and now everyone clambered on board. They quietly slipped away up the farm tracks, across the countryside. John the less and Jo Watts were driving each of the horses. When they had delivered everyone to Bristol they would return and get ready to sail the fishing boat across the ocean. The journey to Bristol took three days. They were well laden and some of the roads were quite muddy causing them to all get off and push themselves out up hill and down dale.

Once they arrived in Bristol, John the less directed them through the city to the warehouse where Ruth and Susan were anxiously waiting for them. There was much excitement when they realised what Uncle John had collected for them to take on their voyage. Equally, the women were amazed at what

Susan had bought in the city shops. It really was going to be a new life with new clothes and many new goods to start them off.

Uncle John made himself known to all of them – he brought some bottles of wine into the warehouse and had a glass poured out for everyone. 'May God bless everyone on all their travels and may God bless you all in New-Found-Land." He raised his glass and toasted everyone. The family and their friends all raised their glasses and shouted; "Thanks be to God."

The goods were unloaded and sorted by Sarah and Nick whilst the larger items were loaded on to the wagons ready to be transported to Christchurch. It was an exciting day with much animated bustle and a degree of chaos on the quay side. The children were running here and there, getting in the way, frightening their parents as they ran along the quay side. Each family were desperately trying to sort their own possessions as they also tried to gain some of the new items for themselves!

Meanwhile, John and Emily were taken by John and Elizabeth to view the 'Bonaventure' as she lay alongside the quay. It was already being loaded with food and other goods. There would be eighty passengers and thirty-four crew to sail the two-master across the Atlantic. To Emily, she seemed a very small ship for so many people. For the first time she realised the enormity of their decision. They were going to sail to an unknown place with unknown people in a ship that was no larger than their row of cottages in Ringwood. John put his arm around her and said comfortingly; "We shall be together with most of our family. God will look after us – just trust in Him."

The next morning the men departed with the horses and wagons. Sarah had given strict instructions about loading the various items onto the fishing boat. John the less assured her that he would look after everything. "That's the problem." said Sarah with a grin. She loved her brother and hoped that everything would be alright on their voyage, so that they would all meet up again soon in New-Found-Land.

As soon as the men had departed, everyone else had to take their own personal bags and clothes on-board the ship and find their own quarters. There was not much space.

For the first time Susan realised what her future was going to be like. Her privacy was almost a thing of the past. From now on she would have no privileges, no servants and no money. But in her heart she was happy, she would be free to serve God and her fellows, just as she believed she ought to do. This was going to be exciting and difficult. But if everyone else could do it – so could she.

In Bristol Docks ...

The ship had three decks. All of the passengers were herded onto the middle deck and each family was provided with a small area. Here they erected blankets as walls to give some privacy and laid out their bedding and stacked their possessions nearby. There was not enough room. In fact there was no space at all. The realisation of what it was going to be like sharing such a small amount of deck with another sixty people in rough seas was beyond imagination. The children thought it just great to be on a big ship and to be sailing across the seas was a dream come true. But for the adults it was a frightening prospect. Nick's dog had now been joined by a bitch so that they would be able to breed their own pups in the New World. But these would be caged on the storage deck along with the other animals.

Sailing had been brought forward because there was a good wind blowing. It was to be a very high Spring tide over the next two days. It was stated by the captain that most people must stay on board and make their chosen space habitable. If there was anything they needed, now was the time to buy it before they sailed. There were tradesmen selling all sorts of goods; from hay sleeping bags to milk and fresh food. Pigs and sheep were being driven onto the ship and penned in the hold. Chicken and geese were also carried on board and caged in chicken coops on the middle deck. It was noisy and very busy as the ship was prepared to sailing.

On the last night before they left Bristol, Uncle John Tilly held a feast in his warehouse which incorporated a short service of dedication. He was not as religious as his nephew but he realised the importance of the families' religious faith. The meal was one fit for a king with bread and pies, roasted beef and mutton, boiled veal and mutton. Salted cod, salmon, cheese, butter and gallons of ale to wash it all down which he supplied for all to share.

A short service was conducted by John Tilly which included the singing of Psalms, Bible readings and Prayers. Finally, they all held hands in a large circle as John gave his last prayer on English soil; "May the God of peace sanctify us wholly; and I pray God our whole spirit, soul and body be preserved blameless unto the coming of our Lord Jesus. The grace of our Lord Jesus Christ be with you all. Amen."

John and Emily were sad yet excited as they thanked John's uncle for all his care and generosity to them all. Without which, none of them would be able to escape to a new life.

On the morning of April 1st 1626, after their first night on board their new home, they woke to find that the ship was about to sail. The wind was good. The tide was high. The sailors were unfurling the main-sail. All of the passengers were kept below deck as the ship began to shudder and shake as she moved away from the harbour wall.

There were shouted commands above as different ropes were hauled across the deck. Slowly, but surely the ship began to move. Through the various portholes they could see the crowd of well-wishers on the quay side. They were cheering and shouting their good wishes to those on board. As the boat slowly crept out of the harbour on the full tide, the passengers could see the city of Bristol steadily disappearing. A few hours later, the boat started to roll as they picked up speed. The mud-banks and reeds receded from view, eventually the land disappeared entirely. They knew that they were on their way, they had left their home behind.

Each person had their own thoughts and prayers as the ship made her way slowly out of the city, along the River Avon and into the Severn Estuary towards the open sea. It was a voyage into the unknown which could bring new life or a disastrous death.

'Worlds Apart'

Thirteen - 'New-Found-Land'

The voyage was a nightmare in more ways than one. There was just no space. Everyone had to get used to having no privacy and no space. It wasn't too bad until they sailed out of the Seven Estuary into the ocean. But once they encountered the buffeting waves, it was awful. The children were petrified day and night. People were sick and had violent diarrhoea. There was no-where to hide. Everything was public for everyone else to see and hear. None of the passengers were allowed on deck. It was just too dangerous.

Each and every passenger sooner or later wished they had never left England. Even the seasoned sailors like John Tilly found it difficult and irksome to be trapped below deck. Tempers became frayed, everyone was miserable and full of despair. People lashing out, at least in words if not with their fists.

Fortunately, the weather was not too harsh. The winds maintained a steady strength. Progress was quite good across the Atlantic. It was however, very cold. Everyone on board found that they were constantly wet from the spray and the running water which percolated throughout the ship. Nothing was dry. No-one was warm. Grandma suffered the most. Up to now she had not particularly grumbled about any of the misfortunes to befall the family. But now she was finding it very difficult. John and Emily feared that she might not complete the journey, that it might be just too much for her. But all she said was; "I be made of strong stuff – I am not easily got rid of, I just wish that it was a bit warmer."

Ruth was also finding it difficult. However, she managed to find a corner and wrapped in a blanket, just sat there. Often talking with Susan about all sorts of things, religion, politics, children and families. Everyone else tended to leave them alone. This was in part because no-one knew how to communicate with 'a lady' and no one could quite understand what 'a lady' was doing in such circumstances.

All of the passengers got to know each other very well during the voyage, they spent hours talking about what they might do when they arrived. Most did not have the equipment or skills which would enable them to start a new life. Most were escaping persecution, many from religious persecution. Some were in debt and had accepted a 'passage' as a way of escape. Two young women were pregnant and their families had paid the fare to send them far away from home, out of sight and out of mind.

There was just one independent man of means travelling to New-Found-Land. He had been appointed to the post of Assistant to the Governor, Sir George Calvert, in order to manage his master's estate. His name was George Thomas Pengellan. Sometimes he had access to the deck being a 'significant passenger', having paid rather more for his passage than anyone else. However, during the voyage he also spent some time on the middle deck with the Tilly family. He struck up a friendship with Susan, much to the interest of everyone else. This friendship was encouraged by John Tilly as he thought that it might be extremely beneficial to them all when they arrived in their new home.

By the beginning of the fourth week of the voyage, the air had become noticeably colder. Everyone found it increasingly difficult to sleep. With no exercise and the constant presence of icy water, sleep was well-nigh impossible. They were shivering for most of the time. Grandma had succumbed to a cold with a hacking cough. The two youngest children of the Watts family were ill and Mary feared for their lives. Another family were seriously ill with sickness and diarrhoea; their constant vomiting kept everyone disturbed.

They had eaten almost all of the food that they had brought with them from England. Some of the families had none at all, Emily shared their own meagre rations with them. Life was getting tough but John knew that it would get even tougher before they reached their destination. From his experience on the high seas, he knew that if they had a storm then it would be difficult to survive.

No sooner had John thought about this and he realised that the ship was beginning to be pounded by the seas in a new and frightening way. He supposed it was his seaman's instinct that told him that a storm was brewing.

The baggage and possessions began to slide across the deck. He shouted for all the passengers to be roped to each other or to the beams of the ship. "Everything must be fastened down, make sure that the children are roped. Wedge yourself in a corner between the ship's timbers and stay there," he shouted across the deck. Suddenly he had taken charge. He looked around and realised that many were crying or screaming as the ship began tossing and turning. Water was pouring in through portholes on one side and emptying out through the other side. He could hear the wind howling through the ship's rigging. Suddenly a splitting of timber and a gigantic crash was heard above them. He knew that a mast had broken. "Don't be frightened", he shouted, "Just hold on, keep calm, we shall survive."

After what seemed an eternity, the storm calmed and the ship settled. No-one had been lost overboard. The crew were all safe, there were only minor cuts and bruises amongst the passengers. Apparently, a mast had broken but quite high-up It was still possible to hoist a sail so that their speed could be maintained. The real effect of the storm was to lower the morale of everyone. Many had lost their possessions. All of their baggage had been washed backwards and forwards across the deck and was now soaked with much of it ruined.

Four days after the storm, when morale was at its lowest ebb and many had despaired of ever seeing land. A cry went up; "Land Ahoy" The whole ship erupted in excitement. The passengers started cheering and many started packing their belongings. But John Tilly shouted to everyone, "We may be days away from landing, we do not know where we are. We may have to travel some distance before we can dock, just have patience." That was wise advice.

They had in fact made land-fall near Plymouth where the 'Mayflower' had landed two years earlier in what was known as New England. They therefore had another week or so of sailing up the coast and across a stretch of open water before they sighted the southern coast of New-Found-Land known as Cape Race. The excitement really mounted as they inched up the coast of the Avalon Peninsula until they rounded the headland and into the bay of St Johns.

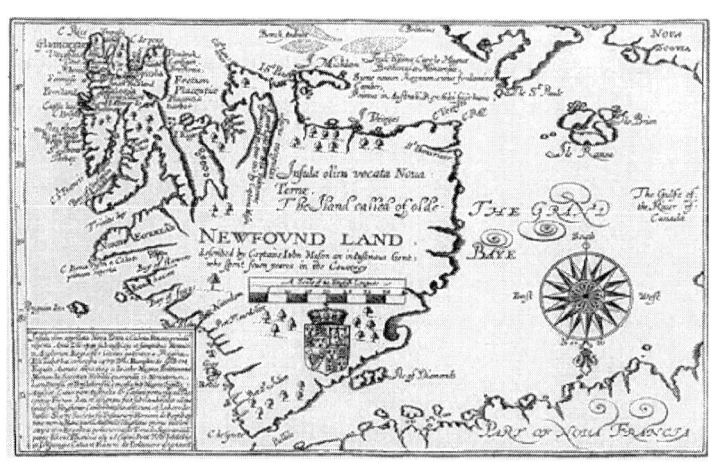

New-Found-Land

As shown by John Mason's map of c. 1617

(N.B. Old maps like this were often inverted in their orientation and drawn with the North at the bottom of the map.)

The passengers were still kept below deck, with the exception of John Tilly. As he was a sea-fearing man and had captained his own boat in these waters, he was asked to assist the captain navigate the ship into port. They could clearly see the harbour wall of Saint John's, but it took a little while before they could dock. The coastline was rocky at this point and the water deep, it was therefore quite difficult to find a channel.

Slowly but surely, they brought the 'Bonventure' into St John's and finally were able to throw ropes to the men on the quay side to secure the ship. George Pengellan accompanied by John Tilly went ashore to meet the port authorities. As John had foreseen, having befriended Mr Pengellan, it meant that they could avoid any lengthy discussion about emigration rights. They were welcomed as citizens of Britain who had come to settle in the New World.

The harbour and quay at St John's was at this time quite basic with a series of wooden jetties with steep pathways leading up to the main town which was perched on the side of craggy slopes. Not an easy place in which to begin a new life.

The passengers were allowed to disembark but they all found it very difficult to walk, let alone carry their wet luggage and possessions up the gang plank and up the steep pathways. As soon as they had done this, it became apparent that they had arrived into the middle of a building site. There were no grand buildings or streets, just a few stone buildings with mainly timber shacks surrounded by a timber palisade fence. There were quite a few soldiers marching about and it felt more like a military fortress than the harbour they had left in Bristol.

Meanwhile, Mr Pengellan had commandeered a horse and was loading his belongings onto it. "I am riding to the English settlement at Ferryland where there are rather better houses and facilities than here at St John's", he explained to Susan as they tried to sort out their respective items of baggage. "You will be welcome to visit me at the Official Residence of the Governor whenever you care to travel across. In the meantime I think your future life is with these fishermen. You will have to leave this compound before nightfall. I believe that you have 'Land Rights' for part of the 'North Falkland' area which is about a hundred and fifty miles away. May you find your new life interesting.

I bid you good-day." With that dismissive comment, he mounted his newly acquired horse and rode off through the gateway of the small settlement of St John's.

As Ruth had heard the comments of Mr Pengellan, she moved across to her friend and former employer, put her arm round Susan's shoulders whispering quietly; "I guess that means you are one of us. It seems to me as if the social classes are as divided over here as they were over there. Welcome sister. Let's pick up our bags and start walking to our new home." Susan looked up to Ruth with tears in her eyes and replied, "Thank you, let's do this together, sister."

The various families were now sorting themselves out with their respective piles of belongings and items that had been stored in the hold of the ship. John Tilly gathered his entire group together and stated what they had to do. "Before we go anywhere, we are going to thank God for our safe journey and ask for his continued care on our fishing boat on the high seas. We shall then leave this compound and start walking northwards. We have to climb up and over those rugged cliffs and find the area known as 'Bonavista'. That is where we shall settle and build our new homes."

As they started to move, they all found it difficult to walk after being cooped-up in the ship for such a long time. However, it was also wonderful to be free. To walk in the fresh air and know that the first part of their ordeal was over. As they moved out of the compound, they started to notice the scenery. The rocky, barren nature of the landscape, the steep drops down to the sea and above all, the air. It felt cold. Although by now it was early May, the air was like a January day back in England. The air was cold and crisp, not damp and moist. A blue sky with a few clouds but the air was still cold.

John and Emily were walking together, hand in hand with their younger children running around them, baby Seth on Emily's back and Grandma being carried in a wooden chair by Nick and Sarah with the dogs bounding around them. Susan and Ruth walking together, arm in arm, more like sisters, joined in a common bond. Peter was fascinated by this new world. He had struck up a friendship with one on the lads on the boat and he and his family were in the company. Peter and his friend were now running ahead excited and challenged by a whole new environment.

"I wonder how the others have got on aboard the fishing boat." said Mother, concerned and worried about the whole of her family as always. "They will be alright," observed Father. "They have experience, John the less and John Watt have both been here twice before. You wait, by the time we have walked to our new home, they will be there waiting for us." As he said this, Peter and his young friend came running back to the rest of the group, "We've seen some weird birds, like little old men strutting across the rocks." Peter cried. "They have a black back and white under-pants, a tall, flattened, brightly-coloured bill. They look funny with red and black eyes and bright orange legs."

Puffins ...

"They're called puffins", Father replied laughingly, "they live here, there are thousands of them."

That night they slept under the stars, the air was cold but they were able to snuggle up close to each other and keep warm. At least their belongings were beginning to dry-out and they did not have the constant drip of water keeping them awake. "Do you realise that it is Sunday tomorrow?" said Nick to Sarah. "No, I did not, I have lost track of time whilst we have been on board." replied Sarah. "That means that we shall be able to celebrate the Lord's Feast in our new land without fear of arrest or of interference. I will have to talk to John about how and when we can do that." commented Nick as he dreamed about his new life in this new land.

The following morning began with all the normal morning activities of a family on the move. They had kept provisions dry for this journey, stored in leather containers in the hold of the ship so they were able to have a good breakfast. At the end of which, Nick stood up and said to everyone; "It is the Lord's Day today, we have been delivered from the storm, we are beginning the journey to our new home. It is right that today before we start walking, that we break bread together, thanking God for his protection and putting our new venture in his hands."

There were many sounds of assent across the group as they formed a circle on the rocky ground and used the bread left from their breakfast and wine kept for this memorial to remember the death of their Saviour. John Tilly began their short service in prayer and leading the singing of Psalm 118 which included these words; "This is the day that the Lord hath made; we will rejoice and be glad in it." And concluded with; "O give thanks unto the Lord; for he is good; and his mercy endureth for ever."

Nick stood and gave his first talk at such a service, which gained many amen's from the villagers. He talked about Israel preparing themselves to enter the Promised Land under Joshua, thousands of years earlier. He ended with these stirring words; "Be strong and of a good courage; for unto this people shalt thou divide for an inheritance the land ... for the Lord thy God is with thee whithersover thou goest."

John Tilly took the bread and wine and after quoting from the Apostle Paul about its significance, passed the bread and the wine from hand to hand for them all to share. After prayer, they silently sat with their own thoughts, reflecting upon the journey so far accomplished and the journey that lay ahead of them.

Eventually, Mary Watts commented to everyone; "We are not going to get there if we stay seated on the ground all day. Let's get going and see what this New-Found-Land really looks like."

As they gathered their baggage and started to move forward, they looked around them and see their new landscape with fresh interest.

It was rocky and barren. At first they could see few trees but then they realised that the short stumpy bushes that they could see all around them were in fact trees stunted by the wind. It was windswept but beautiful. The sky was a brilliant blue reflecting the sea which was wild with waves crashing against the cliffs. Looking towards the horizon they could see hills which would have to be climbed if they were to walk towards their new home. They were amazed at the birds which flew constantly overhead and they frequently disturbed small flocks of puffins from their rocky homes.

Emily was thinking about John the less and the rest of the party still sailing on those tempestuous seas and prayed that God might keep them safe till they were all re-united on dry land. The children were excited as they ran ahead encouraging the older members of the party to walk more quickly. As they walked, they sang the Psalms that all of them knew off-by-heart.

They marched for ten days on stony tracks, camping under the stars and seeing little sign of life. Climbing craggy rocks and crossing peaty bogs until they had crossed a range of hills and could see a large bay of calm water surrounded by flat land. In the bay before them there where several ships and men were busy working, unloading boats and building timber sheds.

Bonavista Bay

John Tilly stood still for a moment whilst he asked Sarah and Nick to unpack the documents from 'The Society of Merchant Venturers' which showed the area to which they had ownership. They unrolled the manuscripts to find the legal title deeds and rough plans of the area. They could identify the bay on their map and were able to point out to everyone the area of the bay which they had been allocated. They all moved forward with excitement and enthusiasm after months of such difficult travel. After another couple of hours walking, they had arrived.

The land sloped gently towards the shoreline. The ground was stony but there were patches of peaty soil. Enough rich soil to grow some crops and plant herbs thought Emily. John already was thinking of constructing a pier out into the bay so that their fishing boat could be moored nearby. Susan and Ruth were dreaming of houses and streets, However, Sarah and Nick being responsible for all the materials, were thinking in more practical terms of how to construct homes without even the most rudimentary tools. Where was their fishing boat with all the tools and equipment?

At least, they could collect timber and get a fire burning. But the first priority was to find a plentiful source of fresh water. They searched the whole area and discovered several springs. They chose one which seemed to be the fastest flowing with the water tasting fresh and good. The children started to build a dam so that the water would collect into a reasonably-sized pool. Some of the children were told to spread along the shoreline and collect pieces of driftwood. These they had to drag back to the pool so that they could start a fire, a fire to keep them warm and cook their food.

However, before they could really get organised, several fishermen from boats across the bay, arrived. They were angry and challenged the Tilly party as to their right to be able to set up camp. Their leader spoke in a foreign language which Nick said was Portugese. He could speak French so he used his expertise to negotiate with them. He showed them the official documents giving them legal right to the land. Their reply was emphatic; "We were here first, that gives us the right to fish and decide who else fishes in this bay during this season." Nick's reply was to invite them to supper and to share a bottle of wine. The visitors agreed and departed for their fishing boats moored across the bay, to return later that night.

The next task was to think about food and shelter. They sorted through the driftwood that that had been collected. They found several large pieces which could be used initially as supports for their blankets, thus providing some shelter from the wind. The women had by this time established a good fire, heated water and were beginning to get the domestic scene organised.

Ruth walked along the shore to find a small creek and had been able to catch some fish which she gutted and brought back for cooking. Susan had constructed a small oven made of stones above the fire. One of the other women who had brought flour from England managed to make some dough and subsequently bake the first loaf of bread. By late afternoon, they had fed the children and were cooking their first real meal for everyone else.

By the time the Portuguese fishermen returned, the camp had signs of permanence. With the smell of fresh bread and cooked fish, the men's former anger disappeared. A wonderful evening was enjoyed by all.

Meanwhile on board the fishing boat, as John the less had anticipated the voyage had been difficult and dangerous. They had loaded the boat with the goods and chattels which had been collected in Bristol This together with the food and pieces of furniture that they had collected in Hampshire made the boat very heavily laden. However, they were experienced seamen and they had travelled to New-Found-Land before.

But this time it was different. In particular, there were several non-experienced passengers who had to be cared-for. These new sailors coped reasonably well with life on board until three weeks after leaving Christchurch. Suddenly they found themselves in the midst of a storm. Some of the cargo moved which made the boat more unstable. They nearly lost two men overboard. They were all desperate for land.

Eventually the winds died down and the seas calmed. They reckoned that they should sight land at anytime. In fact, they took only one week longer than the passenger ship before they sighted New-Found-Land. Because they were more experienced in sailing in the region they were able to steer rather more accurately than the passenger ship. They sighted the cliffs at the entrance to Trinity Bay and sailed around the headland into Bonavista Bay.

The excitement was tangible. Nearly everyone was visibly moved, as their beloved fishing boat slowly moved into the bay. They could see their family and friends on board. The fishing boat dropped its anchor off-shore and they off-loaded their small boat to ferry everyone to land. At last, they were all together on dry land. They had all safely traversed the mighty ocean to their 'promised land'.

John called everyone together and spoke on behalf of them all. "It is by God's grace and his loving mercy that we have been brought to this land without loss of life. We need to give thanks to him and always honour his holy calling. However, the most difficult time is yet to come. We need to build shelters, plant crops and manage the fishing."

That night there was much happiness, the party were together. They had triumphed over tremendous odds and they all felt ready to face whatever challenge they might meet.

The challenge came quicker than they had expected. They were all fast asleep. They were all so tired. Suddenly, a roar of flame burst from the fishing boat.

In an instant, they were all awake. The men shouting to get the small rowing boat afloat, John the less and Nick quickly shipped oars and rowed out to the fishing boat which by then was fully alight. It was extremely difficult to work on the burning ship, trying to extinguish the flames with only small leather buckets to hand.

They managed to salvage the bulk of the goods from the burning ship but some of their prized and essential possessions, which had been brought from England, were now destroyed. It was going to make their lives even more difficult but they had no alternative. More importantly, they could not fish in the deeper waters off the Grand Banks. They were confined to the waters of the Bay itself, they would be competing with many others for limited fish stocks. This event would force them all to think more seriously about farming rather than just fishing. Fortunately, they had been able to salvage many parcels of seed. These they were able to cultivate and produce crops of corn and vegetables.

In the morning Ruth and Sarah talked to Susan about forming a group to look for suitable land and start preparing the ground.

Meanwhile the men held a council of war. They were furious that they would be unable to fish in the deeper water. In reply to this, John the less suggested that as two men were shipwrights that they ought as soon as possible to check on the extent of the damage. If they could repair the fishing boat then they should start immediately.

"I think that the fire was started deliberately by other fishermen," stated Joe Watts; "they don't want us here. They particularly don't want us to set up a base and stay here for the winter. We shall control fishing in Bonavista Bay. I think that they caused the fire to make life difficult for us."

"We shall just have to build a secure homestead for ourselves with a surrounding fence," said John the less, "If we can re-build the fishing boat then we shall have to keep a permanent watch on her. Security is going to be critical for our survival." He stated with concern. "However, I think that we ought to take the initiative. We ought to meet the fishermen again and see if we can establish friendship rather than trying to wreak revenge. We should send two men to make contact with them and also with natives in the area. If they decided to attack us then they could wipe us out overnight." So it was agreed that John the less and Joe Watts should see if they could meet all of the fishermen with Nick and one of the younger fishermen to make contact with the natives.

While this meeting was taking place, the women had traversed the plot of land to which they had title. It was a mile in a radius from the shoreline. The land was rocky and rough. At the furthest extent the forest began – pine trees and heather with a peaty soil. Susan who together with Sarah actually knew quite a lot about trees and plants thought that they would just be able to clear an area of ground of stones, without attempting to clear any of the heather. They marked out an area of ground with sticks and started to move boulders, stones and branches. It was hard work. They seemed to make little headway.

By lunch-time, they had cleared a hundred yard strip of land a few yards wide. Once they had cleared the rocks and stones, the soil underneath was a rich, dark brown colour. Susan commented; "We shall have to get crops sown as quick as possible, so that they can grow. We can then harvest them before the winter frost and snows start which will be much earlier than in England." To which Sarah replied, "I had not realised that, I was thinking that we would have plenty of time but I think that you are right! We need to get the seed into the ground as quickly as possible."

In the afternoon, they were able to commence preparing a seedbed and with the aid of a crude hoe able to sow beans and peas, a patch of wheat and another of oats. At least they had started to prepare for winter.

The two men visited the dozen or so boats moored around the bay, they soon met strong opposition to their plans. The fishermen challenged the policy of the 'Merchant Venturers'. They stated emphatically that they wanted the 'rights to a free fishery'. However, our friends replied that they did not wish to control the market. Merely to escape persecution in England, providing sufficient food for themselves. After long discussion with the English fishermen, the Portuguese and Spanish reluctantly accepted the situation.

Our two explorers set out to make contact with the natives. First of all they put together some food and gifts in back-packs and started walking. After two day they sighted signs of human life. They found the bark of several pine trees removed as if by some kind of instrument. They also encountered the debris of a camp site; a broken spear shaft, some pieces of timber placed together, obviously arranged to form homes. They discovered a small pile of bones which they decided were probably deer. There were several remains of fires, parts of old canoes and more relics of tent frames. They discussed the implications and decided that these were probably the remnants of the previous year's winter camp, that there were no natives around at present.

They walked for a further two days before encountering marshland which stretched far into the distance. Carefully looking at the trees and bushes they noticed what looked like a pathway. This was slightly raised above the surrounding ground. After walking for hours on this firm path they spotted increasing signs of activity. Eventually, they found an area of drier ground with several indentations with the remains of wigwams. They spotted a low wooden hut, constructed roughly of pine timbers but nevertheless recognisable as a home. Outside the hut there were the smouldering embers of a fire which had only recently been extinguished. They decided to set up their own camp nearby and wait for the natives to return. It was an anxious night but in the morning they woke to find that during the hours of darkness, the natives had visited them and left food and water for them. As they were eating, they heard some sounds of people moving towards them but could see no-one

In a few moments they saw a man walking towards them. He was almost naked and his body was painted in red ochre. He carried in his hands a long spear held across his body as if to present it to our friends. They carefully opened their bags and removed several necklaces with semi-precious stones and dried fish which they had carried with them. These they also held out to their hosts as presents. The man walked nearer, laid down his spear and backed away, our friends copied this action by laying down their gifts and backed away. Other men appeared as a group they walked up to the gifts, picked them up, examined them and returned to their families. After a little while the group of men returned and walked to our two friends with open hands as if to welcome them. This action was taken as being one of friendship and not of war. So began a friendship between the men from Christchurch and the men from New-Found-Land. A friendship which would last for several years.

By this time in the season, other ships had arrived from England. As John had envisaged, several were prepared to buy fish and return to home immediately, rather than spend a month fishing for themselves. They were therefore able to sell much of their first catch and went back immediately to fish for more.

The women had not only to care for the children, feed their families and assist in house construction but also to develop their vegetable plots. Susan had initiated the clearance of the site of stones and branches. The seeds had germinated, the crop plants were growing strongly. Other vegetables had also been planted, after a only a few weeks growth, light green foliage was to be seen in the rows of young plants.

As they worked, the women talked, not only discussing the practical matters of life in a fledgling community but also matters of political and religious significance.

During their first summer in Bonavista their first priority had been to provide food and shelter which would enable them to survive their first winter. By the end of the summer they thought that they had achieved their goal. There was a quiet satisfaction that 'things were going well' and that God had been good to them.

Back in the new settlement at Bonavista, buildings were starting to mushroom. John and several of the men had been on a mission to find suitable timber for building. The women had also been been scouring the shoreline for debris washed up after the winter storms. Together, they had been able to amass quite a store of timber which was now being sorted and cut into suitable beams for roofs. Stones were being collected, the larger ones rolled by the children into place. Slowly but surely walls were emerging for their new homes.

They had decided to group their homes in a semi-circle with the village fire in the centre. Behind each house they developed the cultivatable land to grow their vegetables thus providing a space between their encampment and the surrounding countryside.

The open side of the semi-circle faced the sea so that everyone had a view of 'Bonavista Bay'. John had been able to build a small jetty out into the bay by using stones from the shore. They could almost moor their fishing boat alongside. The aim was to make it possible for fish to be carried from the boat directly on to the shore. Once this had been achieved, they decided that they should start fishing out to sea to establish some stocks for selling to visiting boats and for their own food.

They had been able to re-construct their small 'wherry' which they had brought from England but it was difficult to steer on the rougher waters of the Bay. It was agreed that as soon as possible, they would construct a more robust boat for fishing. This did not stop the fishermen in the community getting aboard their existing 'wherry' boat with lines and sailing to the outer areas of the Bay where the fish stocks were considerable. After a day or so, they returned laden with cod, halibut, flounder and 'red-fish' and as before, they gutted and smoked the fish ashore before drying it in the early summer sunshine.

In July, Ruth started her labour pains. The women rallied round and looked after her during her confinement. She gave birth to a bonny boy on the eleventh of July. They were all pleased that Mother and baby had survived the ordeal, that there were no complications as in their isolated situation this could be fatal.

Unfortunately, life wasn't quite as simple as that. A fact they were soon to find out.

The Settlement

Worlds Apart'

Fourteen – 'It wasn't quite as easy as they had thought'

The winter started at the end of September with a vicious gale which quickly took the roofs off several of the newly built cottages. Consequently, everything got wet in those homes. Many of the children suffered immediately from damp and cold. The storm was followed by days and days of incessant rain. It soaked everything. It was difficult to keep the fire in the centre of the village burning. It was incredibly difficult to find dry firewood in such a wet environment. All the other fishing boats had left along with all of their crew members. The nearest human being was probably over one hundred miles way, they were the other side of a barren landscape of rocks, sea and peat-bogs.

By early October, the temperature had dropped considerably and spirits were already beginning to drop along with the temperature. The fog now came each day. As the watery sun rose in the sky so the fog drifted ashore, making their world seem very small and themselves isolated.

After several weeks of cold rain, the older members of the party and the children started to suffer from horrible coughs. Grandma was the first to become really ill, she had survived all of the difficulties back in England, the terrible voyage across the ocean and now this never ending cold and damp.

After a week in bed, she grew weaker and weaker finally her frail body gave up. She was laid to rest in the fourth week of October.

Several of the younger children were also quite ill, including young Seth, the youngest child of John and Emily. They were all worried that the weather would get worse and they had few medicinal herbs to help them. After a few days two children died and were buried near the rocky headland of their cove. Seth seemed to rally and after a few more days recovered.

However, the weather deteriorated further, the first snows came in November, blanketing everything in a thick layer. The night of the blizzard was really the beginning of their test of endurance.

It was also the night that the natives attacked. This fledgling community was totally unprepared. Several warriors ambushed the compound simultaneously, brandishing their spears with flaming torches. They set light to several of the cottages, ransacking the storeroom. One of the fishermen attempted to stop the onslaught but was killed instantly by a slashing knife. Two natives grabbed Sarah and another woman and disappeared into the whirling snow. Another native grabbed one of the other young lads and ran off with him on his shoulders, brandishing his cutlass.

The community was shattered. There was an outpouring of grief that night which only a few hours earlier would have seemed totally unreal.

When Nick had realised that his beloved Sarah had been kidnapped he wanted to seek revenge. He was angry. He was all for setting out immediately. He would find Sarah and destroy her captors. But the others counselled against it, saying that he would be quickly lost and could easily die in the mayhem of the storm.

By the morning, they all realised that it would be well-nigh impossible to find their loved ones. The snow was several feet deep, a cold wind was blowing and more snow was falling They had no idea where the natives had gone. Sadness engulfed them all. Had they come all this way, encountered and triumphed over such hardship now to lose their families through illness and capture?

The winter got worse. Through November and into December there were considerable falls of snow. The temperature dropped by many degrees so that the ice made life raw. They had sufficient supplies of food but fuel for the fires was increasingly difficult to find. Everyone seemed to consume a tremendous amount of time and energy just to keep warm. Without the fire they would freeze to death.

Nick and Susan discussed their plight. They realised that on their own in Bonavista they probably wouldn't survive the winter. They had insufficient stores of wood for the fires. They did not stand any chance of finding the captives. It was obvious that they were ignorant of the Indian ways and that they knew precious little about the countryside outside their encampment.

They needed some help from outside their community to survive. Wood for the fire was critical. Soldiers would help their security situation dramatically. They desperately needed help and guidance from people who knew a little more of the ways of the natives. They needed supplies, particularly fuel for the fires.

After long discussion, they decided to walk over the headland to Trinity Bay and on to the Avalon Peninsular. They might be able to reach the English Settlement at 'Ferryland' and gain support from Mr Pengellan. This would require them walking over deep snow for many miles but once they were there they might be able to negotiate some assistance for their return. It was worth the attempt.

They constructed snow shoes using small pine branches sewn together to form a web-like frame, these they attached to their leather boots. They decided to carry as little baggage as possible so that they could walk reasonably quickly. They had food and clothing with them for a few days. They would sleep in caves and keep walking during daylight hours. If the weather kept clear they could make good progress, if the weather was bad, they were lost.

The journey began early one bright December morning. They walked as far as it was possible in a southerly direction. When they had walked for four or five hours, they were outside the area which they knew and could only walk by noting the sun's position. They had no map, no compass and no real awareness of distance. As the day drew on, they looked for a cave and found a small depression where they could sleep overnight. They made a fire and ate some of the food they were carrying.

The next morning the weather was not as clear, but they agreed on the direction and again, walked and walked. This time they saw signs of habitation and recognised the area through which they had travelled upon their arrival in May. This time they found a rough timber shed in which they could shelter.

On the third day they found their way down the steep slopes to the shore on the side of Trinity Bay. They detected some smoke on the horizon with associated signs of life. After a further two hours walking, they discovered the entrance to the compound where they were met by guards on duty. They explained their quest and were admitted. They were shown warm hospitality and were accepted into the community. They were given food and ale with a place to sleep. They had made contact with other people which gave them a real hope that they could find help for their fellows back in the compound.

The next day they negotiated the hire of a horse and were given directions to find 'Ferryland' on the other side of the Avalon Peninsula. This changed everything; they could ride quite fast and made good progress. Susan was feeling much more confident about their mission. She was now able to prepare herself to meet Mr Pengellan whom she had not met since their arrival earlier in the year. He was in a position to change their whole situation.

'Ferryland' was a mission settlement funded by the Crown and by Church interests back in England. It had stores of food, clothing and building materials as well as a militia.

They had well over a hundred miles to ride through snow covered hills and on slippery tracks. Steadily, however, they made their way across the Avalon Peninsula to the southern coast of the island. It was a hard ride and it took several days to complete. Each night they managed to find a small hamlet where they obtained food and a warm place to sleep.

Eventually they found the 'Ferryland Settlement'. This fortified encampment had been constructed over the past few years by the men of one George Calvert. In 1622, it had been reported that they had been able to construct stone buildings suitable for the 'Governor.' They had 'fortified the harbour, planted a kitchen garden and created a meadow of three acres for horses and cows.' By the time our two friends arrived, there was a population of over one hundred people, both men and women.

When they arrived at the gates of the settlement they asked for an audience with Mr George Pengellan, the Benefactor's representative. When the said gentleman arrived, he welcomed them with an aloofness and coldness that Susan immediately challenged. "We do not come begging your generosity. Rather we come to meet the people of 'Ferryland' and as fellow-citizens of New-Found-Land to share in the development of this fair land."

Nick felt that she was being rather superior when in reality they had come to beg food and fuel. He therefore countered Susan's remarks by adding his own comments; "Actually, we do need your help, we have managed during the summer and autumn at Bonavista. We have established a small settlement and we have been able to support ourselves by fishing and planting crops. However, this early winter weather has caused several deaths and destroyed some of our cottages. We desperately need fuel and some items of food and some help to re-build our homes – we need nails and leather for repairs. We have also been attacked by natives, they have captured three of our people. We need your help to find them and negotiate the safe return of our family and friends."

"I am sorry", said Susan, "Nick is right, we are in a sad and sorry state and we need your help to survive. As we had spent time with you on the boat, we thought that you might be able to help us, seeing that you are in such a responsible position here," said Susan, rather more apologetically than before.

George Pengellen was rather pleased to meet Susan again. He desperately missed female, educated company and realising that as these two were now unaccompanied by uneducated fisher-folk, he could therefore entertain them properly. He could enjoy himself for once. So he replied; "Yes, of course I can help you, I will see that you are fully provisioned for the rest of the winter. In the meantime, I would like you to be my guests at dinner tonight."

That night, all three enjoyed themselves immensely. For Susan it was like the old days, being entertained and being able to enjoy fine wine, good food and a warm house. George was obviously flirting with her and she responded with enthusiasm. It just felt so good to be able to be herself and be treated as be her station. Nick found this hilarious, he just enjoyed watching the obvious chemistry between the two people. He enjoyed the banter of educated company. It was just like life at back in England before he had become involved with the Puritan community. He also realised that without Sarah, he was lonely and missed the social life of his previous existence.

During the evening they talked about religion and politics, as always. Susan explained how she had become convinced of the truth of the 'Puritan' way as opposed to the Catholic or Protestant beliefs.

They stayed overnight at the cottage of a villager within the settlement. On the morrow, George Pengellan instructed the men who kept the settlements' store to provide food; meat, flour and vegetables, timber for fuel and the various metal and leather items they needed. All of this was loaded onto two wagons which would transport the goods as far as possible towards the village at Bonavista. Our two friends rode the horse back to Trinity Bay before making their way with some of the goods overland to Bonavista. Everyone was overjoyed to welcome them home, particularly to hear of their good fortune in obtaining support to their activities in Bonavista and for the stores that they had brought with them..

Before they left 'Ferryland' they were also able to talk about the attack and capture of the villagers. George Pengellan and his military advisers were furious when they heard about the incident. They had established formal links with the Beothukan Indians in New-Found-Land so they were able to send a message demanding the return of the hostages. George said that the attack was probably the work of a break-away faction of Indians. He explained that the vast majority were peaceful and law-abiding. "In the spring," said George, "We will send soldiers to find the Indians and obtain the release of the women, do not fear, they will not have killed them."

In January, they were able to make an expedition to Trinity with Susan obtaining a horse so that she and Nick could return to 'Ferryland'. They were therefore able to establish some social links which enabled both of them to accept the privations back at home.

In February, the weather became very cold again and everything was frozen for several weeks, but this time everyone was prepared. They had sufficient food and timber for the fire. They had repaired the cottages so that each family had a roof over their heads. The children seemed to have gained a resistance to the cold, everyone fared rather better than back in the autumn. There was a more optimistic spirit abroad. The men were looking forward to the spring and being able to start fishing before any of the boats arrived from Europe. The women were looking forward to being able to prepare the ground for their crops, the children to being able to play outside once more.

The Tilly family were in good shape, although Grandma had died, the rest of the family were making good progress. There was still anger and resentment about the Indian attack which had been instrumental in the capture of Sarah and the others. But John, as always was optimistic about the situation and believed that sooner or later his beloved family would be together again. Ruth and her young baby were happy and content. John the less had a new season of fishing ahead of him, he had also found that his friendship with Bess had grown during the winter. They were now planning to get married in the spring. Emily and John were happy that they had made the break to a new life but they both missed William, Miriam and young Richard.

Of course, they had not heard anything since they had left England, nearly a year earlier. However, they were hopeful that by the summer the family would be reunited. Nick was waiting desperately for news of Sarah but he hoped and prayed that everything would soon be alright, that they could marry and have a family in this fascinating country of New-Found-Land.

It was with great excitement that they received a message from George Pengellan via Susan that in the first official mailbag to arrive in the spring of that year there was news for those at 'Bonavista'.

'William and Miriam Tilly with their new baby Anthony and young Richard Tilly are to set sail from Bristol on April 15th 1626 and will be arriving in Bonavista, God Willing, later in the year.'

There was also news for Lady Susan, unfortunately, that was not as exciting, in fact, it was deeply distressing;

Mr Jonathan Sowerbutts, Solicitor for Sir Richard Tichbourne was also sailing for New-Found-Land with a summons for the arrest of Lady Susan Tichbourne who is to stand trial for Religious Dissent and Desertion from her Marriage Responsibilities.

The story of our family and their friends continues ...

Worlds Apart - Yet One Family'

Epilogue

Our story has only just begun. These early settlers were the forefathers of many in Newfoundland. Over the next two hundred years there was a constant stream of people travelling to and from the New World. Fishermen from Hampshire, Dorset and Devon commuting each year to the fishing grounds off the Grand Banks. Some of whom settled, some of whom returned to their homeland.

However, William Tilly (son of John Tilly) settled in Bonavista and his death was recorded in the Newfoundland Census of 1675 "predeceasing him were his wife, seven sons and two daughters, including; Anthony, William, Elisabeth, Richard, George and Joseph".

The Tilly Family continued to prosper in the Bonavista Bay area of Newfoundland with many descendants who live in the area to this day. In Elliston, Newfoundland, one Robert Tilly contributed funds for the construction of a 'Cottage Church' in the 1840's and commenced a 'supplying merchant's business' in the town. In the 1860's he established a small cannery in Deep Cove as well as being a fisherman, farmer and sawmill operator. His house is now a Municipal Heritage Building. Members of the Tilly family lived in the property until 1925.

John Tilly, the businessman from Bristol, may well have been related to the Tilly's of this story. We know that a John Tilly, linen merchant, died in 1656

And was buried in St. Mary Redcliffe, Bristol. The place of burial with a large commemorative plaque can still be seen today.

In Ringwood, England, the family members increased over the centuries. Some of the descendents emigrated to Australia, New Zealand and South Africa. The religious dimension has also been maintained with members of the family being Quakers, Congregationalists, Strict Baptists, Baptists and more recently, Christadelphians. One descendent was the Rev. Robert Tilly, founder of the Forton Road Baptist Church, Gosport, Hampshire in 1806.

In July 1996, the present writer laid one Jack Tilly (a Christadelphian) to rest in Birmingham, England. Jack was aged 97 and was a direct descendent of John and William Tilly of Ringwood and Newfoundland. He was also a relative of my wife who is also a member of this fascinating family.

I was privileged to know Jack personally for some thirty years. He was a unique man who always demonstrated characteristics of determination in the face of difficulty. Particularly, he accepted life with true humility before God. Characteristics that his forbears demonstrated so many years before. He had a favourite phrase which seems to be an appropriate one with which to conclude this book. **'Whatever will be, will be'.**

Colin J Edwards 2009